Killer in [...]

"Brown deftly spins the tale of Reagan's many misadventures while sleuthing, fills her story with Southern eccentrics, and offers up a magnolia-laced munificence of Savannah color."
—*Richmond Times-Dispatch*

"*Killer in Crinolines* is a fast-paced cozy with lots of twists and turns. Brown has a knack for writing dialogue and readers will find themselves so engrossed in the story, it's hard to concentrate on anything else." —*Debbie's Book Bag*

"Great characters, funny dialogue, twists and turns, and a little romance. What more could you want in a cozy mystery? If Agatha Christie lived in Savannah, she would have written this novel. Charming, clever, and sometimes creepy, a really good read." —*Sweet Mystery Books*

"Southern coziness at its finest! A most enjoyable read—mystery fans will love this one. It's the kind of book that makes a bad day good!" —*Socrates' Book Reviews*

"If you have read *Iced Chiffon*, then you'll absolutely LOVE *Killer in Crinolines*. In fact, if you weren't hooked on the series after reading *Iced Chiffon*, you bet your derriere you'll be hooked after reading this one. Its compelling mystery and engaging plot will have you staying up countless hours into the night . . . If you're a fan of Southern mysteries and just cozy mysteries in general, I HIGHLY recommend checking out this new series by Duffy Brown! You won't regret it, I promise."
—*Dreamworld Book Reviews*

continued . . .

Iced Chiffon

"A Southern comfort cozy with Yankee tension . . . A treat. Not to be missed."
— Annette Blair, *New York Times* bestselling author of *Tulle Death Do Us Part*

"An amazing mystery debut . . . Riveting."
— Mary Kennedy, author of the Talk Radio Mysteries

"A delightful world filled with charm and humor."
— *New York Journal of Books*

"This amusing, thoroughly entertaining mystery . . . has perfect accomplices, plenty of suspects, and humorous situations."
— *RT Book Reviews*

"Besides a fabulous look at Savannah, especially the haunts of high society, Duffy Brown provides a lighthearted, jocular amateur sleuth."
— *Gumshoe Review*

"Delightful . . . If I could give it six stars, I would."
— Examiner.com

"A pleasant beginning to a new series . . . A light tone, a quick pace, [and] good old Southern hospitality . . . all come together for a charming read."
— *The Mystery Reader*

"A strong story, fantastic, well-developed characters, and a great mystery . . . *Iced Chiffon* was a stellar read and I can't wait to see where Duffy Brown takes these characters next."
— *Cozy Mystery Book Reviews*

Berkley Prime Crime titles by Duffy Brown

ICED CHIFFON
KILLER IN CRINOLINES
PEARLS AND POISON

Pearls and Poison

DUFFY BROWN

BERKLEY PRIME CRIME, NEW YORK

THE BERKLEY PUBLISHING GROUP
Published by the Penguin Group
Penguin Group (USA) LLC
375 Hudson Street, New York, New York 10014

USA • Canada • UK • Ireland • Australia • New Zealand • India • South Africa • China

penguin.com

A Penguin Random House Company

PEARLS AND POISON

A Berkley Prime Crime Book / published by arrangement with the author

Berkley Prime Crime Books are published by The Berkley Publishing Group.
BERKLEY® PRIME CRIME and the PRIME CRIME logo are trademarks
of Penguin Group (USA) LLC.

For information, address: The Berkley Publishing Group,
a division of Penguin Group (USA) LLC,
375 Hudson Street, New York, New York 10014.

ISBN: 978-0-425-25248-2

PUBLISHING HISTORY
Berkley Prime Crime mass-market edition / March 2014

PRINTED IN THE UNITED STATES OF AMERICA

10 9 8 7 6 5 4 3 2

Cover illustration by Julia Green.
Cover design by Diana Kolsky.
Interior text design by Kristin del Rosario.

~Acknowledgments~

To my Street Team, you all are amazing. Thanks for your support. The very best part of writing is the friends I've met along the way. This book is for you.

Chapter One

"**P**EOPLE are going to hate me if I do this," I said to Auntie KiKi. "They're going to cuss a blue streak and call me names and tell me to mind my own blankety-blank business and then slam the phone in my ear."

"Oh for crying in a bucket, Reagan." KiKi shoved a computer printout at me. "Time to put on your ironclad bloomers and dial the numbers on this here sheet. It's your very own mamma everyone in this room is trying to get elected to city council. Least you can do is tell folks what a fine alderman she'd be, and Lord knows the city needs her instead of the scum bucket running against her."

KiKi held up a plate full of pure temptation. "And keep in mind that we just happen to have pecan shortbread cookies for those who lend a hand."

Mamma and KiKi were sisters. At birth the muses tangoed over auntie's crib turning her into Savannah's dance diva, and they wrapped mamma in a blanket with little elephants resulting in this campaign and me getting the name *Reagan*.

"Why doesn't Mamma just run ads on TV saying what a total jerk Kip Seymour is? That's what he's doing to her."

"Mudslinging is not your mamma's style," Marigold Haber, Mamma's campaign manager and once upon a time sorority sister, offered, drawing up next to me. She had on the unofficial red, white, and blue "Elect Gloria Summerside" hat, scarf, and matching embroidered vest . . . politics belle style. She waved her hand over six tables of volunteers: some with a phone in each ear, others tweeting and Facebooking to keep supporters current . . . politics contemporary style. I reached for the phone and stopped dead with an acute attack of slam-phone phobia. "What if *we* take out the ads and don't tell her."

"Don't tell me what?" Mamma asked from the doorway of the once-upon-a-time HotDoggery now serving as her campaign headquarters. It was filled with banners, signs, and a Lego replica of Mamma from the Garrison Elementary kindergarten class over on Jones Street. Bruce Willis, my four-legged BFF with wagging tail, and I hated to see the Doggery fold, but even we couldn't eat enough to keep the place afloat, though heaven knows we tried. All that remained was a dull yellowish mustard stain in the back corner and a faint whiff of relish.

Mamma had on a black knit suit, meaning she'd come from court where she was known affectionately—or not so affectionately depending on who you were and what you did—as Judge Guillotine Gloria. KiKi gave me a sharp kick under the table and said to Mamma, "Your one and only offspring got someone to mind the consignment shop for her and is here chomping at the bit to get started making those campaign calls for you."

A worried look creased Mamma's forehead, riddling me with bad-daughter guilt, the product of a Catholic education from no-nonsense nuns who took the honor-thy-mother-and-father idea real serious. I snapped up the phone. "Look, look, I'm dialing, I'm dialing!"

Mamma's lips thinned to a fine line across her face in a way that was reminiscent of when I had married Hollis Beaumont the Third. Considering how that turned out, I figured whatever was worrying Mamma today would send us all straight to hell in a handbasket. "I heard that Kip Seymour has a new attack ad coming out about me," Mamma said. "I don't know what it is, but I'm concerned. They say it's a nasty one."

KiKi snapped up a cookie. "Can't be any worse than that ad declaring you're a snotty judge who thinks you're better than everyone."

"Or the one with you embezzling money from the Children's Aid Society?" Marigold huffed. "I do declare the man's lower than a beetle's bellybutton. Thank the Lord no one in their right mind paid any attention to all that malarkey and we survived just fine and dandy, thank you very much."

"Oh, but I can do much, much better," Kip Seymour said as he and his wife, Money-Honey, strolled in through the open doors as if they owned the place. Honey was fifty-something, had been a barmaid in her previous life, and had new money from a dead cousin over in Beaufort. Now she could buy anything from perky boobs to an incredible cream and black suit right out of Nordstrom's catalog to a politically ruthless husband. Seymour was in his early forties, a building contractor of the crooked-as-a-dog's-hind-leg variety though no one could actually prove it. Today he had on wrinkled khakis to relate to the ever-important workingman, the pants making his behind look like two hams flopping around in a Piggly Wiggly bag.

His lip curled. "My, my, it's the pearl-girl set in all their glory. Is this here the best you got? Kind of a sparse crew to win an election, not that you have a snowball's chance in hell of doing that."

The room stilled, all eyes shooting daggers at Seymour and wife. I pulled up next to Mamma, Marigold and KiKi on her other side. The four musketeers plus peeps.

"The polls have us dead even." Mamma said in her best I-am-the-judge voice.

"That's why I'm here." Seymour shoved his hands in his pockets, stretching the khaki material tight across the hams. "I have plans to change all that and thought you might want to hang up your campaign before things get ugly."

"Your half of the campaign's fallen out of the ugly tree and hit every branch on the way down." I took Mamma's hand.

"You ain't seen nothing yet, girly." Seymour laughed and circled the tables like a wolf on the prowl. "I've got a new ad coming out tomorrow that says if Gloria Summerside is elected, she'll require all the restaurants here in Savannah to disclose calorie content right there on their menu and that dishes requiring more than a cup of butter will be banned. Anyone looking at your skinny behind or that has seen you jogging around town would suspect it's true enough."

"Sweet Jesus in heaven!" Auntie KiKi clasped her hands to her chest, her eyes bulging.

"You're going to label Gloria a foodie foe!" Dottie Harrison put the back of her hand to her head and did a very nice Southern swoon. Marigold sank into a metal folding chair, and all the volunteers sucked in a collective gasp.

Washington had monuments, Arizona had the Grand Canyon, and Savannah had food, really good food. No one messed with Savannah restaurants and the delectable dishes concocted within.

"Foodie foe." Money-Honey slipped her arm through Kip's, all cozy like. "Why that's a right-fine sound bite. You should use it, sugar bear."

"It's a lie," Mamma pointed out.

"Like I care," Seymour said as Money-Honey smoothed back her faux-blonde hair. "Folks will picture the Old Pink House being forced to get rid of shrimp and grits and bring in tofu!"

We all made the sign of the cross over the mention of tofu at the Pink House.

"And they'll imagine the Pirate House giving up pecan chicken and serving steamed salmon and broccoli. Zunzi's would stop making their secret sauce! Leopold's will ditch Frozen Hot Chocolate ice cream and serve yogurt."

There was another round of cross-signing.

Marigold banged her fist on the table and stomped her foot with perfect belle precision. "You're nothing but a whoreson skunk, Kip Seymour, you know that!"

Money-Honey held tight to Seymour. "Don't you yell at my husband; he does have a heart condition you know."

"That's assuming he has a heart," Marigold seethed.

"We'll sue. You'll never get away with this. I've got half my life in this campaign like everyone else in this here room, and I won't have you ruining it."

"Election's in two weeks." Seymour sauntered to the door. "No time for taking this to court. You can refute my ad, but I have a boatload of witnesses to back me up."

"That you've paid off." Mamma ground her teeth. Was that smoke curling from her ears?

"But you can stop this all right now." Seymour glanced back over his shoulder, an evil look in his beady black eyes. "Bow out gracefully."

"You'd still have Archie Lee to deal with," I said with a toss of my head. "He's gaining ground every day."

Scumbucket turned, a sly smile on his face. "Feeling a little desperate? I think I can beat a barkeep. Call it quits, girlie. Say you need to spend time with your family. Isn't that the excuse politicians give to run from the line of fire? Consider this your warning shot."

"How about this for a warning shot?" Mamma snagged the plate of pecan shortbreads and flung them at Seymour's fat head, cookies flying in all directions. "I'm going to strangle you with my bare hands, you overbearing, middle-Georgia, low-rent bastard."

Bastard? From my mamma's mouth? Get out the umbrellas and mops because pigs just went airborne and Lord knew what the fallout would be once they hit the skies.

"See you on TV." Seymour snickered. "Make that you'll see me on TV." He took Honey's hand, chomped a cookie that had landed on his shirt, and left, his hams flopping in retreat.

"I shouldn't have lost my temper like that," Mamma's

voice the only sound in the dead-quiet room. "I'll go apologize to him, make things right."

"Fiddlesticks!" Lolly Ledbetter raised her phone in defiance. "That man's in bad need of strangling. I know it first hand after the nasty way he treated my Cazy over at the savings and loan when he was there. Always wanting favors, cases of wine, trips to the Bahamas, or he'd tell his clients to get loans elsewhere. If you don't go and do the deed, Gloria, I swear on my daddy's grave I'll do it myself and enjoy the experience."

Marigold plopped her purse on the table and yanked out a half-empty bottle of Wild Turkey honey bourbon. She thrust it at Mamma. "If you talk to Seymour, I suggest you get him plastered first; that's what I planned to do tonight. I figured he'd already gone far enough with his sleazy campaign, and he and I needed to have a little come-to-Jesus chat. Now the man's gone and made things worse than ever."

Mamma snagged the bourbon. "We're going to win this thing or die trying, and you all can post that all over the Internet." She squared her shoulders and marched out the door clutching the bottle like a weapon.

"I should go with her," I said, an uneasy feeling gnawing at my gut. "What if Seymour gets mean? What if Mamma gets feisty?"

Auntie KiKi shoved another printout into my hand. "Your mamma can handle herself. What you need to do is get a move on and make some calls. We got ourselves an election to win come hell or high water."

But after a half hour of phone duty, Marigold fired me on the spot. Seems I was a natural-born election killer doing Mamma's campaign a lot more harm than good. I suppose calling a few people narrow-minded, pea-brained jackasses if they didn't vote for Gloria Summerside wasn't proper campaign phone etiquette. Well, it should be!

Marigold and Lolly headed off to the Lady's Afternoon Bridge Club. I snagged a pecan shortbread that had landed on the table, broke off the squashed side, hitched Old Yeller, my yellow Target-special pleather purse, onto my shoulder, then headed down Bull Street. In summer I was a capris and flip-flops kind of girl, but the cooler weather had me in an old denim jacket and flats held together with superglue.

I stopped by Mamma's house hoping she'd come to her senses and avoided the face-to-face with Scumbucket. He wasn't about to give up his ad no matter what she said. The house was a small cottage on West York and easy walking distance to the courthouse for Mamma's daily commute. It had a white picket fence I'd painted more times than I wanted to remember and a perfect Southern garden. It was built for Revolutionary War major Charles Odingsells, the three musket balls still embedded in the ceiling proving the point.

When Mamma didn't answer, I continued on to Scumbucket's campaign headquarters, the gnawing in my gut over her going alone getting worse with every step. Mamma wasn't the type to be pushed around. Mamma pushed back.

Afternoon sun sliced through the live oaks draped with Spanish moss in Chippewa Square where James Oglethorpe stood watch over his fair city and—Holy mother of God save us all, was that Mamma yelling at Scumbucket on the sidewalk in front of his campaign headquarters!

"And don't call me girlie," Mamma barked as I ran up beside her. Then right out there in the open air for the whole world to see, text, and Twitter, Guillotine Gloria socked Kip Seymour in the jaw, sending him stumbling backward to land on his two-ham butt.

"Mamma! That was not a good idea!"

"Well, it sure enough felt good," she giggled, and from the twinkle in her eyes she meant every word.

"You'll be sorry," Scumbucket bellowed, waving his fist as I propelled Mamma down Bull Street away from poised iPhones snapping away. "I'm filing assault charges."

"And you'll look like a big namby-pamby bozo if you do for letting some skinny-butt woman get the drop on you," Mamma shot back over her shoulder.

Oh sweet Jesus, things were not improving! I hustled us to the next block where I spied an old white Caddy rumbling my way, pink plastic tulips taped to the antenna and a WWJD sticker on the bumper. I'd know that car anywhere and flagged down Elsie Abbott. Elsie and her sister AnnieFritz lived next door to me. I ran the Prissy Fox consignment shop and sold clothes; the sisters were professional mourners and ground zero for Gossips-R-Us. Guess who had the most likes on Facebook. I shoved Mamma in the backseat. "Take her to my place," I said to Elsie. "Don't let the press anywhere near her."

"But I was just starting to have fun," Mamma insisted, her head poking out the window.

"What's going on?" Elsie asked, clutching her phone, all of Savannah on speed dial. For sure this was not my first choice in stealthy getaway cars, because there'd be nothing stealthy about it. But beggars can't be choosers, and I had to get Mamma out of there right this minute.

"I'll fill you in later," I said to Elsie. She nodded and sped off, leaving me in a cloud of exhaust and with the realization that this was God getting even for all the angst I'd caused the woman who single-handedly raised me after daddy went boar hunting with the good-old-boys and proved beyond a shadow of a doubt that guns and Johnny Walker Red were indeed a bad mix.

I walked back and stood across the street, staring at the headquarters, everyone having gone back inside. I should do something, but what? I tried to come up with a scenario that painted Scumbucket as the bad guy in all this as a navy Beemer squealed up to the curb.

"Oh, honey," KiKi gasped after powering down the window. "Tell me your mamma didn't for real deck Seymour?"

"Flatted him like a fried egg in the skillet." I took shotgun.

"Why do I keep missing all the good stuff," KiKi huffed then added, "But as much as the woman deserves a medal for the deed, you know full well Scumbucket's going to sue her panties off and make a big deal out of this. We need to convince him somehow that would be a bad idea, that it's better to keep this altercation on the down low. Where is your mamma now?"

"Sent her to my place with Elsie Abbott."

"Holy Saint Patrick, we're doomed. I wonder if Savannah has one of those spin doctor people who make catastrophes seem like Christmas morning with presents under the tree." Deep in thought KiKi tapped the tips of her fingers together. "Maybe we can reason with Scumbucket."

I gave her a *get real* look.

"What about Valentine? He's Scumbucket's campaign manager. We need to go in that there headquarters and make

Delray Valentine realize his candidate sprawled on the ground makes him look weak and pitiful."

"Or Valentine will throw us out."

"There is that." Minutes then more minutes rolled by, a brain-numbing migraine pooling behind my eyes. "I got nothing," KiKi finally said, opening the car door. "You'll just have to wing it once we get inside."

"Me?"

"You flunked phone calls. Think of this as redemption."

We crossed the street, people entering and exiting Scumbucket's headquarters, the inside bustling with campaign hoopla, "Happy Days Are Here Again" warbling in the background. I didn't see Money-Honey or Valentine, but a twentysomething blonde in a short pink skirt and a white sweater with a cute little pink poodle pin gave KiKi one of those *where do I know you from* looks. I stuck an "Elect Kip Seymour" button on KiKi and grabbed a hat for me along with a sticky bun, complete with gooey pecans.

"Camouflage," I mumbled to KiKi around a mouthful of total goodness. One of the workers told us Seymour was in his office down the hall, working on a speech, and he didn't want to be disturbed no matter what. We waited a few minutes then headed that way.

"Should we knock?" I asked KiKi when we got to the closed door. In response she turned the knob and strolled right in to the sunlit office full of metal chairs, a desk cluttered with flyers and flags, but no Seymour.

"Look at this." I pointed at a line of creepy life-size cardboard stand-up posters against the far wall. "Here we have sophisticated Seymour in a blue suit and big smile, casual

Seymour in khakis and a polo and doing the thumbs-up we win gesture, working-man Seymour with a tool belt and hard hat, debonair Seymour in fancy tux complete with Georgia flag lapel pin and—"

"Dead as a doornail Seymour right here on the floor next to my big toe." KiKi pointed behind the desk, her cheeks fading to pasty white.

"Dear God in heaven, it *is* Scumbucket!" I said peering over KiKi's shoulder. I made the sign of the cross for maligning the dead and braced for a lightning bolt to strike.

KiKi collapsed down in Scumbucket's desk chair and reached for a half-empty glass by the phone. "Looks like Gloria went with the honey bourbon softening up approach on the old fart, for all the good it did. I sure could use a belt of hooch right now myself."

"You'll get Scumbucket cooties."

KiKi snapped back her hand, and I picked a paper off the desk. "Look at this, it's Scumbucket's speech, and it's all about Mamma ruining Savannah's restaurant economy, a follow-up to his ad, no doubt."

The shock of Scumbucket dead faded away and being plain old madder than a wet hen took its place. I grabbed the receiver and jabbed 911. "Kip Seymour is dead as a frog on the four-lane over here at his campaign headquarters on Bull Street," I said to dispatch. "No, this isn't a joke. He's just lying there staring at the carpet and not in a gee-ain't-this-a-nice-carpet way. I didn't kill him, tempting as it might be, the no-good piece of crud."

KiKi rolled her eyes so far back she nearly fell off the chair. Guess I should have left out the crud part. I gave my name and KiKi's, getting another auntie eye roll.

"Did you have to go and drag me into this? Putter will hear about it and give me one of his what-have-you-gone-and-done-now lectures and want me to call him every hour telling him where I am."

"You're sitting at Seymour's desk. He's dead right in front of you. You're into this up to your eyeballs." And come to think of it KiKi's eyeballs weren't focusing too well at the moment. Maybe I should have left off the last dead reference. I snagged her arm, hauled her off the chair, and ushered her into the main room where life and theme song carried on as usual; a little color returned to her cheeks.

"In two minutes the cops are going to come barreling through that door," I whispered to KiKi, hoping to get her mind off things dead. "Any suggestions how we can prepare all these workers?"

"Yell 'The jackass bit the big one' and run like the dickens before someone recognizes us?"

Translation . . . a little fresh air and Auntie KiKi was back to being Auntie KiKi.

"Ohmygod, Ohmygod!" screamed poodle-pin girl, running out of Seymour's office. "Kip's dead! He's really and truly dead right there in his office and not breathing or moving or anything, and how can this happen, and now who do we vote for?" The girl crumpled into a heap on the floor like that wicked witch when they threw water on her.

Everyone stared for a moment, the headquarters quiet as a tomb, comprehension as to what happened sinking in bit by bit. It was the lull before the storm. Then as if someone had thrown a switch, three guys ran for Scumbucket's office, girls cried and hugged, and sirens blared in the distance that suddenly wasn't distant at all but right outside the place.

Detective Aldeen Ross flanked by three uniformed police rushed in. Ross stopped dead when she spied me, her eyes narrow, frown lines puckering her mouth like she'd sucked on a lemon. "I should lock you up and throw away the key once and for all. Do the city a favor."

I wanted to say the feeling was mutual, but Ross had a gun strapped to her bony hip and knew how to use it. She once possessed the proportions of a fireplug but had developed a crush on Dr. Oz, dropped forty pounds, and with her brown hair and suit now looked pretty much like a stick.

"Every time I see you someone's dead," Ross groused.

Duh, you're a homicide detective was on the tip of my tongue, but again there was the gun issue.

"Heard Seymour and your mamma had an altercation." Ross pulled a notebook from her brown saddlebag purse as the uniforms tried to calm everyone down, though with the arrival of the coroner coach and the press, calm was not happening any time soon.

"Altercation my old tomato," poodle-pin blurted as she struggled to her feet, hair wild, pupils dilated. "It was a knockdown drag out brawl right out there on the sidewalk." She jabbed a manicured finger in that direction. "That old bat judge punched Kip. She killed him as sure as if she stabbed him with a knife. How could she do something like that?"

"Gloria Summerside is not an old bat," I growled, hands on hips. "My guess is Kippy thought bacon was the fifth food group and it caught up with him."

"Is it true?" Delray Valentine said as he huffed his way through the door, his face blotchy and red. "Kip's really . . . gone? What happened? How can this be?" Delray ran his hand though his thinning gray hair. "I was at the printers and got a tweet about the fight and . . ." His voice trailed off, and he leaned heavily against a table. "We had such big dreams, big plans for the city. A vision."

Visions of dollars from bribes and payoffs and a lot of lying and cheating, I added to myself.

Poodle-pin girl swiped away more tears, sniffed, and hugged Valentine tight. "Kippy was a wonderful man, simply divine. This can't be happening. How will we ever survive? What should we do?"

"Celebrate?" Auntie KiKi's eyes brightened and a grin tipped her lips. She did a little jig right there in Scumbucket's headquarters. "Gloria Summerside wins!"

Chapter Two

"WELL, that was about as much fun as getting poked in the eye with a sharp stick," KiKi said to me an hour later as she powered up the Beemer and we headed for the Victorian district after talking to the cops.

"Detective Ross was a lot nicer when she was plumper," KiKi added. "See, that right there is a mighty good reason to not diet. I'll have to tell Putter." Putter was KiKi's husband, Uncle Doctor Putter. He carried a nine iron at all times, defending Savannah against heart and golf ball attacks.

"You married a cardiologist, honey. The big-is-better theory has sailed." Auntie KiKi and Uncle Putter lived in a pristine Queen Ann that had been in the Vanderpool family since Sherman and his merry men set up shop in our fair city. I lived next door in a partially restored nonpristine Victorian. To make ends meet, or at least come a little closer together, I led haunted Savannah tours during tourist season, opened a consignment shop on the first floor of the Victorian, and took in a dog. Bruce Willis didn't help my economic status, but he had a nice smile and shared my love for hot dogs and SpaghettiOs surprise.

KiKi parked the car in her driveway, and we cut our eyes to my place, the Open sign in the bay window, my good friend Chantilly holding down the fort while I did phone and dead-guy duty. "Think your mamma's heard about the Scumbucket mishap?" KiKi asked.

"Does Dolly Parton sleep on her back? This is Savannah; everybody knows everything in ten minutes flat."

"What in the world happened?" Chantilly pounced when KiKi and I came in the front door of the Prissy Fox. A customer perused clothes displayed in the dining room, and Mamma paced behind the checkout counter that was really an old green paint-chipped door I found in the attic and balanced across two flat-back chairs. Chantilly had helped me set up the Fox a few months ago. She was a former UPS driver and an ex–murder suspect. Chantilly led a rich and colorful life. She dropped her voice. "Is you-know-who really you-know-what?"

"As a mackerel," KiKi volunteered.

Mamma braced her arms on the counter and leaned across, her nose nearly touching Auntie KiKi's, her hazel eyes beady. "You danced?"

"Well, maybe a little. Just a teeny-tiny one, I swear," Auntie KiKi said, holding up her thumb and forefinger, an inch of space between them to emphasize the teeny-tiny part. "Barely moved my feet at all. There may have been a twirl or two involved, but I'm willing to bet no one noticed in all the confusion. It was the stress of the day building up inside me. Besides, honey, you win!"

"And you were tickled to your toes Seymour was dead and gone," Mamma added.

"There is that. The police think it was a heart attack," KiKi said after I sold a pair of leather boots that I had my eye on but couldn't afford. After putting the money in the Godiva candy box that served as my cash register, the Fox was customer free. A good thing in that we could talk; a bad thing in that the water bill was due.

"Hard to imagine Scumbucket suddenly keeling over like that," KiKi said. "He was fit as a fiddle when threatening you with ruin and devastation earlier in the day, then bam, he's worm food. Cher says words are like weapons. The way I see it, this was the good Lord's way of getting even for those ads he had coming out."

KiKi was a roadie for Cher back in the day and never quite got off the bus. From time to time she burst into Cherisms whether they fit or not. "It was a comeuppance for sinful deeds," KiKi added.

"Uh, we might want to keep that to ourselves." I nodded toward the front bay window sporting a display of tan slacks, a cream sweater, and a WVXU van screeching to a stop out by the curb.

"Holy mother of pearl, it's the press." Chantilly grabbed Mamma's hand and looked her dead in the eyes. "They found you, honey! Run! Hide. Change your name and get a nose job. I mean it when I say that nothing good ever comes from these people. They twist and turn things to suit their needs and to sell their papers, and don't listen to a blessed word you say. Look how they went and exaggerated me naked on that there horse at my ex's engagement party."

"You weren't naked?" I asked, vividly remembering the story.

"I had on a top hat for Pete's sake, and they never even mentioned it."

"I'll have to face them sooner or later." Mamma pulled her lipstick from her purse, added a swipe. "You all stay here in case someone heard about the jig." Mamma glared at KiKi then strolled out the front door to face cameras, microphones, and busybody neighbors, meaning everyone within a two-block radius with a pulse.

KiKi, Chantilly, and I pressed our noses to the bay window, catching snippets of Mamma's speech about heartfelt condolences, differences with the deceased being purely political, and, no, she would not attend the funeral. This was a time for Honey and family to mourn the loss of a dear loved one. Mamma was an ace at winging it.

"I think that went pretty well," Mamma said when she came back inside, the crowd dispersing and the press driving off. "I'll suspend campaigning till after the funeral. I need to tell the volunteers what's going on."

"I can drop you off on my way home." Chantilly batted her eyes and added a sexy grin. "I happen to have a hot date with Pillsbury. We're going for an early dinner at Café 37. Their brandy cream sauce is to die for. Then he's coming to my place and itemizing my assets."

Pillsbury was the accountant—the doughboy—for the Seventeenth Street gang. He had the brain of Warren Buffett, the body of an army tank, and the hots for Chantilly. None of us were going to touch the assets comment with a ten-foot pole.

After everyone left, BW and I priced and hung up the new batch of consigned clothes that Chantilly had taken in and did the entrepreneur thing of running the Prissy Fox till seven. I scrambled us up some bacon and eggs in case our Southern cholesterol level was sinking into the normal range, and the two of us dined alfresco, parking our behinds on the front porch of Cherry House, named for the old cherry tree in front. The faint outline of *REL* carved in the trunk of that tree was still visible, and I liked to think it stood for Robert E. Lee since he was supposed to have slept here. More than likely it stood for Roy Elbert Lemon who used to live down the street and had a pet skunk.

I fed BW a chunk of egg. He wasn't exactly a hot date, but he kept my feet warm at night and was a better listener than most men, including the one in the red '57 Chevy convertible pulling up to the curb this very minute. Walker Boone happened to be the slimeball attorney who took me to the cleaners in my divorce from Hollis the Horrible. That I signed an airtight prenup made the cleaners part pretty easy for Boone. He also got me out of a jam or three and paid a hefty vet bill for BW, laying claim to his snout and tail. Since I wasn't in trouble at the moment and BW was in the pink of health, that left the slimeball attorney part to deal with. "What?"

BW bounded down the wooden stairs and did the paws-on-shoulder ritual with Boone. Even SpaghettiOs surprise didn't get me that kind of affection. Boone performed the scratch-behind-the-ears routine then sat beside me. He had on worn jeans and a white dress shirt turned up at the sleeves, his face bore a perpetual scruff, and he smelled like expensive brandy. He snagged a bacon strip and chunk of egg and popped it in his mouth.

"In about twenty minutes Ross is going to take your mamma to the police station for questioning about Kip Seymour," Boone said around a mouthful. "Thought you'd like to know." He licked his fingers and eyed the last piece of bacon.

"Nice try. I was there, saw the body, and got a firsthand report. Scumbuck. . . Seymour died of a heart attack pure and simple, so if you came here to rattle my cage, save your breath; it's not going to work."

"Bumped into Ross over at the Pig in the produce section. Taught her how to thump melons. Seymour's heart attack had help."

I snagged the last bacon strip before Boone. "They think 'cause Mamma punched Seymour she caused his death?"

Boone broke off the end, munched, and stood. "Ross must have more than that. She wouldn't go after a judge without something substantial."

"Substantial like what?" The bacon suddenly tasted like wallpaper paste. "Seymour's the one who came to Mamma threatening her with a damning ad. He wanted to ruin her campaign even if he lied to do it. He called her 'girlie' for crying out loud."

A grin played at the corners of Boone's mouth, his black eyes creasing at the corners. There'd been reports of grown women fainting dead away from that very look. "No wonder she decked him," Boone said. "Sorry I missed it. All I know is Ross wasn't happy about the situation. Your mamma is the judge every cop wants to try his case. She's got . . . cojones."

Cojones and Mamma in the same sentence was a little unnerving, but at the moment I had bigger fish to fry. No matter how crazy my life got Mamma was my rock, my true North . . . or South being that this was Savannah. Little prickles of fear crawled up my spine. "I gotta call Mamma."

"I already did. She'll need an attorney."

"You're an attorney, do something." My voice sounded like Alvin the chipmunk.

"I worked on legal stuff for Seymour a few years back; it'll smack of conflict of interest if I get involved. Besides, Gloria Summerside is on a first name basis with half the attorneys in Savannah."

Meaning Mamma had options other than an ex-Seventeenth Street gang member turned lawyer. Chantilly wasn't the only one who led a rich and colorful life. Boone was a good attorney no matter what his origins. He won, a lot. My disastrous divorce was living proof. I followed Boone to the Chevy, pulled back the seat, and let BW jump in the back. I took shotgun. "Drop us off at Mamma's."

"Still no car?"

"Do you know what a new roof on an old house costs these days?"

"You need to stay out of this. Seymour wasn't just two hams in a grocery bag like everyone thought; he had enemies."

"Sure would have been nice if they said something in the campaign."

"They're not choirboys." Boone turned sideways, his eyes black as the night. He gave me his *no-nonsense lawyer* stare that I knew so well. "Ross is a good detective. She has a gun. Let her do her job."

I gave Boone my *loyal daughter* stare. "If you think for

one minute I'm letting my mamma's future rest in the scrawny hands of Aldeen Ross, you've lost your marbles." I pointed to the ignition. "I don't need a lecture. Come on, time's a wasting, floor this puppy."

Boone gripped the steering wheel and let out a sigh. "Reasoning with you is like teaching a setting hen to crow. Ross will put your mamma in the cruiser, and you'll have a hissy right there in front of her house, yell a bunch of stuff you shouldn't, and wind up in jail yourself. You need to cool off."

My hair fried. "I *am* cool, blast you! Drive now!" Maybe I should have left off the blast you part. I dragged BW out of the backseat then slammed the door behind me and kicked the front tire. "You're nothing but a bacon-stealing scalawag."

"On my better days." The Chevy's taillights faded down the street, turned onto Abercorn leaving BW and me alone on the sidewalk, the rest of the inhabitants of East Gwinnett tucked in for the night. Getting a taxi out here at this hour was the impossible dream, KiKi and Uncle Putter were deep into *Downton Abbey* season three, and besides KiKi had had enough drama in her life for one day. If I got the Abbott sisters involved, Mamma would headline the nine o'clock kudzu vine news.

I hitched up BW, grabbed Old Yeller, doggie scoop bags, and a Snickers for dessert to go. I put on my gym shoes that had never graced the inside of a gym and jogged down the street, trying to get to Mamma's before Ross. Usually night was my favorite time in Savannah, kind of magical with the soft glow of the old lamplight through the live oaks, Forsythe Fountain sparkling in the moonlight, strollers out for a late dinner. The only magic tonight was of the black variety with Mamma right in the middle of a big, fat mess.

Panting and sweating I promised God I'd light candles if he let me make it to Mamma's without having a stroke. When she didn't answer my door-pounding, I hung a right onto Habersham and headed for the redbrick police station designed by a teething two-year-old that was ground zero for major in-city offenses and home away from home for Ross. Tonight Officer Dumont occupied the gray Formica welcome desk, the hubbub of Savannah crime and crime stoppers swirling around him as he yelled into the phone and scribbled notes. I knew Dumont from when I swiped a memorial wreath out of Colonial Park Cemetery and the time I found a dead groom facedown in a wedding cake.

"I'm Reagan Summerside," I said to Dumont, taking advantage of the turmoil and hoping he didn't remember me from past offenses. "Is Gloria Summerside here?"

"No dogs allowed." Dumont gulped his coffee and made a face at a baggie of tiny carrots.

"I just want to know if my mamma's okay? Why was she taken into custody?"

Dumont took another call, cradled the phone against his shoulder, wrote with one hand, and pointed to the door with the other. "You and the pooch outside."

Summersides sucked at waiting, proven by the fact that three months ago Auntie KiKi got herself locked in a closet and instead of waiting to get rescued crawled through an attic and out onto a fire escape then proceeded to fall off the building. When Dumont hung up the phone that immediately rang again, I pulled the Snickers from Old Yeller and stealthily slid the candy bar across the desk, stopping right next to the carrots. "Why do the police think Gloria Summerside is responsible for Scum . . . Seymour's heart attack?"

Two officers broke up a fight in the back of the room, a metal chair sailed across the concrete floor, and Dumont ignored it all and the phone. He eyed the prize, fingers inching closer, a droplet of drool at the corner of his mouth. "Suspicious autopsy."

"And?"

"There was a drinking glass at the crime scene with digitalis-laced honey bourbon. Facebook and tweets from the judge's campaign this afternoon said the judge was headed over to Seymour's with the bourbon to make peace and hopefully continue on with a respectable campaign. Then there were online pictures of her punching his lights out. Sorry I missed that. Seymour's crud." Dumont snagged the Snickers, ripped the wrapper, and bit, a glazed euphoric expression softening his face, meaning that on a fundamental level Officer Dumont and I were kindred spirits. Then reality returned, and he grabbed the phone and pointed to the door. "No dogs allowed. Out!"

BW and I stood on the sidewalk under a streetlight, BW in his coat, all cozy and warm against the autumn chill and making me wish I'd brought a jacket, and another Snickers would be nice, too. Dumont didn't say the police had found the tainted bottle of honey bourbon, so right now everything was speculation as far as whether the poison was in the bottle that Mamma brought. Heck, everyone in Savannah knew Seymour fancied honey bourbon. He could be the poster boy for the stuff, and anyone could have poured out a glass of the tainted booze.

According to Boone, Scummy had enemies, and there was a whole roomful of people at Seymour's headquarters who could have done him in. That these same people were working morning, noon, and night to get him elected was a minor motivation flaw I didn't want to consider at the moment.

Something else I didn't want to consider was just how close Auntie KiKi came to drinking that bourbon. Seymour cooties saved the day. Anyone who doesn't think God works in mysterious ways hasn't lived in Savannah.

"Heard they picked up Judge Gloria Summerside for questioning in the Kip Seymour case," a twentysomething guy said as he rushed up. He had a hedge-trimmer haircut and camera with lens attached dangling around his neck. "Is she inside?" Hedge Trimmer hitched his head toward the building. "Did you see her? What do the cops have to say? When are they letting her out? I need pictures and a statement."

The Kip Seymour case? Statement? Pictures? Why couldn't it be Kip Seymour done and over with and hallelujah he's gone? "I haven't seen Judge Summerside," I said. "You must have heard wrong."

Another camera guy pulled up beside him on the sidewalk, a cigarette tucked behind his ear, one dangling from his lips. "I know you. You're Gloria Summerside's daughter."

"I was out for a walk."

"Sure, and you're here to contemplate Savannah's architectural wonder, no doubt. You're here because the judge is inside." Savannah's version of the paparazzi snapped my picture and headed for the door.

After little white dots stopped dancing in front of my eyes, I headed for the parking lot on the back side of the station where Savannah's finest rode up in their cruisers to deposit Savannah's not so finest to be locked away. That I knew such things was due to Hollis being accused of murder some months ago. There were times when I wished I'd let his miserable hide rot in jail. 'Course then I'd have lost Cherry House to pay for his attorney fees.

I had to get a message to Mamma. She needed to come out through the back door and avoid the press. I'd already used my Snickers bribe on Dumont and figured the cop manning the rear entrance had little use for a near-empty can of hair spray, a half tube of Pink Blossom lipstick, or a roll of Life Savers that were the only decent things left in Old Yeller worth considering a bribe.

"Yo, woman," came a voice behind me. "What you doing here at this hour?"

Big Joey was Pillsbury's bro and grand poobah of the Seventeenth Street gang. We met one hot summer day with me intruding on his turf, giving testimony to the direction my life had taken lately. BW flopped over between two unoccupied cruisers and waited for a belly rub.

"My mamma's inside," I explained as Big Joey did the puppy-pat thing. "They're questioning her about—"

"Seymour getting snuffed. Word is she did the deed. Dropped him a left hook." Big Joey grinned, his gold tooth catching the streetlight. "Props to Mamma Judge."

"The press is here. If they get pictures, it could hurt her chances of getting elected."

Big Joey headed for the station. "A brother got himself incarcerated over an unfortunate error in judgment down at Wet Willies. I'll inform Mamma."

I glanced across the parking lot, checking for reporters. "Can you tell her to hurry?"

"Not her choice, babe."

"Why would you help a judge?"

"Ask Boone." Whistling, Joey took the walkway and banged on the door. It opened, the backlight silhouetting the two men. They did one of those fancy handshakes. The Seventeenth Street band of brothers weren't model citizens by any stretch, but they kept guns and dope out of schools and parks and street violence to a minimum, something the cops could never do on their own.

Moths swarmed the dingy light over the back door of the station. I chewed my thumbnail, my stomach doing somersaults. Mamma being hauled in here for questioning would hurt her campaign for sure, and everyone she'd convicted would come out of the woodwork and malign her good reputation. All her hard work and dedication to truth, justice, and the American way would go right down the drain because of Kip Seymour. The man was a true pain in the rump even from the grave.

The door opened, and this time Mamma's poised silhouette was framed in the doorway. She shook the policeman's hand and walked toward me.

"How do you know Big Joey?" she asked as I hustled her and BW between cruisers toward Hull Street, high heels and doggy nails clicking on the blacktop.

"I'm on his health insurance plan. We've got to get out of here; the reporters are hot on your trail. If they get your picture by the station, they'll have you tried and convicted before morning." Voices and footsteps approached from Habersham, and I yanked Mamma and BW down between empty cars in the lot. I made the *shh* sign across my lips at Mamma and fed BW a cherry Life Saver to keep him occupied and not do the pet-me belly flop for our pursuers—worst guard dog east of the Mississippi.

"I don't see her," one of the guys huffed, fighting to catch his breath.

"This way," another added. "She's here somewhere."

The reporters ran past us, and I counted to ten then poked my head over the edge of the hood. "We'll stay in the shadows," I whispered to Mamma. "Cut across Hall and take the alleyways to my house. There's no hard evidence linking you to Seymour's demise, so by tomorrow some other mayhem will have befallen our lovely city and be page one news instead of you."

I gave Mamma a quick once-over. This was my hazel-eyed brainy parent of perfect hair and suit who spent her days making wise decisions and giving guest lectures at luncheons and graduations. "Are you okay? Being on the lam isn't a normal kind of night for you."

"It isn't for you either." Mamma chuckled then sobered. "Is it? How do you know about these alleys, and what's this about Big Joey and insurance?" Her brows knitted together like that time in the third grade when someone who shall remain nameless released the classroom hamster into the wild and played "Born Free" over the PA system.

"I'm pleading the fifth." I held tight to the leash, took Mamma's hand, and ran.

Chapter Three

"Good God in heaven, who died now?" Auntie KiKi asked as BW and I hustled into her kitchen at seven A.M. the next morning. KiKi had on an autumn ensemble of pumpkin-colored housecoat, matching slippers and hair rollers, and a green facial mask, meaning Uncle Putter had already left for his symposium up in Charlotte.

"It's either that or you're out of food and hungry for breakfast," she added. "After yesterday I'm wishing mighty hard for hungry."

"I can work with hungry." At the moment my fridge contained BW's hot dogs for his daily treat and a grocery list for when I paid the water bill and could actually afford groceries. I turned on the kettle, snagged china cups from the cabinet, and put a bowl of apples on the table to give the appearance of a healthy breakfast in case somebody peeked in the window or one of us weakened and gave into a pang of good-nutrition conscience.

KiKi pulled a lemon/blueberry crumb cake from the antique pie safe that in my opinion beat the heck out of any other kind of safe. With Mamma being a single parent, Auntie KiKi and Uncle Putter were more Mamma and Daddy part two. I knew their house as well as the one on York. "Have you checked your tweets this morning?" I asked KiKi.

"Clara Martin didn't leave Reverend Sweetwater's house till well after midnight, but we all know the man's gay as a tree full of monkeys so that puts the kibosh on any hanky-panky going on, and Seymour's kicking the bucket is still top billing, but that's about it." KiKi stopped the knife slicing halfway though the cake, her lips pursing tight, drawing her face up like a shriveled kiwi. "Uh-oh, why are you asking?"

"Detective Ross picked Mamma up for questioning last night. Someone spiked that glass of honey bourbon on Scumbucket's desk with digitalis, bringing on the heart attack. Everyone and his brother knew Mamma was ticked off at Scumbucket and headed to his place with the liquor bottle to try and smooth things over, and then she decked him on the sidewalk. Someone's out to frame her."

"Glory be." KiKi sank into a chair, the knife still sticking out of the cake. "The old boy went and got himself done in." We both made the sign of the cross to counteract any feelings of just deserts we might be experiencing. "Where's Gloria now?"

"At the courthouse doing business as usual as a judge. No one's found the bottle she brought, so there's no actual evidence to link her to the murder. Right now everything's speculative. Mamma said she left the bottle on the desk, but it sure wasn't there when we showed up."

I took KiKi's hand. "You nearly drank from that very same glass. The cootie scare was the only thing between you and being there on a slab right beside Scummy."

Deep in thought, KiKi finished the slice, put the cake in my cup, then poured tea onto the sugar bowl. "Except there is a mighty big difference between my healthy self and Seymour. My ticker's fine as can be thanks to the superior Summerside gene pool and eight generations of Southern cholesterol adaptation."

KiKi tapped her finger against her lips. "Let's see, how does this go? The digitalis would have caused me problems sure enough, and I would have skedaddled off to the hospital to get checked out, but I could have been treated and been fine as frog's hair. Seymour had heart problems, and everyone knew about it, one foot on a banana peel so to speak. The alcohol dumped the digitalis in the bottle straight into his bloodstream and stopped his heart like hitting the brakes on a freight train. Bam!" KiKi clapped her hands together like a gunshot, making me and BW jump a foot. "The old coot was dead as a fence post in forty minutes, probably less."

I stared at KiKi wide-eyed, my heart still pounding. "You've been watching *Criminal Minds* again, haven't you? How do you sleep at night?"

"Forget TV." KiKi fluffed her rollers know-it-all style. "You can't be married to a cardiologist for thirty years without picking up a thing or two along the way."

"Well, that's it, then. Don't you see?" I said, jumping up suddenly happy as a pig in mud. "Mamma's innocent. Where the dickens would she get digitalis? She's a judge for crying out loud, not a doctor or a pharmacist. You don't just buy digitalis over the counter like bubble gum. Maybe someone who had access to Seymour's medication did the deed. Why did Ross go after Mamma at all? It makes no sense. Ross is on a witch hunt."

KiKi pulled me back down onto the chair and nodded out the bay window. "What do you see?"

"Grass."

"Oh for pity's sake, look a little harder."

"Sky, clouds, walkway, birdbath, garden maintained by delish Italian gardener with a great butt that every woman in Savannah wants to sink her teeth into."

KiKi gave me a long slow stare. "Where in the world did the gardener come from?"

"I have no idea." Actually I did, but I wasn't about to fess up about my sexless life in front of my dear, sweet auntie.

"Every single garden in Savannah is just like mine except for the delish gardener part," KiKi went on. "Why my oleander bush alone could wipe out all of Savannah."

"It's nothing but a bush."

"That's what you think. Nearly ever part is poisonous. If you even drink the water oleander flowers sit in, you're off to that great garden in the sky. If you mash up foxglove leaves, you have digitalis. The garden club did a program called Pretty Poisonous Posies last spring, and I couldn't eat anything green for a week. My guess is when the police crime lab autopsied Scumbucket the overdose of digitalis popped up, and the honey bourbon was the last thing he had to drink. Anyone wanting to get rid of the Scumbucket had the perfect opportunity with Gloria heading over to his place with a bottle of hooch. Scumbucket was high profile, and anyone who watches TV these days knows there'd be an autopsy. The killer pops in and poisons Seymour easy as can be, and Gloria Summerside winds up suspect number one."

"Mamma and Scumbucket argued, took it out onto the sidewalk, someone dumped in the digitalis, poured the drink, took the bottle, and left. How would they know Scumbucket would leave with Mamma?"

"It was a good possibility no matter how the meeting went that Seymour would leave his office sooner or later. He had stuff to do. Anyone with a button and a smile could mosey in just like we did."

"Boone said Seymour had enemies. My guess is one of them did him in."

"Oh, honey, your mamma has enemies, too, and their mean-looking ornery pictures once graced the walls of our local post office. They have families who aren't fond of your mamma one little bit. Framing her for murder would be sweet revenge indeed for the whole bunch. Either way, when the police find that bourbon bottle hidden somewhere, but not too well hidden, Gloria's goose is cooked. Her fingerprints will be all over it. The route from her campaign headquarters to Seymour's takes her right past her own house with foxglove foliage aplenty. Doesn't take much to mash up a few deadly leaves and be on her merry way. She has motive, means, and opportunity."

"But so far it's all circumstantial. There's no smoking gun or in this case bourbon bottle." I glanced at the clock trying to think of a good escape plan. I had an idea and didn't want KiKi in on it. "I've got to get the Fox ready, and you better get that green stuff off your face before it sticks permanent like. Don't you have some dance lessons this morning? I bet you have classes booked up all day with the Christmas cotillion right around the corner."

"Uh-oh. You're babbling and you're flipping your hair. You always flip your hair when you're into something you shouldn't be. Signing that prenup with Hollis nearly made you bald."

I grabbed a chunk of cake and stuffed it in my mouth to prevent more babbling and hurried out the door. The problem with family is they know all your quirks and you can't get away with squat. Whoever killed Scumbucket ditched the bottle somewhere it could be found like in Dumpsters, trash-cans, black plastic bags with smelly God knows what inside.

This was not the first dead-body event KiKi and I had encountered. Lately the two of us had an abundance of dead-body juju. I tried my darndest to keep dear auntie out of harm's way and spare her angst. Gross black bags and Dumpsters fell in the angst category. That KiKi got trapped on a rooftop and leaped from a fire escape meant I failed miserably in the harm's way category.

The cops would be looking for the liquor bottle, and they'd be doing it early before trash pickup. I didn't have much time to find that bottle! I gave BW a quick potty break, did the scoop thing, dropped the baggie in the trash, and stopped dead in my tracks. The heavens parted, a bright light shown down, and a choir of celestial angels sang the "Hallelujah Chorus." There, right in my very own garbage can, was a half-empty bottle of honey bourbon. I'm not one of those who believe God controls every little detail of our lives, but once in a while, the Big Guy above reaches down and saves the day.

I snagged a piece of paper towel from the garbage and plucked out the bottle. All I had to do was wipe it clean of fingerprints and throw it in the river for good measure and—

"Well, well what do we have there?" came Detective Ross's voice behind me.

My heart stopped dead. "Honey bourbon," I said. "I love the stuff." I faced Ross and two cops. "Need to get to an AA meeting." I was in babbling mode again and had no cake to save me.

"I'll take that bottle."

"Not without a search warrant you won't." KiKi had her cardio hubby, and I had my legal-eagle Mamma.

Ross reached in her purse that probably weighed as much as she did, pulled out a paper with the Chatham County seal on top, *Warrant* in the middle, and my address below signed by Judge Crooksy. Crooksy never did like Mamma. Ross snagged the bottle out of my hand and dropped it in a big plastic baggie. Her face morphed into a frown. "You should know that I hate doing this; I truly do. Your mamma is a fine judge and would be a terrific alderman. I get why she knocked off Seymour. If dirty politics were an Olympic event, he'd win the gold. Your mamma should have hidden the bottle in a better place, is all."

"See, that's just it," I said, trying to reason with Ross. "Don't you think it's a little odd that a criminal judge would make a stupid mistake like hiding damning evidence in such an obvious place as her daughter's garbage can? After all her years on the bench she'd know how to commit a perfect crime, right? This bottle was planted by the real killer; you've got to see that. Besides, Mamma would never toss glass into the garbage. She recycles!"

"Maybe she thought Seymour's death would be attributed to an accidental overdose of his heart medication and wouldn't go any further than that. Maybe she intended to come get the bottle later today. Maybe she thought the trash collectors would be here by now. And maybe you're right as rain. It's up to the DA and lawyers to prove what's what and sort out the facts. I'm just doing my job."

"But you're wrong."

Ross and cohorts drove off with the damning bottle, and KiKi hurried across her perfect Kentucky bluegrass and onto my Georgia weed grass. She was barefoot, orange hair rollers still in place, red dancing skirt swirling around her knees, and a blotch of green still clinging to the tip of her nose. "Why was Ross here? I saw her out the bedroom window. I do declare the woman's like the plague. Having her around wreaks havoc and mayhem on us all."

"There was a honey bourbon bottle in my garbage of all places, and my guess is it's the one Mamma brought to Scumbucket's place. Now Ross is off to match fingerprints, and then she'll arrest Mamma."

KiKi plopped right down on the grass, red skirt billowing up, giving her a stuffed-tomato appearance. "Oh, honey. Jail's a mighty bad place if you're a cop; it's got to be even worse if you're a criminal judge."

My mouth went dry. I hadn't even thought of that. Mamma's situation had just gone from bad to disastrous. I hauled KiKi to her feet. "You get to Mamma and protect her somehow till I get there. I'm going to see a man about life insurance. Hurry."

I locked BW inside then hoofed it down Gwinnett. Ross was gonna do what she had to do, and I had to get Mamma help from someone experienced with the inner workings of jail. My knowledge about the place came from watching *Law and Order* when I had a TV and playing Monopoly when I was a kid.

Without wheels I was on first-name basis with the drivers of the Savannah mass-transit system known as Old Gray. I stood in the street and waved my arms over my head. The bus growled to a halt, double doors folded back, and a woman resembling Ice Cube—the younger years, minus the facial hair—peered down at me.

"Girl, you know this ain't no taxi that picks you up when you feel the need. You're supposed to get yourself to an official stop and wait like everyone else in this here city for the bus to come to you."

"Earlene." I jumped inside so she couldn't motor on without me. "I have a situation."

"You always got a situation." She tipped back her navy uniform cap and drummed her fingers on the steering wheel, waiting for me to deposit my fare.

"I sort of ran off without my purse, and I need to get to Seventeenth Street."

"Seventeenth Street?" Her eyes arched over her sunglasses, and the four passengers on board scurried out the rear door. "You need to get yourself somewhere else."

"I'll pay you twice tomorrow, I swear."

More finger drumming, eyes on the fare box, no bus movement.

"I'll bring you a meatloaf sandwich from Parker's, throw in a pickle and two chocolate chip cookies."

I got a tapping foot and a finger jabbing where my money should be. Time was of the essence, and I was getting nowhere. Mamma could be in big trouble right this very minute. "I'll . . . I'll fix you up with Big Joey." Did I really say that?

The finger drumming stopped. Earlene sat back in her cushy seat. "You wouldn't be stringing old Earlene along just to get your way, now would you? I have brothers. I know where you live."

"Big Joey and I are tight." I held up two fingers, crossed them good-buddy style. "I'm going over to his place to ask a favor right now."

"Well, tickle my giblets and call me Butterball." Old Gray lurched forward. I grabbed for the nearest silver pole and held on for dear life. "Girl, you done got yourself a deal. Always wanted to be hanging off that man's arm. He is one fine-looking stud. For some quality time with Big Joey, I can make this baby fly like the wind."

Ten minutes later, after jumping curbs and scaring the dickens out of a flock of tourists, I arrived at the corner of Seventeenth Street and got me the heck off this thing.

"So when's Mr. Hot-Stuff going to be giving me a call?" Earlene asked as I leaped to the ground, sheer willpower keeping me from kneeling down and kissing the sidewalk.

"Soon, very soon." I pictured St. Peter putting a big *X* next to my name for when I got to the Pearly Gates after Big Joey tossed my lifeless carcass in the nearest alligator infested swamp. But I'd deal with all that later. I gave Earlene a little finger wave as she motored off, then headed down Seventeenth Street.

The houses were smaller in this part of town, closer, rougher. Yards were more red clay than green grass. Massive limbs of live oaks draped a green awning over the streets and cracked sidewalks. Spanish moss gave a touch of tired quaintness. Three brothers fell in step behind me. Well, gee whiz, my very own private escort complete with politically incorrect comments accompanying totally gross slurpy sounds.

This would be a little unnerving to a novice Seventeenth Street invader, but I'd been here before. Sometimes it worked out better than others. Big Joey's house was nestled between two pink crape myrtle trees that would make the Savannah garden club salivate. I climbed the gray weathered stairs to the porch and rapped on the door.

"White woman. What you doing here on my porch?" Joey asked, giving my companions the it's-cool nod. Today Joey had on Diesel jeans, a green T-shirt that fit like a second skin, showing off well-tuned biceps polished to an Armor All sheen, and sideburns trailing onto his chin. Seventeenth Street Savannah does *The Wire*.

"I need another favor."

"Do tell." Joey came out on the porch and parked his very nice backside on the porch railing. "What I get?"

"The gratitude of a criminal judge or at least a criminal judge's daughter. Ross is arresting Mamma as we speak. She'll get out on bail, but she'll be in jail for a few hours, and it may not be good for her health if you get my drift."

"She should get private accommodations; she's a judge."

"But if she doesn't and she's in with others who have it in for her . . ."

Big Joey shoved his hands in his pockets. "My cousin's doing a nickel upstate 'cause of your mamma."

"Did he deserve it?"

"There is that." Big Joey slid an iPhone from his pocket

and punched around on the screen. "Done. Mamma bear safe and sound. Guillotine Gloria is one hardass, but fair. Besides, she and Boone are tight, and you got to respect that."

Before I could ask, respect what?, Big Joey looked at his phone and read, "Says Ross is at the courthouse now and some woman is having herself a flat-out hissy fit." He turned the phone screen my way, showing me the picture.

"That's my auntie KiKi. I gotta go."

Big Joey grinned as I hopped down the steps. "Your family never disappoints. Later, babe."

I headed for West Oglethorpe. To save going around the block I darted in the back door of Ma Hanna's Chicken and Waffles and out the front door, snagging a chicken leg along the way thanks to my giving Hanna a good price on a Coach purse the other day. I cut across the Civic Center and arrived at the courthouse half dead from overexertion but well fed with my drumstick. Usually the center of our local judicial system was a hubbub of subdued activity, the guilty of Savannah content to keep their sins on the QT. Today, "Leave my sister be!" echoed through the corridors.

Oh sweet Jesus! Kiki had herself spread-eagle across Mamma's courtroom doors.

"I have to do my job," Ross said. "That's why the taxpayers pay me. Back away, Miss KiKi. You're only making things worse."

"Never! Like Cher says, 'Someone has to pay for the frogs and dancing fairies.'"

"What are you doing?" I asked KiKi after I elbowed my way to the front of the crowd. "What do frogs and fairies have to do with anything?"

Auntie KiKi cut her eyes my way. "It's a mite tense

around here in case you didn't notice. That's the only Cher quote I could think of. You told me to protect Gloria, and I'm protecting her best I know how. Should have brought along Putter's nine iron for good measure."

"I need a doughnut bad," Ross muttered on a long sigh while rubbing her forehead. She nodded to the officers beside her, and they peeled Auntie KiKi off the doors and put her in handcuffs as Mamma erupted into the hall, black robes trailing behind.

"What in heaven's name is going on, KiKi? Why are you here? What is this all about?"

"Judge Gloria Summerside," Ross said, pulling another set of handcuffs from her purse for those days when two bad guys—or gals—had to get hauled off to the poky. "You are under arrest for the murder of Kipling Seymour. You have the right to remain silent . . ."

I lost the rest in a flurry of gasps, picture taking, and the swelling multitude of kibitzers reveling in the irony of a judge getting arrested.

"You can't do this." KiKi's voice ricocheted off the walls. "I'll sue. I'll protest. I won't teach your kids the fox-trot."

I grabbed Ross's arm and looked her dead in the eyes. "That's my mamma and my auntie you've got there. You can't put them both in jail."

Ross glared at my hand. "You looking to join the party?"

"I don't care what you do to me, but you can't lock up my fam—" I was yanked backward into the crowd, my protests dying in my throat as I struggled not to fall on my behind while Ross, the cops, Mamma, and Auntie KiKi paraded on to the slammer.

Chapter Four

"LET me go!"

Boone hustled me out of the courthouse through the arched doorway and around the corner to the parking lot. Yanking open the door of the Chevy, he pushed me in. "For your mother's sake, calm down."

I shoved against the door, but with big, bad, and ugly leaning against it the door didn't budge. "What are you doing here?"

"Keeping you out of jail. Any more Summersides arrested today and Ross loses the paperwork and you all spend the night in a concrete room sharing facilities with the underbelly of Savannah society. And Big Joey wants you safe and sound. Something about settling a score over a bus driver sitting on his front porch."

It wasn't even ten, and I had my family behind bars and Big Joey less than thrilled with my matchmaking efforts. I gulped in some breaths to clear my brain and get my blood pressure below raving lunatic. "How long will it take Mamma and KiKi to get out?"

"A few hours with the right attorney. Go home. Run your shop. You can ride shotgun or in the trunk. Your mother's done me a couple of favors over the years, and I'm doing likewise getting you out of the way."

Boone took the driver's side, and I stayed put. He'd toss me in the trunk in a heartbeat. The Chevy circled Franklin Square, named after favorite son Ben, and headed across West Congress. It would be a great day to be cruising in a convertible if my world wasn't crumbling down around my ears. "Can we at least stop at the Cakery Bakery?"

"You had a chicken leg. Quit whining."

"Okay, since you're such a smartass and know about Mamma and my chicken leg and Big Joey, maybe you know who knocked off Seymour. In case you didn't get the memo, things are looking particularly bad for Mamma, and best I can figure, it's someone who didn't like Seymour and is using Mamma as a patsy or someone out to get even with Mamma."

We stopped for a light, a campaign poster of Gloria Summerside adorned with mustache and devil horns staring back at me, activating little gray cells in my brain. "Or maybe . . ."

"Forget *or maybe*, Blondie. Nothing good comes from you and maybe."

"Or maybe someone who doesn't want Seymour *or* Mamma elected. It's just two weeks till the election. There's got to be a connection between the campaign and Seymour's death. Why not just off the jackass any old time."

I felt instantly better with an actual alternative suspect in my sites. "Archie Lee! He's the third candidate. Mamma and Scumbucket are out of the picture, and Archie Lee wins the election. Bingo! Perfect fit."

"Scumbucket?"

"If the shoe fits . . ."

Boone pulled up in front of Cherry House, put the car in neutral, and turned my way. "Archie Lee was put on the ballot one fine Saint Patrick's Day by a city full of inebriated individuals as a tribute to their favorite bar and bartender. At the time it seemed like a good idea."

"You were in on it?"

"Green beer makes people do strange things. Seymour's death doesn't have to be connected to the election. Might be a murder of convenience with Gloria showing up mad as a hornet. Seymour bites the dust, and the police have their suspect. All very neat and no one poking around because the killer is obvious."

"Or maybe Archie Lee likes the limelight that goes beyond serving drinks at the Cemetery and has his eye on being alderman. Kill two birds with one honey bourbon bottle, and he's sitting on city council."

Boone did the dismissive-shrug thing. "I'll look into it."

"No you won't; I know you. *I'll* look into it."

"You start poking around and everyone will clam up."

"I'll be discreet.

"Getting run into a swamp, dragged into an alley, trapped under a bookshelf, and strangled by a pissed-off boat captain doesn't happen to people who are discreet. You don't have a discreet bone in your body. Staying off your mother's case is the best way to help her."

A growl crawled up my throat. "This is the woman who changed my diapers, kissed my boo-boos, and didn't say I told you so when I caught Hollis doing the Hokey Pokey with Cupcake. If it were your mother, would you do nothing?"

Boone's face went instantly blank, not one readable flinch or blink. During my divorce, while sitting in Boone's cherry-paneled office grinding my teeth and visualizing his head on a silver platter, I learned a few things about the guy. He was hardworking, arrogant, conceited, a pain in the butt, and liked a little coffee with his cream and sugar. I knew Boone the lawyer and considered Big Joey and Pillsbury his siblings of the hood. I knew zip about Boone in the early years, how he wound up a lawyer, but somewhere I hit a nerve.

He didn't look like he wanted to chat about it at the moment. I got out of the car and parked my hands on my hips. "We have different ways of doing things is all."

"I have connections; you rattle everyone's cage till something escapes and has you for dinner. Stay away from the courthouse." Boone put the car in gear and motored down Gwinnett.

I trudged up the sidewalk, got the daily cash from the safe that was actually a rocky road ice cream container in the freezer. I let BW out to irrigate the front yard then sat down on the top step of the porch . . . alone. Usually Auntie KiKi was with me along with coffee or a martini or two or three as we dished the dirt on Savannah society or lately tried to figure out the latest murder. Right now I had no KiKi or martini or suspect . . . except for Archie Lee.

The Cemetery was a watering hole for locals with the best boiled peanuts on the planet. Using Old Bay spice was the secret that wasn't really much of a secret, but Archie Lee had fine-tuned the technique. The bar was across from Colonial Park Cemetery, a convenient location if things got out of hand and ended badly, and two doors up from Urgent Care if things just got marginally out of hand. Having a face-to-face with Archie Lee about motives and murder may not be a prudent idea on my part, but I'd never been a slave to prudence, and Archie Lee was the only lead I had at the moment.

That gave me a plan, something to work on, something to cling to in finding the killer. The day would improve, I convinced myself as I flipped the Closed sign in the bay window to Open. Least that's what I thought till I spied Marigold Haber in full election regalia of vest, pin, and straw hat strutting her way up my sidewalk, huge cardboard box in hand.

"I do declare what a morning this has been." Marigold plopped the box on the green checkout door and swiped a stray curl off her forehead. "Gloria's arrested and the owner of the HotDoggery just evicted us. Do you believe such a thing! Said he's not having a murderer for a tenant, that it'll give the place a bad name."

Marigold held out her hands in total disbelief. "They sold processed meat, for crying out loud, with enough added nitrates to kill a small army. Now that's a bad name if you ask me. I was beside myself with worry not knowing what to do or where to go with your mamma's campaign head-quarters, and then it came to me clear as a bell."

Marigold gazed around my shop, a euphoric grin tripping across her face. "You have a parlor and a kitchen that's empty as a schoolhouse in summer since you sold off all your furniture to pay your bills on this place, such as it is."

Gee, thanks. "I have kids clothes in the parlor now."

"Why this here hall is plenty big enough to accommodate

those little bitty things, and there's nothing around but used clothes anyway, so it's not like we're upsetting anything important. We'll be setting up shop and working from here. We can store the banners and placards in the kitchen."

Marigold grabbed my shoulders, her eyes moist. "You're such a good daughter, Reagan. Your mamma will be mighty proud of you helping out like this in her time of great need." She kissed my cheek. "Mighty proud indeed."

Jiminy Christmas, Marigold was playing the proud parent card. She'd just insulted my business and me and my house, but any child south of the Ohio River will do whatever it takes to make Mamma and Daddy proud. *Mighty proud indeed* are the magic words that get kids to play football instead of chess, attend church on Sunday mornings even if they sleep through the sermon, take dance lessons instead of skateboarding, and apply to the University of Georgia instead of Stanford. I was toast, and Marigold knew it.

"We'll all have such a fine time together in this old place, don't you agree?" Marigold beamed, a twinkle in her eye. "Keep up each other's spirits till the real killer is behind bars where he or she belongs. I already called the phone people, and they should be here any minute now to run more phone and fax lines for us to get things going."

Marigold poked her head out the front door, stuck her thumb and finger in her mouth, and let go with a piercing· un-belle-like whistle. Three cars screeched to the curb.

"Now that I think about it," Marigold said to me, "getting evicted is a blessing in disguise. We won't have to pay rent and rely on donations that are sure to dry up with all this bad publicity circulating like it is." She raised her right hand, looking a bit like Paula Deen and the Statue of Liability all rolled into one. "We're not giving up, no siree Bob. Onward and upward in the election polls."

Marigold headed for the parlor located off the dining room followed by a string of chatty women trooping in the front door lugging more boxes, chairs, laptops, and a cappuccino/espresso/latte machine.

"This way, ladies, follow me," Marigold called over her shoulder as a U-Haul truck parked in KiKi's driveway. Since KiKi hadn't mentioned anything about moving and Savannah burglars had more smarts than to fleece a place in broad daylight, this was more campaign stuff headed my way.

"Oh and, honey," Lolly Ledbetter said as she passed me, adding a schoolteacher finger wag for emphasis, "you might want to take care of those dark roots you got going on. Not attractive at all for the candidate's daughter."

"And for heaven's sake," Dottie chimed in, "stand up straight." Dottie went to high school with Mamma and used to be Miss Six o'clock News on WSAV. She knew all about standing straight. "The press and TV reporters come calling around, and you don't need to be slouching around like an addle-minded teenager."

My left eye started to twitch as I spied Chantilly entering through the kitchen, steps slowing, eyes widening at the continuing chaos. "What's going on around here?" She dodged two men lugging a table, BW hid under the checkout door, and three customers coming up the walk took one look at the confusion and fled for their lives.

"I got to find Scumbucket's killer and do it quick," I said, my voice shaky. I grabbed Chantilly's hand and dragged her over to the parlor doorway, the volunteers fixing up, setting up, and plugging in. "They got kicked out of Mamma's campaign headquarters over on Broughton. This is me having a roomful of mothers."

"Mothers like in PB and J sandwiches with the little crusts cut off?"

"Like mind your manners, no kissing on the front porch, what time did you get in last night, and don't trust bad boys." I felt my eyes start to cross. "I can't take it. We need to go to the Cemetery tonight and see Archie Lee. I'm hoping he's the killer; he's got the most to gain with two opponents out of the way."

"And you intend to tell him that to his face?"

"I was thinking of wording it a little better."

"How do you get into these messes?" Chantilly asked. Then we both made the sign of the cross.

AT THREE O'CLOCK THE PEARL-GIRLS ALONG WITH some of the good-old-boys were in full campaign mode; the Prissy Fox not so much. Ringing phones, cranking fax machines and printers did not add to the ambiance of a shopping experience and were killing dead what was gearing up to be my best month so far for Prissy Fox sales. But an even worse problem was that there was no sign of Mamma or KiKi. Boone said it would take a few hours to get bail arranged, but five was more than a few. Five was many . . . too many. I was done with being cautious and standing around doing nothing. I didn't care what Boone said; I was headed straight for a full-blown panic attack and the police station to get my family out of jail if I had to rent a backhoe and level the place to do it.

Grabbing Old Yeller I made for the door as the Beemer

squealed into KiKi's drive. She jumped out, grinned, held up to-go cups with Jen's and Friends stenciled in blue on the sides, then cha-chaed her way across the grass/weed patch separating our properties.

I threw my arms around her. "What happened? What took so long? Are you and Mamma all right?"

KiKi sipped from her cup and handed me the other one. "I got us strawberry martinis to celebrate my new do." She did a little twirl. "What do you think? I'm plum gorgeous, don't you agree?"

I plopped down on the top step of the porch. "You stopped off to get your hair done?"

KiKi parked next to me. "Didn't have to. Mercedes did it right there in the slammer. Your mamma looks terrific. Got rid of that old bob thing she had going on. We hung around for a while so Mercedes could show us how to do the curling part. She's coming over tomorrow to put in highlights. I'm going to teach her the rumba."

I took a sip of martini, little gray brain cells starting to function. "Waitaminute. You stayed in jail on purpose because you wanted to? What happened to shivs and dope and being somebody's bitch before noon?" I took a big gulp of martini. "Where the heck's Mamma?"

"Oh, honey, even Martha Stewart taught knitting while incarcerated. Must be a new trend these days. Mercedes took a liking to us right off, and we passed the time away. Your mamma's back at her house safe and sound without a reporter in sight thanks to Betty Lou Harris and her marital difficulties. Seems she found her Dwain with two prostitutes over there at the Weston, and she went and shot his do-da clean off. I'm here to tell you that a dismembered private part trumps fingerprints on a liquor bottle any day of the week. Sorry I missed all that hoopla, had to be some sight. Heard tell Jerry Springer is headed this way. He's gearing up to do a show about using it and losing it."

KiKi finished her martini, eyes not focusing as she sucked two strawberries right off the toothpick and nodded at the open door. "So what's going on around here?"

"Business sucks. Mamma's campaign headquarters moved into the Prissy Fox, and I've been told to stand up straight and put on lipstick like I'm an addle-minded teenager. I should have gone to jail with you."

KiKi gave me a kiss on the forehead. "Come up with any ideas on who polished off Scumbucket?"

I did the clueless hunch and KiKi tsked. "Poppycock. You're lying like a rug. I can tell a mile away. You should be ashamed of yourself, fibbing to your dear auntie that way after she just got out of jail."

She snatched my martini right out of my hand. "But I got to lay low tonight anyway, so don't go snooping around on your own. Putter's coming home, and it's going to take all my womanly wiles to explain away me being in jail. Thought I'd go with 'I was just there waiting for Gloria to get sprung.'"

"And leave out that you were in the pokey with her while waiting? I suppose that's not exactly a lie."

"The way I see it, this falls under the category of selective absentmindedness. Anyone in AARP has the right. I do believe it says so right there on the bottom of the card." KiKi winked, gulped down the rest of my martini, followed by an appreciative burp, then sashayed her way across the yard to Rose Gate.

Lolly Ledbetter came out the front door, the guys and

gals of Campaigns-R-Us in tow. They gave a little wave as they left, and Lolly said, "We're meeting up at your mamma's tonight to talk damage control. She's calling a press conference first thing tomorrow morning before Seymour's funeral to say her being at the police station was a misunderstanding."

"Think they'll buy it?"

"Not for a minute, and that's what they'll write, but we're not giving up. All of us will be back here tomorrow except me. It's my day to run the trolley."

Lolly sat down beside me and heaved a weary sigh. "This isn't the way it was supposed to be, you know. Nowadays, Cazy takes Monday, Wednesdays, Fridays, and I do Lolly's Trolley the rest of the time. Used to be the trolley was just a hobby of mine for when the kids went off to college, and I liked sharing the wonders of our fair city with visiting folks. Since Cazy lost his job at the savings and loan the trolley's turned out to be our bread and butter."

Lolly took my hand and grabbed tight, a steely glint in her eyes. "I'm sorry your mamma got nailed for whacking Seymour, but no one deserves being whacked and buried more than that man. He was evil clear through to the bone. Amen, hallelujah, and good riddance, I say."

Lolly headed for her car, and BW gave the yard a good sniffing in search of squirrels, rabbits, or chipmunks daring to invade his space. Boone said Scumbucket had enemies. I never considered the fact that Lolly was one of those enemies and working on Mamma's campaign to make sure Scumbucket didn't get elected as alderman.

I went back inside to finally enjoy a moment of peace and quiet till I heard the printer grinding away in the parlor and found Marigold Haber sitting alone at one of the long tables stuffing envelopes. "You should be the one running for office considering all the hours you put in on this campaign," I said to her.

"Oh, Lordy, no. Put a microphone in front of me, and I sound like a cracked record. Besides, Butler's a dinner-on-the-table-at-five and did-you-pick-up-my-blue-suit-at-the-cleaners kind of husband."

"Honey, it's after five."

"Imagine that." Marigold forced a tight smile, but her eyes looked more sad than happy. "Where does the time go?" Seemed like she meant that for more than just today. She turned off the printer and snagged a handful of flyers and her black purse that was showing a bit of wear.

"I'm off to see your mamma," she said. "We're going to win this here election if it's the last thing I do. Gloria deserves it, she's worked hard all her life, and I'm going to make it happen for both our sakes. See you tomorrow, honey, and pick out something a little more fashionable than shoes held together with glue. You can see it oozing right out the side."

Business picked up a bit without the hubbub of the campaign buzzing in the background. As I scurried around taking in clothes to consign and ringing up sales, I thought about the good old days that were less than twenty-four hours ago. Life turned on a dime . . . or a honey bourbon bottle.

At eight sharp two honks at the curb heralded Chantilly's arrival, and I hurried out to the Jeep idling under the street-light. "Great outfit," I said as I climbed in, eyeing Chantilly's green skirt, short boots, and tan suede jacket. "Win the lottery?"

The Jeep turned for Abercorn, night settling in over the city and tucking it in for the night. "It's part of last year's splurge when I was gainfully employed with UPS. I so need a job. I go on interviews, and employers take one look at me and say, 'Hey, you're that girl.' Being tied to Simon's murder isn't helping my chances one little bit."

Riding a horse naked on YouTube didn't enhance Chantilly's resume much either, but she felt bad enough at the moment without me throwing that in the mix.

"I told Pillsbury you and I were headed for the Cemetery," Chantilly added. "Said he'd stop on by, doesn't want anyone infringing on his territory. That means me. Isn't that the sweetest thing you ever heard? And another big reason I need a job. I need rent. Moving back in with my parents is out of the question. If ex-cop daddy gets wind of Pillsbury and me together, that there conflict with the Yankees a while back will look like a tiny skirmish in comparison."

"Your daddy thinks you sit home knitting?"

"Told him I was dating an accountant and that part happens to be the God's honest truth. Pillsbury's a full-fledged certified public accountant for Pete's sake. What more could Daddy ask for, right?"

"That Pillsbury's *public* wasn't the Seventeenth Street gang? But then I married Hollis the horse's patoot when everyone told me not to, so I'm not one to be giving advice or throwing stones."

Chantilly found a parking spot, and we hoofed it the few blocks to the bar. The Cemetery was old as dirt. Many moons ago Sherman's soldiers downed a few pints at the place, and more than one wound up poisoned, buried in the basement, and left wandering the halls of this fine establishment to this day . . . or so we haunted Savannah tour guides liked to elaborate. The present day Cemetery was known for beer cocktails such as Black and Tans. Translation: pale ale, Guinness, with a taste like burnt tar with a dash of roadkill.

The place was long and narrow; wood bar lining one side; mismatched tables; ESPN on the tube; neon signs for Miller, Samuel Adams, Heineken, and the like dotting the wall; peanut shells on the floor. It was always in various stages of busy and tonight even more so because right above the old mahogany mirrored bar was a big red, white, and blue sign proclaiming "Archie Lee . . . wins!"

"What do you think about that?" I asked Chantilly, both of us staring at the proclamation.

"In hopes of a nice, peaceful night how about we go with this here sign being the power of positive thinking, and confidence is a virtue?"

"What about overconfidence? Sounds suspicious if you ask me. A little too overly positive considering Mamma hasn't been found guilty. I wonder what Archie Lee has to say for himself?"

Chantilly headed for the bar. "Sweet mother in heaven, it's gonna be one of those nights, I can tell."

Chapter Five

CHANTILLY and I commandeered two stools at the end of the bar and ordered Miller Lights. "This seat taken?" Pillsbury sallied up to Chantilly, draping his piggy bank–tattooed arm around her, followed by a kiss on the cheek. He and I exchanged pleasantries, but the lovebirds were soon lost in their own little world, leaving me to come up with a tactful way to accuse Archie Lee of knocking off Scumbucket and framing Mamma. Archie Lee had the looks and temperament of Danny DeVito, making him one popular barkeep . . . usually. Heard tell the flipside was Archie Lee provoked.

"So," I said over the din as Archie Lee refilled my bowl of boiled peanuts. "The election's looking pretty good for you with Seymour and Summerside out of the way."

"Need another beer?"

"How do you like campaigning?"

A barmaid called out an order, and Archie pulled the spigot on two beers, foam running over the top and dripping down the side.

"We don't serve champagne here. We're a beer and whiskey joint," Archie yelled back to me and handed off the mugs to the waitress as another patron elbowed in with an order for three Black and Blues, another one of those burnt tar drinks.

Okay, this was going nowhere. The place was crowded, Archie Lee was busy as a one-armed paperhanger in a windstorm, and I needed someone who liked to chat. I tossed a few bills on the bar, dumped the nuts in a basket on the nearest table, and went in search of a boiled-peanut refill along with information. A hallway with chipped green paint and century-old dinged chair rail led out the back, and I followed it, taking a detour toward some racket and a small kitchen area.

"What are you doing back here?" a guy with Popeye muscles and Dr. Phil hair asked. Using a canoe paddle, he stirred a huge pot boiling over an old black stove propped up on one side by a two-by-four chunk of wood.

Being all Little Miss Dazed and Confused, I held up my empty basket. "Looking for a peanut refill. They're kind of busy out front, thought I'd try back here. Well, my goodness gracious, is this how you make them?"

"They don't make themselves, sweetheart. You got to leave. This is no place to be."

"Everyone thinks you all make the best boiled peanuts in Savannah. Hope that doesn't stop now that Archie Lee might wind up an alderman. You think he's really serious about taking the job?"

"Looking forward to it as best I can tell. I can handle things around here when he's off being mister good citizen." Popeye popped the tops on twelve bottles of Guinness, dumped them into the caldron, then added boxes of Old Bay seasoning. He stirred the brew, yellow flames licking up the sides, spicy steam wafting over the top.

"Why get involved in politics when he has the bar? He's already got enough work just like this to keep him busy."

"Got that right." Popeye added a behemoth bag of green nuts and gave another swirl with the paddle. "Got to cook them for a long time to kill the toxins, and you need a big old stove like this to get things hot enough. Archie Lee's got this down to a science."

Popeye glanced at me through the haze, little droplets of sweat collecting on his unibrow. "Why do you care about Archie Lee anyway? You think he's not smart enough to be with those knuckleheads down at city hall? He didn't finish high school, but he's plenty smart enough. He'll be great in politics; he's honest and works for the little guy, not like that rich snotty judge or a hotshot builder with all his mountains of money and . . ."

His voice trailed off as a spark of recognition lit his black eyes. "Hey, I know you, you're that judge's daughter." A sinister tone crept into Popeye's voice. "What are you doing back here? What do you want from me?"

"Nuts." I made my blue plastic basket do a little dance in the air and added a sugar-sweet smile. The smile never worked with teachers when I forgot to do my homework, but I was hoping for a better outcome now.

"You're not here for nuts; you're here for trouble. You're thinking Archie Lee knocked off Seymour then framed your mamma. Archie Lee said that might happen. He figured that judge and her police friends would try and pin the murder on him. All you rich people stick together and screw us little guys, and you don't care who gets hurt."

"You want little guy, I'll show you little guy." I slid off my shoe and held it up. "Are you wearing stuff held together with super glue? You call that rich? I'm not rich, and my mamma is not snooty."

Popeye stepped around the two-by-four holding up the stove and pointed his paddle to the door. "Get out while the getting's good." He backed me toward the hall, me hopping in that direction on one shoed foot. "Archie Lee and I are brothers, and don't you forget it. Mind your own beeswax if you know what's good for you and your mamma."

I stopped and stood my ground. "No one threatens my mamma."

"And who's going to stop me? The scrawny likes of you?" Least he said I was scrawny.

"Hey," came Archie Lee's voice echoing down the hall. "What's going on back here?"

"We got ourselves a pest problem," Popeye said over his shoulder, giving me the chance to dart for the door, yank it open, and hobble out onto a rickety loading dock in the alley. Safe at last, except that Big Joey was crossing the street twenty feet away. I wasn't in the mood to deal with the Big Joey/Earlene situation. Heck, I had just escaped the Archie Lee/Popeye situation.

Hopping again, I ducked behind the Dumpster till something with beady black eyes, twitching whiskers, and a long skinny tail scurried across my one and only foot on the ground. I slapped my hand over my mouth and tried not to scream. I really did try, but the scream jumped out anyway, and I leaped from behind the Dumpster. Big Joey looked up, frowned, and headed my way. This was all Chantilly's fault, I realized. She said it was going to be one of those nights. She'd jinxed it.

A lonely bulb lighting the back alley silhouetted Big Joey, proving beyond all doubt how he got the *big* attached to his name. Not that I was actually afraid of the guy, but I hated being on his bad side, and the Earlene state of affairs put me there big-time. On more than one occasion he had saved my butt; my reciprocity consisted mostly of comic relief and getting in the way.

"I'm sorry," I said at the same time Big Joey blurted, "Apologies, babe." We stared at each other for a beat, both of us confused.

"Why are you apologizing?" I said. "I'm the one who dropped Earlene on your doorstep."

Big Joey nodded toward the back entrance of the bar. "Hanging with Earlene presently. No bird but true and tight, and that counts." Meaning Earlene wasn't a hot young chickie, but she was someone you could count on and she was nice. My bilingual skills were improving.

"How Mamma make out?" Big Joey asked. "My inside man buzzed to a new area. Not cool."

"You didn't arrange for Mercedes?"

"The ride?"

"The woman. She looked out for Mamma and my auntie KiKi, and I thought you got her there somehow."

A flicker of recognition sparked Big Joey's eyes, a slow smile on his lips. "*That* Mercedes."

"Meaning . . . ?"

"It's all good." He eyed the shoe and basket, the grin expanding. "Troubles?"

"A little misunderstanding."

"Keep it real, babe. Gotta bounce." Big Joey took the backdoor into the bar, and I slid on my shoe and hung the basket from the doorknob. I headed for Mamma's house. The campaign meeting had to be over by now, and I needed to check that she was okay with my own two eyes. Besides, I was dying to see her new do.

A stiff breeze off the ocean made me button my denim jacket and turn up my collar. Thank the Lord Savannah never got beyond jacket cold. Snow was an occasional fluke, and icy conditions were found only in sweet tea and drinks on the veranda.

I cut across Oglethorpe Square catching a glimpse of the Owens-Thomas House and wondering if Miss Margaret strolled the gardens tonight. She died back in '51 of course, but that didn't mean she didn't take a stroll now and then. This was Savannah after all.

I turned onto York as Walker Boone ambled down Mamma's front sidewalk and got into the Chevy. Okay, what was with Mamma and Boone? There was a connection, but what and why? I did my stop-the-bus routine of standing in the street, waving, and looking ridiculous. Considering the night I'd had so far, the ridiculous part fit right in. Boone hit the brakes, and I took the passenger side.

"You and Archie Lee have a nice visit?" he asked.

"Don't know if I'd jump right to nice. You do realize he has a victory banner right there in his bar? He knows liquor, and his brother knows about toxins from plants. Sounds like a murder suspect to me, and the Cemetery is sure in a party mood. I think he did it; he knocked off Scumbucket and framed Mamma."

"You really think Archie Lee would advertise winning if he killed off the competition?"

"It's genius. He looks innocent and simply the beneficiary of an unfortunate . . . or fortunate, depending on your point of view . . . occurrence that just happened to fall his way. He's just one lucky guy, real lucky. I wonder where Mr. Lucky was when Seymour got knocked off."

"You going to ask him?"

"Is there some reason you're at Mamma's?"

Boone pulled the convertible to the curb. "There's a new sheriff in town, and it's going to muddy the waters. They're bringing in a detective from Atlanta. Ross is second fiddle on this case. You're mother's well liked by the police here, and this new guy is to make sure there're no cover-ups. It's good in that when Gloria's found innocent, the prosecuting attorney can't cry foul play, because there's an outside source."

"Putting a judge away could be a feather in Atlanta boy's cap. Did you ever consider that?"

"He'll be fair."

I made a strangling sound of disbelief.

"Keep in mind he won't think twice about throwing your meddling butt behind bars for obstruction of justice."

I got out of the car. "And what if Atlanta boy catches you snooping around?"

Boone gave me a fat-chance eye roll and motored off. The porch light was still on at Mamma's, meaning she hadn't gone to bed. I gave a little knock and went inside. Mamma met me in the front hall. Her hair was flipped out instead of tucked under, her bangs swept to the side and tucked behind her ear. I touched a strand. "You look mighty fetching, Judge Summerside."

Mamma smiled, then sobered. "What in all that's holy happened to you? You're all dirty. What have you been up to? More alleys?"

"It's all Chantilly's fault. Do you know this detective from Atlanta?"

"Bet you didn't have dinner." Mamma led the way to the kitchen, updated last year with marble counters and white cabinets. "I haven't met the detective, but I'm sure he'll be fair."

"That's what Boone said." I sat at the old yellow pine table where Mamma and I had shared meals since I was two and that had thankfully escaped the upgrade.

Mamma smiled. "You got to trust the system, honey."

Mamma was all serene and peaceful as she took ham and roast beef from the fridge like when I was in grade school bellyaching about math class. She pulled out a loaf of sourdough bread and the mayo. "You really do mean it, don't you? About trusting the system."

"What kind of judge would I be if I didn't?" She added lettuce and cheese, and sat the sandwich in front of me, a blue linen napkin beside it. Sometimes you can go home again . . . at least for a little bit.

"How did you know I was hungry?" I got up and washed my hands at the sink, and Mamma nodded at the pile of campaign posters.

"I have spies. Your refrigerator's empty, and your dog eats better than you do."

"Who do you think killed Seymour?" I asked, and

reclaimed my seat. I snatched the sandwich and chowed down.

"Hard to say."

"Who's your attorney?" I mumbled around a mouthful of sublime comfort food, thankful for a break in the action. I plucked up a slice of Swiss that had escaped and plopped it into my mouth. How could something with holes taste so good?

Mamma rewrapped the cold cuts and cheese, and cleaned up crumbs that weren't there. "I'm working on that one."

"Any front runners?"

"I'll get somebody good. This could be dangerous. Seymour was a dangerous guy. I don't want to involve just anyone in my problems." Mamma folded then refolded the kitchen towel twice, and I put down my sandwich—so much for peace and calm. I wasn't the only one with idiosyncrasies that gave me away. With Mamma it was making busy work when she didn't want to give straight answers. The time she donated my favorite jeans to the Goodwill by mistake she arranged all the pens in the house by size and color.

"Sweet Jesus in heaven." A sickening feeling settled in my gut. "Boone's your attorney."

"I don't want you to be part of this, Reagan." Mamma opened the cabinet door and turned all the cup handles to the right.

"What happened to trusting the system? Boone sidesteps, ducks, twists, and dodges the system every chance he gets."

Mamma took the chair across from me. "Honey, sometimes the system needs a stick of dynamite up it's behind to get it going in the right direction. Walker knows how to do that. I see what happens in a courtroom every day. It's the best system out there to be sure, but it isn't always pretty."

"My divorce wasn't pretty, and Boone was the culprit."

Mamma gave me a sideways glance that suggested otherwise, like me signing that prenup was the otherwise. Okay, she won that point, but there were others. I poked myself in the chest. "Boone can help you and I can't? What's with that?"

"If things fall apart, I don't want to take you down with me. For better or worse Walker's used to the rougher side of life. You're a—"

"Wuss?"

"You're my baby." Mamma added a little sniff for good measure. "What would I do if anything happened to you? Promise me you'll let Walker handle this."

Lord have mercy and sweet Jesus above, here we go again. *My baby* was right behind *mighty proud*. And there was even a sniff involved. When giving birth, at the hospitals there must be a list of guilt phrases given to new parents to bring their offspring in line. *My baby* was one of the top five on that list to be sure.

Well, that was just fine and dandy, but kids had their list, too, and it was usually learned on that big yellow bus or the playground. *Tell them what they want to hear and do as you darn well please . . . just don't get caught,* was tops on that particular list.

"Boone's good at what he does." I ground my teeth so hard I think I chipped a molar. I crossed my fingers under the table. "I'll stay out of his way." *Unless he gets in my way, then all bets are off,* I added to myself.

Mamma smiled then patted my cheek. "That's my good

girl, and if you don't get involved, neither will KiKi. I'll rest so much easier knowing both of you are safe."

I left Mamma's feeling as if the wind had been knocked right out of my sails, but that didn't mean I couldn't row the boat. Not that I didn't see her point. If I were the one in trouble, I wouldn't want Mamma to put herself in danger for me. But she would . . . and so would I.

I headed for home, cutting across Madison Square and rounding the statue of William Jasper. Why there wasn't a statue of James Madison, Father of the Constitution and fourth prezy of the USA, in Madison Square was one of those little Savannah mysteries of life. A more current mystery was how to find who killed Scumbucket and do it on the down-low when I was more of an in-your-face, front-and-center kind of girl.

AS ALL DOG OWNERS KNOW, THERE IS NO SUCH THING as sleeping in. Dogs want out when they want out, and they don't really care diddly if you tossed and turned all night, have the hangover from the Black Lagoon, or slept like the dead, which happened to be my present condition. BW used the suffocation approach to get me out of bed, sitting on my back till my lungs quit working and I woke up gasping for air. Worked like a charm.

I crawled into jeans, ran a toothbrush around my mouth, and added a hoodie and socks against the seven A.M. nippiness. BW was already at the front door doing the can't-wait doggie dance as I stumbled down the steps. I opened it and sat on the porch to make sure he didn't chase something into the street. I waved to Uncle Putter as he backed down the drive, another day another dollar in the life of Savannah's numero uno cardiologist.

I looked over to his house. There were lights on in the kitchen, Auntie KiKi was sitting at the table laden with pastries, and my chocolate-icing-with-sprinkles doughnut alert was fully activated. She was chatting with a lady in a red floppy hat with a tan lacy shawl across her shoulders. Mercedes? Highlights and doughnuts were the only things I could think of that would get KiKi up and going at this hour.

My stomach growled, the sprinkles beckoning. In a few hours the pearl-girls would again take over my house. I needed fortification to make it through the day, and I needed to thank Mercedes for taking care of Mamma and KiKi the way she did. I was no expert on prison protocol or the life and times of Martha Stewart, but there was more going on than Mercedes being there when needed and Beauty Salon 101.

"Well Jeez Louise, you must be little ol' Reagan I've been hearing so much about." Mercedes jumped up and flung her arms around me bear-hug style. She was about as big as KiKi and Uncle Putter put together and had the personality of a Golden Retriever. She looked me over, head to toe, like a long-lost relative. "Well goodness me, aren't you just as cute as a bug's ear? I can fix those roots you got going on and then hook you up with Mr. Boone. He could do with a nice woman in his life."

"You . . . you know Boone?"

Mercedes sat down and using KiKi's sterling silver tongs carefully selected a cinnamon doughnut and put it on one of Grandma Summerside's blue china plates. "I've been cleaning Mr. Boone's house for the last six months, what there is of it. The man's in fearful need of furniture; he rattles around in that big old place like a BB in a box. Can't imagine why he bought it in the first place."

Without the benefit of high-octane caffeine it was hard to fight through my morning brain cobwebs and make sense of how this all came together. "Why were you in jail with Mamma and KiKi?"

KiKi gave me the auntie kick under the table and the *how rude* stare. Mercedes broke off a piece of doughnut and took a dainty nibble. "Mr. Boone agreed to pay me double if I'd spend a few hours in that barred establishment and make friends with two ladies who had no business being there in the first place. Said I'd know right off who they were. Seems the police were more then happy to oblige. Your mamma has some fine friends on her side."

"Boone set this up?"

"Said he owed the judge and wanted to keep her safe, and I was good for that. No one messes with Mercedes." Mercedes dabbed her lips with the napkin and stirred her tea. "Honey, you best sit down for a spell and take a load off. I declare you're the color of pea soup."

I took the chair, and KiKi handed me the blue china teapot, older than the house we sat in, and asked, "So you have a beauty salon?"

Mercedes took another nibble. "Once upon a time I was owner and operator of Mercedes's Mane Event over on Green Street. It was also the main event for some of our male customers when business got kind of slow, if you get my drift. The police didn't exactly cotton to my business diversification plan. The good part is two of the girls are marrying their acquaintances this very month; don't that beat all? The way I see it, Mercedes's Mane Event was sort of a Match.com with a little pizzazz. Nowadays I just do house calls."

KiKi's eyes shot wide open, and she dropped her doughnut in her cup, splashing tea everywhere. Mercedes added, "You know how all those ladies and gents look fine as can be when laid out for their final viewing on this here earth? That's my doing."

"You mean you fix people up at the funeral homes?" I asked. "Do their hair?"

"And makeup. Pays good, and they sit real still." Mercedes laughed. "A little funeral home humor."

"Well, I certainly do appreciate you watching out for Mamma and KiKi."

"Mighty glad to do it, honey, mighty glad indeed. None of my customers at the Event cared for Seymour at all, I can tell you that. More than once Dozer came in spitting nails over something Seymour did. Seems he was always pulling a fast one on Dozer to make a buck."

"Dozer?"

Mercedes took a sip of tea. "Dozer Delany. Short for Bulldozer. He runs a construction company. When Seymour outbid Dozer for building that library addition, it was the last straw. Dozer's blood pressure went haywire right there in the shop, and we had to go and call in 911. One of the paramedics was a regular customer, so they knew right where to come; otherwise, I think Dozer would have been a goner."

Mercedes picked up her pink tote and said to KiKi, "We best be getting to those highlights so you can squeeze in the rumba lesson. I always wanted to learn how to rumba. At noon I'm due over at House of Eternal Slumber to give

Seymour himself a little spiff-up. If you like, I could nose around and see if anyone has unflattering things to say about the old boy. Your mamma didn't do him in, but somebody sure did, and not speaking ill of the dead is a big old fat myth. When a no-good rotten creep bites the dust, everyone who kept their mouth shut when he was alive and kicking comes out of the woodwork to give their two cents why he deserves to be dead and buried."

I took Mercedes's hand. "I would really appreciate that, but you can't tell Boone. He thinks snooping is man's work and wants me to stay out of looking for the real killer. But this is my mamma we're talking about."

"Honey, I know hair and I know men, and best I can tell, men are good for two things in this world, and one of them is opening a door for a lady. The other, well, I'm going to leave that one to your imagination."

Chapter Six

BY ten sharp the pearl-girls were brewing up lattes and cappuccinos, and pestering the heck out of everyone who answered a phone or was plugged into some type of social network. I braced for another day of no sales and grinding fax machines as Lolly's green and red trolley bus festooned with bouquets of plastic chrysanthemums and streaming ribbons pulled to the curb in front of the Fox.

Lolly climbed out, her flowered Lolly's Trolley hat dancing in the breeze. "I'm on my way to pick up a tour group over at the Olde Harbor Inn," she said, coming in the front door. "But first I need a black dress. I'm going to wear it once and burn the thing in celebration. Seymour's wake is tonight, and I plan on seeing for myself that the piece of dog excrement is dead and out of my life for good. I'm packing Cazy's .38 to put a bullet through Seymour's heart just in case."

"He's embalmed, honey. I think all the bases are covered. Besides there might be a law against shooting a dead man."

"Don't much care. I'll sleep better knowing I did my part and maybe do a little celebrating." Lolly sauntered over to the little-black-dress selection hanging on a painted-white broom handle suspended between matching stepladders. I was going for the shabby-chic look and hoping it didn't fall into the bargain-basement look.

"Now *this* is a dress," Lolly said, a smile breaking across her face as she ambled over to another dress rack. She held up a red silk with sequins at the neck and a little flounce at the bottom.

"What happened to black and burn?"

"The .38 and celebrating have more appeal if I have a red dress to do it in. What do you think?" Lolly held it against her front and propped her hand on her hip. "Red's my color more than black, don't you agree?" She thrust the dress at me. "I like it, ring me up."

"Don't you want to try it on?" I nodded at the cute yellow and white dressing room that was once my kitchen pantry. Considering that the most the pantry ever held was a box of mac and cheese and a can of SpaghettiOs, losing the kitchen space wasn't much of a hardship.

"It's a size four," Lolly said reading off the tag. "I'm an eight. My boobs will puff over the top and my behind can stick out the back. I'll look downright slutty. Seymour messed up my life; I can mess up his demise. It's perfect." Lolly opened her wallet and pulled out her American Express. Far be it from me to come between good taste, a woman's scorn, and the first sale of the day.

"Bet you're not going to the wake," Lolly said to me as

I ran her credit card through the machine. "The daughter of Seymour's accused killer showing up at the funeral would not be good for Gloria's campaign or her reputation." Lolly picked up her bag and gave me a wink. "Mighty sorry you're going to miss it. I intend to make a big fat old scene, be embarrassing as all get out. I'll give you a blow-by-blow tomorrow. Keep your eye on YouTube; it's bound to pop up."

I propped open the front door to let a few hours of warm sun in and BW and the campaign racket out as AnnieFritz and Elsie Abbott ambled up the sidewalk, their flowered dresses swaying, sprayed hair not daring to budge, their steps slowing the closer they got to the house.

"Lord have mercy, what's going on in that there place of yours, Reagan honey?" AnnieFritz asked, her face pulled into a frown. "Usually we come over here and shop a bit, sit a spell, and have ourselves a chat and a nice cup of tea. We can't shop and chat with all that racket."

The sisters were retired school teachers and came to live next to me three years ago when their uncle Willie told Dr. Oz to take a long walk off a short pier, cancelled the subscription to *Cooking Light*, bought a Fry Daddy at Walmart, and six months later went to that great cream-gravy gathering in the sky. The upside was he left his pristine Greek revival to his two nieces. They supplemented their pensions and social security checks as professional mourners. No one got a room sniffing and sobbing like the Abbott sisters, and every mortuary in Savannah knew it and paid dearly for the privilege.

They turned to leave, the unpaid water bill on the steps catching my eye, the threat of no hot water giving me the willies. I rushed out onto the porch. "Today's twenty percent off day," I blurted. "Lots of good deals on fall clothes. Mamma's campaign is sharing the house till the election's over is all."

"Well now, twenty percent, you say?" Elsie exchanged looks with AnnieFritz. "Sister and I are in desperate need of new attire for the Seymour wake. We'll be front and center tonight. If we don't have new duds, it'll be bad for business. We have to keep up appearances, you know. Everyone's going to be there. Should be a real wingding affair with the burial tomorrow being for family only. This here event is everyone's last chance to get a good look before Seymour gets shipped off to that great campaign in the hereafter."

We all made the sign of the cross, and AnnieFritz added, "I suppose we can put up with a little racket for twenty percent. 'Course 25 percent would be better."

The sisters climbed the steps and headed for the dresses, Butler Haber coming up the walk behind them. Butler owned Haber Lumber LLC out on Old River Road. Butler made it big back in the '90s when building houses was king and bought the Philbrick-Eastman House over on Chippewa Square. I had the feeling when the housing market tanked, it took the Habers right along with it. The Philbrick-Eastman House was looking a little dodgy these days, and Butler's Buick was far from new with something dripping from the bottom. "I need to speak to Marigold," Butler said to me.

I stepped aside. "It's a consignment shop and campaign headquarters all rolled into one. Take your pick."

Butler ran his hand over his head, messing up his carefully arranged, dyed comb-over. He looked pale, gaunt. "Just give Marigold a message. She won't pick up her blasted phone. Don't know why she has the thing if she isn't going to use it. Cost a bundle. Tell her she needs to get herself home in time for that wake tonight. This will be the last of it. It's done now. Over. We need to keep up appearances." He added the last part as if talking to himself as much as me. "She'll know what I mean. Don't forget, you hear? It's important."

I gave a little two-fingered soldier salute instead of the one-fingered salute I really wanted to give him. No wonder Marigold didn't like going home; who would like to have that waiting for them? Butler turned on his heel and stormed off, and I headed inside enjoying my economically challenged single status more than usual.

The volunteers chatted on phones and stuffed envelopes. Dottie handed me a box of Nice 'N Easy champagne blonde along with another lecture on appearances, and Marigold sat off to the side stretching Gloria-Summerside-for-alderman plastic sleeves over wire frames that would get stuck in front yards.

"These are the last ones," Marigold said to me as I came over to deliver Butler's message. "Donations are scarce as deviled eggs at a church picnic, and we are now fresh out of funds."

"When we get the real killer, things will pick right back up, just you wait," I said in my best Little Miss Cheerful voice. Not that I actually believed it, but the volunteers had put in too much time and effort for me to rain on their parade, and Mamma had put in too much time and effort not to win. But the ugly truth was that the campaign couldn't go on with Mamma's tainted reputation, making Archie Lee a shoo-in.

"Butler stopped by," I added. "Said you have to go to the wake tonight and this is the last of it and it's all over or something close to that. What's over?"

"Me! I am so over him!"

The office stopped dead, and the Abbott sisters did the wide-eyed stare from the dining room. Marigold pulled off one shoe and flung it against the wall, then the other, and did the stomping-tantrum routine right there in the office. It was pretty much the same routine I did when I found Hollis playing hide the salami with Cupcake. Men have that effect on women sometimes.

"Fine! I'll be there," she spluttered, shoving tangled hair off her flushed face. "And it better be the last time or else, I can tell you that."

I took a step back and slapped on a smile. "Wanna shop for a little black dress? Twenty percent off?"

BY SIX THE PEARL-GIRLS HAD LEFT, AND I TOOK UP roost on the front steps in celebration. KiKi slunk across the yard barefoot, martinis in hand, and dropped down beside me. She handed off a glass, downed hers in one gulp, then switched drinks with me. "Three teen dance classes this afternoon to get ready for the Christmas cotillion. Next week I'm bringing in a whip and a chair. Maybe a cattle prod."

KiKi rolled her eyes upward toward her hairline. "This morning I looked fantastic after Mercedes worked her magic. You wouldn't have recognized me, ten years younger and twenty pounds thinner."

"All that from hair?"

"I was adorable." She plucked up a limp strand. "Now

I'm a big old rat's nest and look ten years older and ten pounds heavier. When kids get to twelve, they should do everyone a big favor and skip right to twenty." She nodded to the open front door. "How's business and the campaign going?"

"Had a nice run on black dresses, at least Scumbucket's good for something, but the campaign's belly up. No one's interested in backing a murder suspect. I don't have a lot of ideas on how to fix that situation, but I sure enough can't let Mamma lose to Archie Lee. Right now he's my prime suspect for knocking off Scummy, and that's based on a banner hanging over a bar. Lolly Ledbetter's wearing red tonight, so something's going on there with her and Scummy, and I bet that Dozer guy Mercedes told us about will show up, and I'd like to get a look at him and find out who he is. For sure the kudzu vine will be on super-charge all night with gossip. You know how tongues wag over a casket. 'Did you like the jerk? Neither did I. Tell me your Scumbucket story, and I'll tell you mine.' I need to be at the wake."

KiKi patted my leg. "Not unless you want to add Savannah's riot squad to the list of attendees. We can talk to Lolly any old time, and I bet the only way Dozer shows up is if he's wearing glasses and a black mustache with a plastic nose." KiKi cut her eyes my way. "Uh-oh. What are you thinking? You ate your olives and then went and ate mine, too. What now?"

"Is Uncle Putter home tonight?"

"He's at the senior center talking heart attack avoidance, and *we* can't do anything. The man hasn't fully adjusted to the jail incident."

"This has nothing to do with jail, and it's completely

safe." I ignored the KiKi eye roll. "I've got two ugly black dresses left. I intended to cover the dining room chairs with them for a kind of black-and-white sophisticated look. Instead we can pad them up, add hats, sniffle into hankies all night like the Abbott sisters do, and listen to what's going on at the wake. Do you still have those Cher-in-the-70s wigs?"

"Maybe."

I jumped up. "See, it's a sign. We're two little old ladies with wild hair stuffed under big hats. We'll blend into the sea of black clothes, hushed voices, music to die by. They'll have cookies."

"I have cookies."

"I need some leads, and I'm not leaving this all up to Boone. What if he overlooks something? What if he takes too long? Sooner or later the real killer will be exposed, but we have to do it sooner. You know we can't let Mamma lose this election to Archie Lee, and the longer she's a suspect the worse it looks for her. She wants to be an alderman, and she'll be great at it. What kind of daughter would I be if I let Archie Lee win instead of Mamma?" I gave Auntie KiKi the *raised eyebrow* look. "What kind of sister would you be?"

"Lord have mercy, you're playing the guilt card."

"You always play the guilt card; it's my turn. I'll even teach one of your teen dance classes."

"You can do two classes, and I'll bring the hankies."

FORTY-FIVE MINUTES LATER I TOLD KIKI TO PULL the Beemer to the curb. "We can't park here," she said to me. "It's two blocks to Eternal Slumber. We need to get closer. I can't walk that far, or my butt will fall off. It's only got two pins holding it in place."

"Take small steps. We can't park in the Eternal Slumber lot; your *Foxtrot* license plate is a dead giveaway." I checked the mirror on the visor and shoved a few more curly black strands of my Cher-hair—the Brillo-Pad-on-steroids era—under my black hat left from Grandma Summerside. I got out of the car and smoothed my black dress over my 38Ds. So this is what it felt like to have boobs. I jutted my chest a bit, feeling sort of powerful with my new tissue-enhanced womanliness.

Dusk faded to night, the soft glow of wrought iron street-lights marking the way for two old ladies hobbling their way along the sidewalk. We passed Walls' BBQ, the spicy aroma of sauce and grilled meat straight from heaven wafting out onto the street.

"Maybe we should grab some ribs," KiKi said, her foot-steps drifting off course toward Walls' green front door. "We didn't do dinner, and I'm starved. We need sustenance to get us through the night."

"We just can't buy a slab of ribs and eat it on the hoof. Barbecue dribbled down our fronts isn't very little-old-lady-like at all." I cupped her elbow. "On the way back we'll get takeout with a side of slaw. We have to hurry. You don't want Uncle Putter to beat you home, do you?"

"Oh sweet mother, if he sees me dressed like this, I'll be in one of those ankle contraptions like they put on that guy in *White Collar* so they know where he is all the time. Now there's some mighty fine eye candy if you ask me. Where did they find him is what I'd like to know. Hubba-hubba."

"Hubba-hubba?"

"Hormone replacement therapy. I think it's kicking in right nice."

The viewing started at seven, and a line spilled out onto the lit porch and down around the manicured boxwoods. "This is never going to work," KiKi said, pulling lacy hankies from her black purse big enough to stash cookies since I sort of promised BW. "We need to get inside and set up by the casket now and not miss anything. The casket is where the good talk is. People see a dead body stretched out proper and feel the need to spill their guts. It's sort of like cramming for finals; they confess everything for when their time in the big box comes along."

"I thought gossip central for this event would be the cookie table."

"That's where everyone talks about everybody else who shows up and how they've gained weight or lost hair and who's sleeping with who."

"How do you know this? Is it another one of those AARP things?"

"I taught Elmer Merryweather to cha-cha last month. He owns that Peaceful Endings place over there in Garden City. He always smelled like flowers and mints when he came in, and he gave me the funeral home 411." KiKi handed me a handkerchief. "Here's what you do. You act like you're crying your heart out, make a bunch of blubbering sounds, keep your head down, and follow me. I got this covered."

KiKi buried her face in her hankie and let loose with something that sounded like a cat with his tail caught in a door, sending chills clear up my spine. People parted like Moses and the Red Sea, probably scared half to death of what was headed their way. We scurried around the line, went right in the doorway and past the black-suit-and-black-tie-clad owners of this fine establishment.

We weaved between baskets and vases of lilies and carnations saturating the place with the fragrance of the dearly departed and steered clear of the Abbott sisters by the picture display of Scumbucket in all his trumped-up earthly glory. From time to time the sisters burst into tears, half the room following suit.

KiKi pulled up beside a stand supporting a wreath of yellow roses adorned with *May he rest in peace* from Jill and Bob Decker. I had no idea who Jill and Bob were, but they dropped a pretty penny on flowers.

"This will do just fine," KiKi whispered as we staked out a spot next to a display of ferns, our backs to the casket as if we were in our own little state of sorrowfulness. Money-Honey and Valentine, both draped in black, greeted the mourners.

"I do declare, did you happen to catch a glimpse of Honey?" KiKi whispered again. "She looks a fright, big old raccoon eyes from smeared mascara and a red blotchy nose. Never figured her for the grieving-widow type, but she sure seems distraught over the ordeal."

The line wound past the casket, everyone offering condolences and saying how Seymour was such a fine man and would have made a simply wonderful alderman and my oh my doesn't he look peaceful.

"There's nothing here," KiKi muttered into her hankie a half hour later. "I'll go check out the cookie table and see what's going on there."

"You just want a cookie."

"They have those ones shaped like maple leaves. I love

maple leaf cookies. If I don't go now, they'll be gone for sure, and since you pooh-poohed the ribs, I need a cookie to keep my energy levels up."

I told KiKi to get one for BW, and she wandered off into the crowd. I took up roost behind a palm at the head of the casket. I didn't want to look like a little old lonely lady and have someone be tempted to do the Southern hospitable thing and come chat. I had my flowered hat pulled low and the wig close to my face, but one good look at me and it wouldn't take Sherlock to figure out I wasn't a little old lady. Or even worse, what if they didn't figure it out?

Scumbucket did look good, mostly because his mouth was shut, his eyes were closed, and he was not moving a muscle. He had on a blue suit with a campaign button stuck on the lapel, and there was something pink tucked under his left shoulder. It wasn't obvious from a front view. What the heck was it?

I shuffled my way to get a better angle and bumped into a middle-aged woman with wild gray hair and crazy eyes. She folded her arms and glared down at Scummy. "I'm glad he's gone, and I don't mind saying so. And that Judge Summerside is going to fry for doing the deed is the icing on the cake. The universe finally aligned itself, and all is well. These two finally got what they deserved."

I was with her all the way up until the fry-Mamma part. I watched the crazy-eyed woman exit through the side door, and when I looked back, Honey was hurrying off in the direction of the ladies' room. As much as Money-Honey wasn't my favorite person, burying her husband had her truly distraught. KiKi was right. Honey looked plum terrible and then some.

With Honey out of the picture Valley continued greeting the mourners with four basic phrases he used on a rotating basis. He sounded sincere enough, but you'd think he'd be a little more genuine over losing a friend. He and Scummy were in a campaign together; they had to have a basic camaraderie, right?

KiKi hustled up to my side all out of breath, her cheeks flush with gossip. "You're not going to believe this. Marigold and Butler are in the side yard doing battle royal and drawing a bigger crowd than Seymour is in here. And . . ." KiKi wiggled closer still. "When I was in the little girl's room trying to re-pin things back up where they belonged, Money-Honey came in. She must have thought she was all alone 'cause she threw water on her face to get her mascara running and added blush to her nose and drew circles under her eyes. Let me tell you, my hindquarters and your boobs aren't the only fake things around here tonight, sweet pea."

"Maybe Honey's just not a crier but wants to look like she cares?"

"Or maybe she's happy as a pig in mud Seymour's gone, but she doesn't want to let on?"

"Speaking of a pig, there's something pink tucked under Scummy's left shoulder."

KiKi parted the fronds to get a better look. "Well, I'll be; there is something there. It's kind of sparkly best I can tell. Not men's jewelry for sure. Bet I can reach in and get it if I just—"

"No!" I growled deep in my throat, adding a good deal of stern to my voice. "If we cause a scene, Mamma will kill us and . . . Oh good grief, here comes trouble."

I nodded to Lolly Ledbetter next in line at the condolence

meet and greet. She had on the red dress all right, along with red shoes, red hat, and even her eyes were bloodshot.

"Well, finally." KiKi rubbed her hands together, a smile tripping across her face. "Be a pity to have a wake this size without a little excitement at the casket, and I do believe Lolly's drunk as a skunk."

Lolly parked her hands on her hips, tossed her hair, and said to Honey, "Well now, the old boy sure looks a lot better in there than he ever did out here where he caused nothing but trouble for the rest of us."

Everyone gasped, then the room went dead quiet, not as much out of respect for the dearly departed as not wanting to miss a single word of what was going on. Honey's mouth pinched tight, two black suits hurried over to Lolly's side, and out of the corner of my eye I saw KiKi lean in toward the casket. She grabbed for the pin as her faux butt slid down around her ankles. Eyes bulging, KiKi wobbled, losing her balance. I grabbed for her; she grabbed for a fern, missed, and knocked it plant side down, dirt side up onto Scumbucket's head.

Everyone stared at the casket. My heart stopped dead in my chest. If Mamma got wind of this . . .

I kicked KiKi's fake rump under the casket display as she stepped out of it and slowly pulled her backward. "Count to three and run," I whispered. Tucking our heads down, we turned slowly then beelined for the hallway, voices picking up in the main room, the thick-padded carpet muffling our getaway.

We dashed out the side door, and KiKi yanked me behind a hedge of magnolia trees. We froze perfectly still in case someone followed in hot pursuit of the funeral crashers, but the only sound was from the traffic on Price and enough mayhem inside to rattle the windows. "What happened to completely safe?" KiKi finally said to me.

"Hey, you're the one who went and lost their butt." Did I really just say that? I closed my eyes to get a grip on the situation then turned KiKi around to look at me. "Head for the car," I told her. "If you're not home watching *Dancing with the Stars* when Uncle Putter walks in, he'll know in an instant who caused this commotion."

"You think he'll hear about this?"

"The Abbott sisters are inside." I nodded toward the funeral home. "In five minutes flat all of Savannah will know about Scummy wearing a fern on his head, complete with pictures. I'm going to hang around and see if I can find out anything on Marigold and Butler and what that's all about. They're tied to Scummy some way."

"I don't know Butler all that well, but I can't see Marigold killing Seymour. Why that girl's sweet as pie."

"You weren't at the Fox today." I pealed off KiKi's hat and wig, and fluffed up her hair and smoothed out her makeup. "Better." I smiled. KiKi's eyes twinkled. Batman and Robin do Savannah. "Keep in the bushes and go around the back to the sidewalk on the other side."

"I'll get us some ribs."

"If you smell like BBQ, the jig's up with Uncle Putter. He'll inform Mamma, and I sort of told her I'd let Boone handle the Seymour mess and find the killer so she wouldn't worry about the two of us."

"You think she bought it?"

"I gave her my best *sweet little girl* look and lied my heart out." I kissed KiKi on the cheek then lost sight of her rounding the corner. Hard to believe no one followed in hot pursuit. Then again, the black-suit-and-black-tie brigade had their hands full with cleaning up Scumbucket and dealing with the fainted-dead-away faction that was sure to accompany such a social nightmare.

I took off my hat and wig and unstuffed my upper dimensions. Pulling my dress down over my now 32Bs, I tightened the belt for a long black dress appearance; at least that was the plan. My hair was always a disaster so nothing new there. I wadded up the undercover outfits and wedged them into one of the bushes, as I heard the sounds of sirens approaching. Taking two calming breaths, I squared my shoulders, stepped into the open and right into the path of Walker Boone.

Chapter Seven

"WHAT the heck were you doing in there?" Boone asked. Tonight he wore jeans, a navy jacket, and a really pissed-off expression. He herded me back into the magnolias, the uproar emanating from Eternal Slumber not subsiding one little bit. Two ambulances screeched to the curb, and Boone jabbed a finger in their direction. "What happened to you butting out and me handling things?"

"How'd you know I was here?"

"*Foxtrot*'s parked up the street, Seymour's wearing a plant on his head, and the EMTs have landed. Doesn't take Einstein to connect the dots."

"Who's Dozer?"

Boone gritted his teeth and muttered something colorful, a few capillaries popping in his eyes. "Seymour rubbed shoulders with some unpleasant people, and Dozer's one of them. You sniffing around in his life guarantees to make yours a short one. Keep that in mind and go sell some hats and dresses and stay out of the way."

At first I felt really guilty for lying to Boone about not getting involved in investigating Seymour's murder when I knew all along I would, but the go-sell-hats crack was instant absolution. "I have leads, you know. Good ones, and I'm not sitting on the sidelines and twiddling my thumbs when I can help my own mother."

"You call adventures from the crypt help?" Boone ran his hand over his hair; the sound of gurney wheels rattling on the sidewalk drifted our way. "No one's going to talk because God knows where the disastrous duo will strike next and cause a scene. You have everyone diving for cover, and people don't want to get involved. Your mother's worried you'll get hurt trying to clear her, and she's got enough on her mind without you adding to it."

"How will Mamma find out? You gonna go all Mr. Goodie-Two-Shoes and tattle on me like we're in kindergarten?"

Boone stilled, his stance relaxed, a slow smile creasing his face. "Goodie-two-shoes?"

"Trust me, it wasn't a compliment."

"I'm not the only one who knows you're stirring up trouble, Blondie. There's a whole city out there tuned into the kudzu vine, and you've got top billing these days."

A spark of devil lit his black-as-night eyes, and he tucked a strand of hair behind my ear. My stomach got all squishy, and it had nothing to do with the tucking and everything to do with the devil. Boone on the warpath was one thing; Boone scheming and conniving and aiming it all at me was a whole other matter. "What?"

"Your mother won't be trying any cases with all these allegations hanging over her head, and we both know her campaign's in the toilet. She needs something to keep her busy, occupy her time in a meaningful manner."

"Volunteer work at the hospital?"

"I was thinking more like helping you at the Fox. You're screwing up my life. I'm returning the favor. Having Judge Gloria Summerside around will keep you and KiKi off the streets and out of my hair."

"You wouldn't"

The grin broadened.

"That's pretty low even for you."

"What happened to goodie-two-shoes?" Boone shoved his hands into his pockets, gave me a little wink, then stepped into the foray of people exiting Eternal Slumber. A gurney rolled to the front door, attention-whore Blanche Woodside buckled in tight, waving to the crowd Pope style.

"You're not going to stop me," I yelled at Boone as he headed down the sidewalk.

"But I can slow you down plenty," he called back over the crowd.

I winged a pinecone at Boone's big fat head, missed by a mile, and knocked Elsie Abbott's hat cattywampus. With all the commotion she didn't even notice. I was more determined than ever to snoop around and not just because Boone ticked me off. I had suspects on my list that Boone didn't have, really good suspects. Oh, I could inform Mr. Pighead that Marigold had a big old hissy over going to the funeral with her dear husband, and Lolly Ledbetter wearing a red dress to the wake tonight meant something other than she liked the color red. Boone wouldn't get that these two gals were beyond infuriated and more than capable of dumping poison in Scummy's drink without a moment's hesitation.

Archie Lee was still a front-runner on my who-killed-Scummy list. Popeye had a working knowledge of poisonous plants, and now there was this guy Dozer to consider. Two people had warned me about him being a badass, and Dozer had blood pressure problems, meaning he knew something about heart meds and what they did. He was also a working guy, not a fan of Seymour's, and probably one of the original Saint Patty's Day signers of the declaration of Archie Lee for Alderman.

The ambulance carrying Blanche motored off down Price with sirens blasting, at the request of Blanche no doubt, as Lolly's Trolley minus its passengers charged our way. It swayed precariously from side to side and jumped the curb, chasing weary mourners screaming onto the porch. The trolley finally came to rest between two lampposts.

"Is that Lolly?" Cazy asked, stumbling down the trolley steps and pointing a shaky finger at the retreating ambulance. "A few minutes ago Twitter lit up like a Christmas tree, saying some ruckus happened here at Eternal Slumber. I knew it must be my Lolly. I told her not to go and wear that red dress. What happened to her? Is she going to be okay? I told her she shouldn't come here. Seymour's dead, and our troubles are over once and for all. What happened?"

I sat Cazy on the bottom step of the trolley and fanned him with Old Yeller. "The what-happened part covers a lot of territory tonight, but Lolly isn't in the ambulance."

"Blanche Woodside again?"

"The one and only. Lolly is probably headed home. Last time I saw her she was fine, but you best move this trolley;

the police are in a bad mood tonight. Seems someone dumped a plant on Seymour's head, causing quite a stir, and no one's been quite the same since."

Cazy's jaw dropped. "Lolly did that?"

"Two little old ladies with wild curly hair. Sort of disappeared into the night; no one's seen them since." I pulled Cazy to standing. "Officer Grumpy-Pants is coming this way. You better get a move on."

Cazy climbed behind the wheel. I stepped into the street, holding out my arms to stop traffic. I did the come-on-back wave to Cazy, directing him where to go, and after a few back-and-forth K-turns he straightened the trolley. Hoping Cazy was in a chatty mood, I took the seat behind him when he pulled into the flow of traffic. It was a chance to get a little information, enjoy the open-air ride over cobblestone streets with downtown Savannah all lit up and nighttime happy.

"Why did you think Lolly would be at Eternal Slumber?" I asked Cazy, a Little Miss Oblivious lilt in my voice as we rumbled along.

Cazy stopped for a red light and glanced my way, eyes widening in recognition. "Well heavenly days, you're Judge Summerside's daughter, aren't you? I was in such a state back at the Slumber I didn't recognize you. Lolly sure wanted your mamma to win that election, and she worked real hard on the campaign. Too bad the judge had to go and get accused of knocking off Seymour. Crying shame. Lolly didn't suspect for a minute things would turn out the way they did."

The light changed, and the trolley chugged forward. I leaned closer. "So how did Lolly want things to turn out?"

"That your mamma would win of course, and Seymour

would throw himself under a fast train. Lolly even followed your mamma to Seymour's the day he croaked to make sure she was okay. Then Seymour wound up dead as a carp in a cup of spit." Cazy slowed as a group of tourists meandered across the street to Colonial Park Cemetery for a night tour called Ghosts in the Graveyards.

"What happened to make Lolly hate Seymour so much?" I asked as Cazy started up again.

"Mostly it was the way he treated me at the savings and loan." Cazy's voice was strained, and he had a death grip on the steering wheel. "Always making demands on me, he was."

The trolley picked up speed. "Belittling me in front of other employees," Cazy growled, the trolley rumbling faster and faster still. "Saying I was old and no one would ever hire me." The trolley took the next turn on two wheels, sliding me right out of my seat and sending pedestrians in a crosswalk diving for the sidewalk. "Telling me I didn't know what I was doing and—"

"Holy Toledo, slow down!"

Cazy jammed on the brakes, the trolley stopping inches from a phone pole.

"Sorry." Cazy flopped back in his seat and puffed out a lungful of air. "Talking about Seymour gets me a little riled up is all. Now where can I drop you?"

I scrambled down the trolley steps. "Thanks for the lift." I gave Cazy a long look. "Are you sure you're okay? You seem a bit upset. Maybe you shouldn't be driving."

Reaching in his pocket, he pulled out a brown prescription bottle and shook two blue pills in his palm. He tossed them in his mouth, closed his eyes, and relaxed. "Om shanti,

shanti, shanti," Cazy chanted in a calm voice. He pried open one eye. "Means 'peace prevail everywhere.' I go to Amy's House of Yoga over there on Whittaker twice a week. I'm getting really good at inverted turtle."

"Amen." I made the sign of the cross.

"The little blue pills are pure magic." Cazy gave me a friendly grin, and I watched the trolley amble on down the street.

Sweet Jesus in heaven, the whole freaking city was medicated! Cazy was on the blue-pill regimen, Dozer had high blood pressure and was taking stuff for that, and the way Marigold flipped out at the Fox my guess was she needed to up her dose of Prozac. Tomorrow I'd find out more on Marigold. Tonight, as much as I didn't want to revisit the Cemetery, I figured it was a good place to get the skinny on Dozer above and beyond his medical history. Besides, I'd already had my run-in with Boone, so I doubted if he'd be there to get in my way.

I didn't know what Dozer looked like but guessed someone at the Cemetery would. Mercedes seemed to think he had a real problem with Scummy underbidding him on projects, and with the construction business taking it on the chin these days Dozer might be in a world of financial hurt and have Scummy to thank for it. Just how much he wanted to *thank* him was the question. Funerals might get people talking but so did sitting at a bar with a few longnecks. The trick was to steer clear of Popeye and be inconspicuous. Hey, I could be *in*conspicuous. I figured I'd used up all my conspicuous for a while.

The Cemetery was packed and loud, the banner declaring Archie Lee winner still on display along with "Archie Lee

Wins" posters on the walls in case someone didn't get the message. I spotted Big Joey with Earlene—who would have thought?—and some guys I knew from high school. The Cemetery was Savannah's melting pot of all sorts of beer-loving people, especially with Archie Lee in the limelight as the city's new and future alderman.

I found six inches of open space at the far end of the bar. Somebody put a mug of beer in my hand as Archie Lee raised his, everyone following suit. "To the little guy in city hall," Archie Lee bellowed. "This one's for us."

Everyone cheered, added congratulations of their own, and downed their brews. I asked the twentysomething guy sitting next to me if he'd seen Dozer here tonight, that we were supposed to meet up.

He gave me a *duh* look and pointed to a dude the size of a bulldozer in an Atlanta Braves ball cap standing in the back. I took my beer and elbowed my way in that direction, trying to think of an opening line that was idle conversation, basic chitchat. I needed information but needed to be subtle about it. Something like *On a scale of one to ten how much did you want to kill off Seymour?* was definitely out.

I sidestepped the guy in the leather jacket with a snarling Georgia Bulldog on the back and a girl in a brown corduroy skirt that would sell in no time at the Fox. "Great party," I said to Dozer, holding up my glass in salute.

"You bet, sugar," Dozer slurred. He took a swig from his longneck and wrapped his big arm around me, pulling me close to his side. He smelled of beer and cigarette smoke, another candidate for Eternal Slumber.

"Guess you didn't like Seymour much?" I prodded.

"Seymour thought he was so darn smart." Dozer leaned

on me for support. "Wheeling and dealing to get his way all the time. You know what?"

"What?"

"The Lord works in mysterious ways, and sometimes He needs a little help from his friends, and I got lots of friends here. Archie Lee's a real good friend, a bartender who listens to everyone's troubles, and we all got troubles, now don't we?" Dozer clicked his beer to mine. "I figured out what Seymour was up to all by myself."

Dozer laughed deep in his barrel chest, pulling me closer still. I eased out from under the crushing weight of Dozer's arm and came face to chest with a white T-shirt splashed with red barbecue sauce. My eyes traveled up to shoulders— the guy didn't have a neck—and I recognized the face.

"Get out of here," Popeye bellowed at me, the bar getting instantly quite.

"Hey, buddy," Dozer cajoled, looking at Popeye. "Don't you be talking that way to my friend here." Dozer snagged my arm and yanked me back to his side. "She's a cute little addition to the place, don't you think?"

"This here ain't no friend," Popeye sneered. "This here is trouble, Summerside trouble, the worst kind. You don't want nothing to do with her, man." Popeye hoisted me up by my other arm, Dozer not letting go of my neck. I couldn't breathe, the room swimming in front of me. I swore if I ever found the real killer, I'd strangle him or her with my own two hands.

I dropped my beer and shoved at Dozer, gulping in mouthfuls of air. Popeye didn't give a hoot about my near-death experience and hauled me toward the back hall and the rear door I was getting to know all too well.

"Getting tossed out of here once wasn't enough for you?" Popeye shoved me into the alley again. I stumbled, tripped, and landed on my backside, jarring every bone in my body.

"Is this any way to treat a lady?"

"Ladies don't come around here accusing my brother of murder."

"For your information I was here tonight to accuse some-one else of murder."

"Dozer?"

"Maybe." Open mouth, insert foot.

"I'll be sure to let him know." Popeye slammed the door hard enough to rattle the frame, the party inside picking up where it left off. So much for me being inconspicuous.

"Honey, are you all right down there?" A woman gazed at me, the alley light catching in her gray hair. She juggled two big white boxes with *Cuisine by Rachelle* stenciled in blue on the sides. One of the boxes started to slip, and I caught it before it hit the ground.

"Why thank you kindly for that." She nodded at the boxes. "I'm the Rachelle on this here box, Rachelle Lerner, and I'd hate to walk inside with a banged-up delivery. Archie Lee's a good customer, and I aim to keep him happy as best I can. I need the business." She cut her eyes to the door. "Guess you two don't get along so well?"

"I criticized his boiled peanuts." I got to my feet and helped Rachelle adjust the boxes.

"He's mighty proud of those peanuts. Concocted the recipe himself from what I hear. He's serving up shrimp po'boys tonight with special sauce in honor of being the new alderman. I got the buns right here and two more boxes waiting out in the van. He sure is tickled about winning this here election."

"Do you need some help?"

"I can manage on my own. Been doing a lot of managing these days. Used to be my Parnell made the deliveries for me. 'Course that was before a no-good, rotten judge sent my baby boy to prison. So he sold a few drugs; everyone's on something these days. I hope that Summerside judge rots in prison herself now, I truly do." Rachelle drew up close. "She's the one they're accusing of knocking off Seymour."

"No," I said on a gasp. The gasp was because I realized the woman was the same one who had stood beside me at Eternal Slumber, happy as a clam Scummy was history.

"Yes indeed, and it's just what that woman deserves if you ask me. Someone sure fixed her little old red wagon, now didn't they?"

Fixed her wagon? "You don't think the judge really killed Seymour?"

Rachelle gave a who-cares shrug. "She's getting accused of it, and that's what matters. Fact is, a lot of folks didn't like Kip Seymour, and I'm right at the top of that list. Now if you could hold that there door open for me, I'd be mighty grateful for the assistance."

Rachelle wobbled inside with the teetering boxes, and I headed for home, the long walk giving me a chance to pick up a to-go meatloaf sandwich with extra provolone from Parker's deli and gas station, and time to think about the evening. I licked a glob of cheese from my thumb and decided Rachelle had a bad case of what Mamma often referred to as the Baby Jesus syndrome, meaning *my child can do no wrong*.

But was Rachelle just plain old mad at Mamma for sending her darling Parnell off to jail, or was she mad enough to do something sinister about it, like frame Mamma for murder? Why knock off Scummy in the process? What was her gripe with him? She said there was a list of people wanting Scummy dead and she was on it.

What did Dozer mean by Scummy wheeling and dealing? What was he into? By the time I got to Cherry House, I was full and frustrated. I had a lot more questions than answers, and my night of keeping on the down-low hadn't exactly gone according to plan. I fed BW a chunk of meatloaf sandwich and the last hot dog in the fridge. I promised him I'd go to the store on the morrow for a hot dog refill if he'd stop with the *poor pitiful neglected pup* look. I let him outside for a nightly round of sniff-and-sprinkle, and Auntie KiKi waltzed her way across the grass, martini glass in hand.

"Heard you had quite a time over there at the Cemetery and figured you might need this."

"Twitter?"

"And Facebook. The pictures are suitable for framing. Cher says, 'Until you're ready to look foolish, you'll never have the possibility of being great.' Honey, after tonight I think you're gearing up for the presidency."

We both sat down on the porch, and I took a sip of martini. The cool sliding down my throat and alcohol buzzing in my bloodstream took some of the sting out of the fact that in one single night my not-so-great sleuthing skills made top billing on two social networks. "Did Uncle Putter suspect you were part of the Eternal Slumber fiasco?"

"The seniors had a pepperoni-pizza-and-cheesy-breadstick delivery from Vinnie Van GoGo's right there in the middle of his healthy heart talk. He was so spitting mad when he got home that nothing else mattered."

"God bless Vinnie, double cheese, and speedy delivery." We both made the sign of the cross and then KiKi dropped a pink sparkly pin in my lap.

"Holy cow, you got it? I forgot all about this being tucked under Scummy's shoulder."

KiKi fluffed her hair and flashed a superior auntie smile. "I'm not only smart and mighty good-looking; I'm sneaky as all get out, too."

I picked up the poodle, turning it in my hand, the faint streetlight reflecting off the pink rhinestones. "I know this pin. One of the cute young chickie volunteers at Scummy's campaign headquarters wore it on a white sweater when we were there. You think Scummy was diddling with the help and the pin was a little present?"

KiKi made a sour face and shuddered. "Sweet mother in heaven, he's old enough to be her daddy. Then again women like men with power, and men like . . . well we know full well what men like."

Kiki plucked the skewered olives from my drink, handed them to me, and took the martini. Some days were like that, I realized. Just when you really needed the martini, you wound up with the toothpick.

"You know," KiKi said, her brow creased in deep thought. "Maybe Money-Honey found the pin too and realized what was going on with hubby and the volunteers. That's why she faked the running mascara and looking all upset at the funeral. Deep down she was glad he was dead and gone. But Money-Honey being ticked off at her dead husband doesn't get us any closer to finding who killed him. Right now I'd say Archie Lee is the obvious choice since he gained the most, and then there's that Dozer guy that Mercedes told us about."

"I met a caterer who has it in for Mamma and didn't like Scummy, and then there's Marigold and Butler on the kill-Scummy list. I don't know what's going on there, but something sure is. Cazy Ledbetter and Lolly hated Seymour, and if you open up an account at the savings and loan where Cazy worked, we could ask around and see what the employees have to say. I think the savings and loan is giving away toasters. Everybody can use a toaster."

"I already have a toaster." KiKi stood and finished off the last gulp of martini. "Besides, tomorrow morning Putter's in a golf tournament over there on Hilton Head Island. I'm driving the golf cart for luck, and you, my little sweet pea, have a dance lesson with a bunch of juvenile delinquents. Cazy, the savings and loan, and the toaster are just going to have to wait their turn."

WAS I REALLY THIS OBNOXIOUS AS A TEENAGER, I wondered while standing in KiKi's parlor staring at ten kids who wanted to be here as much as I did. "You need to turn off the phones and pay attention," I said for the third time.

"What if something happens?" Kelly Ann Randolph asked with her eyes still fixed on the screen.

"It's Saturday morning in Savannah, honey. Nothing's happening."

"You mean it's not like last night when you got thrown out of that bar?" Linton Parish gave me an arrogant look. All the other little darlings of notable Savannah families snickered, making me wonder if Uncle Putter still kept that Smith and Wesson in the hall closet.

I heaved a sigh. I had promised KiKi I'd teach her class, and I'd do it if it killed me . . . or them. Right now it was a toss-up. I selected an Adam Levine song from KiKi's iPod. The guy sang like no other and was delicious enough to make any woman forget her troubles, and I had ten big ones.

"Take your partner like this," I said, claiming Linton Parish as my guinea pig. Give *me* a hard time, and you pay for it. Linton was my height, rail thin, and considered himself God's gift to Savannah thanks to his parents who knew beyond a shadow of a doubt that he was and, given half a chance, informed everyone else in the city of that fact.

The dear boy's left clammy hand took my right one, his right hand went to the small of my back, then it slid right down to my butt. He grinned and gave a squeeze. After last night I didn't think my life could sink any lower, yet here I was, at nine o'clock on a Saturday morning being groped by a pimply faced teenager with hot chocolate breath.

A large hand suddenly closed around Linton's scrawny neck. "I don't think so, kid," came Boone's deep voice.

Linton's eyes nearly popped right out of their sockets, and Boone steered him over to Kelly Ann. "Ditch your phones. Get your partners. Move it!"

Immediately, ten reprobates lined up, and Boone was my partner, his hand firm at my back, his right hand holding mine.

"Now dance," Boone ordered, and we all did, "One More Night" playing in the background.

"Why are you here?" was all I could manage, my brain trying to compute what was going on. Boone and I battling it out I understood as business as usual. The possibility of

Boone and me dancing in Auntie KiKi's parlor had never crossed my mind.

He gave me a lopsided grin, a smug glint in his eyes. "After last night's escapades at Archie Lee's and you winding up as gossip fodder yet again, your ass belongs to me, Blondie, not some snot-nosed kid. Any leads out there on Seymour's murder are dead ends thanks to you, and lighten up a little, you're like a Mac truck out here."

Boone had on faded black jeans molded to a nice package in front and the state's best buns in back. His mussed blue T-shirt felt soft under my left hand. He was unshaven, his dark chin close to my cheek, a lingering woodsy scent of soap and shampoo drifting my way. A hint of danger hummed under the surface as always with Boone, even when dancing. There was never a doubt as to who led whom, and Boone was good, really good. The kids sucked.

"Pay attention," he ordered again. All eyes focused on us gliding around the room, Boone throwing in a little swing. He gave me a wise-guy smile and held me a little tighter, not rough tighter, just . . . tighter.

I missed a step, our hips touching, thighs brushing. His smile faded, and Boone missed the next step, his eyes now black as midnight.

"How'd you learn to dance?" I asked, needing to say something, anything, to get my mind off . . . dancing.

"Either that or off to juvie."

"You're kidding."

"Do I dance like I'm kidding?"

"No." I swallowed. "You don't dance like you're kidding at all." My voice was barely a whisper. It was suddenly hard to breathe. The song drifted off, the last beat dying before

Boone took a step away. His hand fell from my waist, the absence unsettling.

"You're . . . a good dancer," he said, his voice low, ragged. "I didn't expect . . . this." Then Walker Boone turned around and walked out the door.

Chapter Eight

A LITTLE before ten I finished the dance lesson, the kids more angel than devil with the possibility of Boone returning at any moment, and if he had, I probably would have peed my pants.

My heart had been doing the slow-thud-and-flip-flop thing since he had walked out the door forty-five minutes ago. I hadn't been able to concentrate for beans. What was wrong with me? It was a simple foxtrot, not even a rumba. It was Walker Boone for heaven's sake, the bane of my existence through divorce hell and beyond.

It had to be the Adam Levine influence I told myself. "One More Night" was one of my favorite songs, and Levine's voice could turn any situation, even a teen dance lesson and Walker Boone into something . . . hot. I took a few deep brain-cleansing breaths as I locked up KiKi's house and headed for mine. Mamma's Caddy was parked at the curb.

"You're all flushed," she said to me while getting out of the car.

"Taught one of KiKi's dance classes is all." We started up the walk together. "Are you here for breakfast?" I asked, needing to get my brain focused on something else besides Boone and midnight black eyes. "I was just going to the store. I can fix pancakes, I'm getting better at pancakes, they're not so gooey in the middle, and if you add enough syrup, you don't even notice."

"You're rambling. What happened now?" Mamma stopped and looked back at me, a quizzical expression on her face. "Walker dropped by my place a half hour ago. He looked upset and all out of sorts, too."

"Really?" My mouth went completely dry.

"Did you do battle again?"

"Not exactly."

"I declare, you two are oil and vinegar."

"Sometimes."

"You're always at each other over that divorce or whatever else is in the wind. Savannah's not that big. You're going to keep running into each other." Mamma headed for the steps. "One of these days you'll have to bury the hatchet and kiss and make up, you know."

I tripped on the top step and landed on all fours.

"Oh for goodness' sake," Mamma said, helping me up. "It's just an old expression, but it would be nice if you two got along. You're going to drive each other crazy."

"Did he say anything?"

Mamma pushed open the front door. "He said you needed me to come right over and lend a hand. That fall was a mighty busy time at the Fox and you couldn't keep up. Said you needed me to pitch in for a few weeks and help out."

Mamma held out her arms, showing off her white blouse and black tailored slacks. "I'm dressed for work. You just tell me what to do. I'm all yours."

Well, there you go. Boone and his out-of-sorts were about carrying out his plan to get Mamma here as watchdog and being all pleased with himself that he pulled it off. The dance was just a dance and nothing more. Why would I think otherwise? It was Adam Levine's fault, pure and simple.

I plastered a big smile on my face for Mamma. "I'm glad you could make it. November is hectic. The change of seasons makes people want to change their wardrobes. I'll show you the ropes. You'll love working at the Fox. I have terrific customers."

BW trotted down the steps after having hogged the whole bed in my absence. He did the paws-out-butt-up stretch and yawned so wide I could see clear back to his tail. Oh, for the life of a dog. I let him out the back where chasing critters would lead to KiKi's yard or the Abbott's and not the street.

When I came back from the kitchen, Mamma was staring at the deserted campaign headquarters, no volunteers scurrying about, no phones ringing or fax machines grinding. A stack of flyers sat lonely and forlorn on a table, yard signs in the corner, discarded "Elect Gloria Summerside" hats on the floor, and more stuff back in the kitchen.

I came up beside her and took her hand. "Boone's going to find the killer, and then it's full steam ahead for your campaign. We'll make up for lost time. You'll be a wonderful alderman; everyone knows that."

"Scandal, even if it's later proven bogus, pretty much kills any chance of winning an election, honey. I think it's over for me."

"But Savannah needs you."

"I've been thinking about this," Mamma said with a smile, but it was one of those forced ones like when I got a D in chemistry after studying for a week. "Archie Lee will be okay as alderman. Getting on the ballot was a joke to him at first, but from what I hear he's taking it more seriously now. My fear is he'll be swayed by his beer-drinking buddies and not do what's best for the city, and you truly need to stay away from his bar. I hear his brother is mighty protective, almost as protective as my daughter is of me."

Mamma gave me a little wink and kissed my cheek. "Did you really land on your behind right out there in that alley?"

"I had a hankering for boiled peanuts, is all, and Archie Lee's brother thought I was there to cause trouble with me being your daughter. A little misunderstanding, there's nothing to worry about."

I hated Facebook. I hated that Zuckerberg guy and the Twitter guy and any communication device with a lower case *i* in front of it. The goal to connect the whole freaking world was making my life a living hell. How was I supposed to find Scummy's killer, keep Mamma from fretting over my well-being, and keep Boone off my back . . . or the dance floor?

BY NOON SALES WERE UP, AND I'D TAKEN IN A NICE batch of fall clothes for consignment along with a floral folding screen that we set up in front of the campaign headquarters in the parlor. We didn't need customers going in and poking around, and Mamma didn't need the constant reminder of what almost was.

In no time Mamma knew how to check people out and record the amounts so I could pay my consigners when they came in, and she'd really gotten into the swing of things by rearranging all the displays. Sweet saints in heaven, now the purples were in with the lime greens, orange with turquoise, and gold mixed in with pinks. A black scarf adorned a brown sweater, navy shoes sat next to black skirts, and an orange shoulder purse crossed a purple stripe coat.

Mamma had no color sense! Not one lick. Thank God she always wore black! I figured it was destiny along with a big dose of divine intervention that made her a judge, and she pretty much always dressed the black-and-white part. That she hired decorators to redo the house when she got the urge was a blessing from above. Thank you, Jesus!

Chantilly came in the front door, exchanged wide-eyed looks with two other shoppers, and held up her hands in astonishment. "What in the world is—"

"Is my mother doing here?" I cut in, pointing to Mamma behind the counter. "Mamma's come to help me, and she redid all my displays. Aren't they incredible?" I did the toothy-grin nod, hoping Chantilly would catch on.

"That's one way of putting it," Chantilly said. "Actually the displays are amazing. I don't know quite how she accomplished such a feat."

Mamma smiled, a little blush in her cheeks. I guess as a judge you don't get many compliments on sending people off to the pokey.

"Now that Chantilly's come to visit," Mamma said to me,

"and you have the extra help you need for a few hours, I'm going over to the courthouse. I won't be trying cases for a while, so I need to get things ready for the other judges taking my place starting on Monday."

Mamma nibbled her bottom lip for just a second, a hint of worry sneaking through. Then she was her bright, sunny self again. "I'll be back here tomorrow right after church and for the rest of the week," she added. "I can do the display in the front bay window. I'll make it special."

Mamma collected her purse and hustled out the door, and I felt my heart squeeze tight. Mamma was more worried than she was letting on. I hated that anything upset her. Baby bear protects mamma bear; at least that was my plan, and I wasn't doing all that good of a job.

Chantilly grabbed my shoulders, snapping me back to the moment. She looked me dead in the eyes. "What happened to this place? It's giving me a migraine. Isn't it giving you a migraine? You've got to find the . . ." She eyed the shoppers and mouthed the word *killer*. "And you've got to do it right fast."

"I know." And I meant it for more reasons than arranging displays. "I may have a lead, and it'll help you out, too. You can be my mole, my inside person."

Chantilly took a step away. "Uh-oh."

"It's a job. You said you needed a job."

"Uh-oh."

"You'll make some money, listen to what's going on, and maybe pick up why this particular person didn't care for you-know-who and maybe did you-know-what. It's the best of both worlds. Great idea, huh?"

"You want me to take a job with a you-know-what?"

"Well we don't know for sure, it's just a possibility, and best I can tell she only gets upset when you cross her; otherwise, she's a lovable little old gray-haired lady. She's a caterer."

Chantilly leaned across the checkout door, eyes thin slits, nose nearly touching mine. She whispered through gritted teeth, "You want me to work for someone who poisons people, and she's a cook!"

"Cuisine by Rachelle," I whispered back. "She's a caterer and needs a delivery person because Mamma sent her son to prison and he did the deliveries before. Since you know the city so well, being a UPS driver like you were, you're perfect. We know why she dislikes Mamma. All you have to do is find out why she dislikes Scummy and whether it is enough of a dislike for her to kill him and frame Mamma for it."

"In other words you want me to see if she's crazy as a loon."

"It's Saturday, and my guess is Rachelle is in her kitchen right now cooking for some event tonight. You should go see her. Tell her you were at Archie Lee's when she dropped off the buns and heard she needs a delivery person. She likes Archie Lee. You'll be able to pay your rent, not move in with your parents, and keep seeing Pillsbury. This is all in the name of love. Tell me, what do you think of that song 'One More Night'?"

"Lethal. A girl gets dancing to that and she could fall for an orangutan."

"That's just what I suspected. Rachelle will never figure

out that you know Mamma, but just in case she does don't eat anything."

I CLOSED THE SHOP AT FIVE TO MAKE GOOD ON MY promise to BW to bring home the bacon, or in his case the hotdogs. I grabbed Old Yeller and the denim jacket that should have been donated to the Goodwill years ago. It had a frayed right sleeve from my arm rubbing against the desk while scribbling all those notes during my college days. The pink smudge on the bottom was from the time KiKi and I sampled different nail polishes at the local CVS, the stain by the pocket was from picking strawberries with Mamma, and the yellow splotch was from painting the shutters of Cherry House for the first time. It was a stonewashed diary. How could I give this jacket to the Goodwill?

Kroger's was right around the corner, an easy walk from my house. I remembered my two reusable market eco-friendly bags so I could carry one in each hand, the trick being not to overload them so my arms were two inches longer when I got back from the store than when I left. The night air was crisp, a hint of wood smoke lingering from fireplaces in use to take the chill off the house as KiKi would say.

As I crossed the street, a red BMW slowed beside me, and the window powered down, framing Hollis's face in the opening. Hollis was in his mid-forties, a touch of gray at the temples, and *GQ* handsome. You know the saying *don't judge a book by its cover*? That went double for Hollis.

"Nothing better to do on a Saturday night than grocery shop?" Hollis quipped. "Thought you'd be hobnobbing out at the country club with the rest of us. Billy Bob Sayer's annual birthday bash. Headed there myself after picking up Judy Rollins; we're an item now."

"What do you want, Hollis?"

"I hear your mamma's moved her campaign headquarters to Cherry House. Gee, that's got to be real good for business." He laughed. Actually it was more of a sneer; with Hollis it was hard to tell one from the other. "Bet you're not making a dime with all that confusion. That big old house is going to have you in bankruptcy, Reagan, mark my words."

"And you want to sell it for me and spare me all that unnecessary aggravation. We've been through this, Hollis. I saved you from an orange jumpsuit wardrobe and mystery-meat cuisine for the next twenty to twenty-five years. Cherry House is mine free and clear."

"For old times' sake I can help you out in your time of need."

"I'm not in need, and old times was you bedding anything in a skirt and me too dumb to know what was going on."

"I can get a pretty penny for Cherry House now. If you wait till the holidays roll around, the market dries up. No one wants to move during the holidays."

"Bye, Hollis." I walked on, the BMW keeping pace, Hollis's head poking out the window turtle style.

"If your mamma can't shake this murder charge, you won't have any business; you realize that, don't you? A scandal like this gives everyone in the family a right bad name. Who will want to associate with the daughter of a murderer and that includes buying merchandise? You should sell now before things get worse. When Gloria goes on trial, things will get much worse, I promise."

"You have a buyer, don't you?"

"Loan's preapproved and everything. They have big plans for that house. Think about it, Reagan."

I gripped the window opening, and Hollis stopped the car. Expensive cologne oozed from the interior, and his minty-fresh breath fell across my face, devil horns neatly concealed under his hundred-dollar haircut. He probably had his pitchfork stashed in the trunk. "Judge Gloria Summerside would never kill anyone, but that doesn't mean her one and only daughter wouldn't if you get my drift."

An icy contempt flashed in his eyes. "I should never have listened to Boone."

Hollis floored the BMW, laying rubber like a teenager with too much car and too little brain. I cut across the parking lot. As much as I disliked Hollis Beaumont the Third, I had to admit our divorce was not all his fault. I was the stupid idiot who married him in the first place, and what did he mean about not listening to Boone? The only connection between me, Hollis, and Boone was the divorce that still gave me nightmares.

Saturday evening at the grocery store was pretty Zen with most people having better things to do than squeeze the tomatoes and read the ingredients on a cereal box. I loaded up on the essentials of life like SpaghettiOs and toilet paper, and wrote down a recipe on the back of my receipt for meatloaf that the checkout gal guaranteed even I could make and would impress Mamma to no end.

I stuffed the recipe in my pocket, hoisted Old Yeller onto my shoulder, and snagged my now full eco-friendly market bags. On the way out of Kroger's I picked up a free copy of the *Savannah Pennysaver* and met Mercedes coming through the door. Tonight she had on black slacks, a cream blouse, and a blue jewel-toned pashmina scarf with matching pumps I'd seen in the Nordstrom's fall catalog. Obviously spiffing up the dearly departed paid well.

"What's a fine girl like you doing here on a Saturday night?" Mercedes asked. "You should be out making whoopee with some young stud."

"I did the stud thing once, and it was a disaster."

"Honey, that's because you went and got yourself the wrong stud. I still got my eye on Mr. Boone for you. Now there's a fine-looking man and then some. You should give him a try."

Both grocery bags slid from my hands, the contents spilling out onto the sidewalk. Mercedes shifted her weight to one foot and looked me over head to toe. "You got something going on with Boone?"

"Nothing good."

"Uh-huh." Mercedes laughed and helped me with the items. She handed me the copy of the *Pennysaver* that I'd dropped along with the bags.

"Why there's Dozer on the front page of this here paper doing some advertising. My guess he's trying to recoup some of that business he's lost to Seymour."

"I met up with Dozer last night."

Mercedes arched her left brow high enough to touch her red bangs. "So that's what got you tossed out of the Cemetery? You got to be careful with Dozer. A few drinks and he gets real unpleasant, and if you're to keep winding up on the Internet, we need to do something about those roots you got going on."

I stepped off to the side and out of the way of shoppers coming and going, Mercedes following. I dropped my voice.

"You mentioned that Dozer was upset with Seymour outbidding him on projects. Last night when I was talking to him, he said he'd found out something about Seymour, something he was hiding. Something big. Do you think Dozer is capable of killing Seymour? But then why would he when he could just go to the police with this information he has and get rid of him that way? Do you have any idea what's going on?"

"Dozer couldn't turn in Seymour to the cops because Seymour probably had something on Dozer. You do me, and I do you kind of thing. Dozer runs a pretty big operation, and best I can tell Seymour was driving him into the ground financially. Building new houses is dead in Savannah and has been that way for a few years now. My guess is municipal projects are where the money is, but with cities being cash poor that's got to be mighty tight too and the competition stiff. I haven't had anything to do with Dozer in months, but if he came across some information that gave Seymour the edge in these municipal bidding wars, he'd be crazy mad about it."

"Crazy enough to kill him?"

"You can only push a man so far. You think someone was letting Seymour know the lowest bid on a project and then he'd turn in an even lower one."

"But then how could Seymour make money if the bid was so low? Something was going on between Seymour and Dozer, and Dozer was on the short end of the stick."

Mercedes pointed to the little map in Dozer's ad. "Delany Construction is a few blocks over from here. We could take a look around."

"It's Saturday night. He's closed."

"There's all kinds of closed, honey. The thing is, I like

your mamma. She's not one of those uppity snobs who think she's too good to talk to the likes of me. We both know she didn't kill Seymour, but somebody sure enough did. Dozer is as good a candidate as any. He wasn't nice to my girls back when I had the Mane Event, and I don't forget something like that ever."

"You should know that I have a way of attracting the wrong kind of attention lately. Well, actually, more than lately. I don't want to cause you trouble."

"I look at dead people all day long. I need something to liven things up a little. That's some more of that funeral home humor," Mercedes said on a laugh. "I was stopping here for ice cream for my cousin Scooter's birthday party, but he don't need that anyway with his cholesterol being off the charts the way it is. I got my car in the lot, but two women out walking, talking, and toting grocery bags is pretty ordinary stuff, unlike a pink Caddy circling the block and casing the place out. I say we get a move on and head on over toward Delany Construction."

Before I could protest, Mercedes snagged one of my bags and crossed onto Lincoln, heading in the direction of East Broad. A stiff breeze kicked up, sailing clouds across the sky and tumbling leaves and the occasional Starbucks cup down the sidewalk. I snuggled into my jacket, and Mercedes wrapped her pashmina tighter around her shoulders. Big Victorians gave way to basic clapboard domiciles with narrow pockmarked alleys in back. Streetlights were of the glaring blue-white variety, and fences were chain link instead of ornamental wrought iron. Mercedes told me stories from the Mane Event that would make a terrific HBO series.

Traffic was sparse, no one out strolling on a blustery autumn evening. Residential morphed into light industrial. Buildings sat farther apart now with security lights scattered here and there. Oglethorpe Marble and Granite sat on one corner, Delany's on the other.

The office was brick with white shutters and matching window boxes overflowing with orange and yellow chrysanthemums. A green awning with "Delany Construction" in white letters sheltered the front door, and there was a line of decorative boxwoods by the street. The gravel road ran back to a warehouse, bulldozers, backhoes, cranes, and other earthmoving equipment men salivate over from childhood and beyond. And everything was safe and secure behind industrial strength chain link and a growling, drooling guard dog.

"Guess this is as far as we get tonight." I shifted my bag to my other hand.

"There's a gap where the gates are padlocked together in front." Mercedes pointed in that direction. "Bet you could squeeze your skinny behind through that there opening."

"And wind up being Killer's midnight snack."

Mercedes put her hand to her ample hip. "Girl, where's all this negativity coming from?"

"I've had a few setbacks lately."

"Then it's time for a change of luck. What we need here is some sort of dog distraction. Get that bad boy's mind off guarding and onto something else, and we can get inside. Since we don't have a sexy little poodle to strut her stuff around, we'll have to come up with plan B."

Mercedes held her black patent leather purse under the streetlight and rummaged around. "I got a pack of Juicy Fruit in here and some of those sour Icebreakers. Love sour

Icebreakers. Maybe Killer does, too. Had a dog once who couldn't get enough brussels sprouts. Smelled something fierce and would bring tears to your eyes."

I pulled the package of hot dogs from my eco-friendly bag. "Better than brussels sprouts."

I plucked out a cold chunk of processed meat, and Mercedes and I crept toward the fence. "Here doggie, doggie, doggie," Mercedes sing-songed as I stuck the hot dog through to the other side, keeping my fingers out of snapping range. Growling and snarling, Killer trotted over, eyes mean, lips curled back, teeth bared. He sniffed; he ate; he wagged.

"Well, I'll be. Now we're in the money," Mercedes said as I pulled a handful of hot dogs from the package. "Women like their jewelry, but for men it's all about food; they cave every time. Feed Killer some of those things now and stuff the rest in your pocket. You got to get yourself back out of that there office, you know."

I gave Killer a wary look.

"He's harmless," Mercedes soothed. "Nothing but a big old pussycat now that we fed him."

I slid the flashlight from my purse and sat Old Yeller beside the two grocery bags. "I don't see any security cameras mounted on the office, but I bet there are plenty back by the warehouse and equipment. You know, I don't have a clue what I'm looking for."

"Sometimes you just have to take a leap of faith, honey. Do what comes along next, and trust in the Lord to lead the way."

"You think the Lord's leading the way to breaking and entering Dozer's office?"

"He got us this far with hot dogs and an opening in that there gate, didn't he?"

She had a point. I tossed a hot dog on the ground for Killer and stuck my head then the rest of me through the opening. Killer looked up, a what-the-heck-are-you-doing-here expression on his face. I swear it really was that kind of expression. He licked his chops, suddenly more interested in me on this side of the fence than the meat on the ground.

"Uh, maybe you should come back out of there," Mercedes said. "That dog's getting himself an attitude."

Except Killer growled and circled around, cutting me off from the exit. Mercedes's gaze fused with mine. "What should I do?"

"Give him another hot dog. Hurry. He's looking real upset."

I dropped another hot dog then another, Killer gobbling as fast as I dropped. I ran backward toward the office, dropping more meat, Killer gaining on me till I crashed flat against the door; it only now occurred to me that I didn't have a key to get inside.

Chapter Nine

"I DON'T know how to get in," I yelled to Mercedes, every hair on my body standing on end. "There are more hot dogs in the bags."

Mercedes pulled out the second package and kicked our purses and the bags behind the boxwoods. She put an expensive suede shoe against one side of the opening, pulled back on the other side Superwoman style, and wedged her head and shoulders through. She looked like a piglet stuck in the rabbit hole till she gave a final wiggle and popped out like a champagne cork from a bottle.

Killer looked up at the racket, zeroed in on Mercedes, and licked his chops. She ripped the package and flung it out into the yard, hot dogs flying in all directions. Mercedes galloped my way, Killer deciding between fast food on the ground and two-hundred pounds on the hoof. Hot dogs won out, and Mercedes pulled up beside me on the step huffing and puffing.

"Now we're both stuck out here," I said, Killer devouring package number two.

"The Lord will provide, honey."

"Provide Killer with dessert, and that would be us."

Mercedes laughed. "Chocolate and vanilla." Then she reached behind, turned the knob, and miracle of miracles the door opened! Killer charged as Mercedes and I scrambled in and slammed the door, and a hundred pounds of totally pissed-off dog hit solid wood.

"How'd you know the door would open?" I wheezed, sinking into an overstuffed chair, my heart beating a million times a second and Killer serenading us with growls and snarls.

Mercedes grinned, looking calm as a heifer in clover. "If you had a big old fence and Killer the dog on retainer, would you bother to lock your door?"

"Why didn't you just tell me that while you were standing on the sidewalk?"

"Didn't occur to me till I was running this way."

I smacked my palm to my forehead. "How could I think of the hot dogs and remember the flashlight and forget about getting inside the office? Bet 007 never had days like this."

Mercedes patted me on the head. "Honey, you're 008 in my book. You're trying to save your mamma. Nothing's better than that. Now we better get a move on before that dog claws his way in here."

Street light sliced through the blinds marking rows of dark and light on the carpet, couch, chairs, and the tables decorated with artificial flowers. A little kitchenette with an eating bar sat toward the back.

"Smells sort of musty in here," Mercedes said, walking around. "Not that nice new smell of success. Dozer's in a hurt all right. This here area in front is for customers picking out things for their dream home. I'm guessing offices are down the hall."

I flipped on my flashlight, keeping it trained at the floor so as not to draw attention from anyone passing by. Mercedes followed. There were offices on each side, one furnished with basic Ikea, the other an antique desk with comfy chair and a row of file cabinets.

"Doesn't take a genius to figure out which office is Dozer's and which belongs to the hired help," Mercedes said, heading inside. I handed her the flashlight. "How about you take the file cabinets, and I'll take the computer." I sat behind the desk and powered up the old Dell.

"Over here it looks like customer files on houses and projects," Mercedes said, drawers sliding open and shut. "I got nothing but pictures of appliances, cabinets, and carpeting and lists of products, manufacturers, and catalog numbers. Here's the Alcamps' beach house out on Tybee, the Andersons' house on Skidaway, the George Boifeuillet Warehouse on Washington Square when they converted it over to the Mulberry Inn. These are all from years ago."

"Nothing's password protected on the computer," I said. "Guess Dozer's not a techy kind of guy." There were folders labeled *Alcamp*, *Anderson*, *Boifeuillet* that corresponded to the cabinet files and right at the end was *Seymour*.

"Find anything?" Mercedes wanted to know as she came up beside me. "I got nothing over there."

I pointed at the screen. "There's a Seymour file on Dozer's desktop, but it's just a list of the projects that I'm guessing Dozer lost out on because the library project is listed at the end."

I opened the top desk drawer to chewed pencils, Tums, Pepto-Bismol and a manila folder marked *Seymour*. I flipped it open. "Newspaper articles? This one's on that porch collapsing at Shady Haven Senior Center, this one's on the roof at the SPCA leaking like a sieve, and here's one on that new floor needed over there at the library. What's with that, the library's not even two years old?"

Mercedes picked up the articles, a picture sliding to the floor. She retrieved it and held it under the flashlight. "It's a picture of a bunch of numbers and abbreviations on a piece of wood."

"It's a lumber stamp. They use them at the mills so you know what you're buying. The numbers and letters are code for grades, sizes, species, and moisture content. Construction grade lumber and standard grade lumber are for residential building. Utility grade has about a third the strength, so using that to hold up your roof may not be a great idea. This stamp says this piece of lumber is grade two. It's for roofs, floors, load-bearing walls, 15 percent moisture content, fir, and the BHLC with Mill 10 means it's from Butler Haber Lumber Company number 10."

"Yo, girlfriend, you've been watching way too much of *This Old House*?"

"Honey, I own this old house. You should see me change out a faucet."

Mercedes snatched up the folder and headed for the Ikea office. "I'll make copies, and you are in desperate need of a life."

"Hey, I have a life."

"Uh-huh."

I emailed KiKi an attachment of the Seymour folder, my

name in the subject line, then deleted the action from Dozer's sent folder so there'd be no record. If Uncle Putter saw an email from Delany Construction, he'd think I was fixing up my place. When KiKi saw it, she'd be ticked as all get out she missed the action, knowing I was up to something. I had no idea what either of these folders meant, but Scummy's business in Dozer's files meant something was going on between these two, and one of them was dead.

Mercedes rushed back in, her eyes huge. "Sweet Jesus, a cop car just drove by. You know faucets; I know cops. They drive up the street, and they'll be driving back down. We got to get out of here before they realize Killer's at the door for a reason."

I powered down the computer, Mercedes slid the copies under her pashmina, and we slid the folder back in the desk drawer. She doused the flashlight, and we scurried toward the main room, Killer still barking his head off.

"He's sounding kind of hoarse," Mercedes said. "Giving himself a bad case of canine laryngitis. Bet he feels right poorly tomorrow. How many hot dogs you got left?"

I pulled out an empty wrapper.

"We'll have to fake it. Women are real good at faking lots of things." She grabbed the doorknob. "I open, you toss the wrapper, and we run like the devil. On three. One, two." Mercedes whipped open the door, completely throwing off my timing.

"You said on three. That was two."

"That was on three. Throw the wrapper!"

Killer charged inside leaping for the airborne plastic. Mercedes and I tore out the door, slamming it closed behind us, Killer now growling and barking on the other side. We hustled to the gate, and I squeezed through, then Mercedes as a police cruiser pulled to the curb, red and blue lights flashing in the night.

"You weren't kidding about attracting the wrong kind of attention," Mercedes said as Mr. Uniformed Officer got out, rattled off his name, and blinded me with his flashlight. Another guy in a suit got out on the passenger side. Uniformed guy was bald and beefy, suit guy young and scrumptious.

"What are you doing in there?" Beefy asked, nodding to the office.

I glanced back to Killer barking and snarling like the banshee from hell. "Well, you see—"

"That's what's going on," Mercedes said, pointing at the office and taking over like someone who'd encountered the police before. "That poor little doggie is in some severe distress, I tell you. We were out for a night walk and heard the thing carrying on something pitiful and thought he might be in trouble, so we took ourselves right over there to have a look-see. But he's okay," Mercedes added with a bright-eyed grin. "Gotta take care of our furry little friends now, don't we?"

Uniform put his hands on his hips. "Dozer has that dog outside to watch the place. What's he doing inside the office?"

"See?" Mercedes added. "That's exactly what got us all worried."

"What's your names?"

"Ann . . . Ann Taylor," I said, thinking of the pile of fall catalogs on my counter and the fact that the police did not need to know Gloria Summerside's daughter was in on this. "And this is Donna Karan."

Suit folded his arms. "Donna Karan's a designer."

I nodded at Mercedes. "Her mamma has good taste."

"You always carry a flashlight on your walks? You two sure you're not out here for no good," Suit said, rounding the cruiser.

"Not unless we're going to drive off with a backhoe or crane." My smartass remark got me a *don't poke the bear* look from Mercedes. She was right; the bear might look handsome, but his eyes said he was trouble. He was Hollis with a badge.

"Kind of dark back here," I said. "But we like the solitude when out walking. Om shanti, shanti, shanti," I chanted in a calm voice. "Means *peace prevail everywhere.* We go to Amy's House of Yoga over there on Whittaker twice a week. We're getting really good at inverted tortoise."

Uniform pushed his hat back on his head as if trying to picture Mercedes doing inverted anything. "Guess the dog's okay till tomorrow. Dozer must have forgotten to let him out. I'll give him a call."

The officer and the suit got back in the cruiser, and Mercedes and I started for the grocery bags, the cruiser following us at a snail's pace.

"Donna Karan?" Mercedes hissed in a low voice. "Do I look like a Donna Karan?"

"Better than L.L.Bean."

"I'll get the grocery bags and put these copies of the news articles in your purse. I'll drop them off later tonight. Right now we best keep walking."

"I'M GONE FOR ONE DAY, AND YOU REPLACE ME," KiKi said, pacing my bedroom in an aqua housecoat, matching curlers, and velour slippers.

I pried one eye open. "It's seven A.M. on a Sunday. What are you doing up at seven A.M. on any day?" I put my pillow over my head, BW burrowing his head under the covers. I so needed to find a better hiding place for my spare key.

"I was sleeping all peaceful like, and Putter was on the computer," KiKi went on. "He said there was an email from Delany Construction with your name on it. I knew you were up to something and then remembered seeing Mercedes's Caddy dropping bags at your house last night. One measly day I'm not around, and you go off without me." She sniffed.

Oh dear Lord in heaven, KiKi was playing the martyr role. I pushed myself up on one elbow and flipped my hair out of my face. "We were just trying to get some information on Seymour and Dozer, and since it was a Saturday night, we just sort of headed toward his office."

"I bet there was breaking and entering involved. You never include me in breaking and entering. I do all the boring stuff like go to funerals and get locked in closets."

"You went to jail, and you've jumped from a fire escape—that was pretty cool—and if Uncle Putter finds out you're into B&E, he'll have you tethered to the front porch."

Auntie KiKi stopped pacing, a twinkle dancing in her eyes. "I got nothing going on tonight. I'm free, bored to tears, and Putter's driving up to Augusta for a seminar on obstructive hypertrophic cardiomyopathy."

"Sounds impressive."

"It's really an excuse to play at the Augusta National Golf Club where they hold that there Masters tournament every year, and I'm sure there will be new golf clubs involved. This is your big chance to make it up to me; let's do something risky tonight."

My one hard and fast rule with my dear auntie KiKi was not to get her involved with things blatantly against the law and obviously risky. That didn't mean breaking the law and risky didn't happen en route, but at least I started out with good intentions.

"What about church?" I asked.

"What about it."

"It's Sunday morning; we should go."

KiKi leaned over my bed, a huge scowl on her face. "Your answer to leaving me out in the cold and taking up with Mercedes is hauling me off to church?"

"We need to meet up with Marigold, and she's a lector at the ten o'clock Mass. I think Butler may be involved with Seymour, and I want to see if she knows anything about it. Talking with her is a whole lot easier than chatting it up with her storm trooper husband."

KiKi put her hands to her hips. "You're patronizing me, aren't you? You have yourself a new buddy, and I'm just yesterday's news. Church?" She added a harrumph for good measure.

How could I feel so guilty about not including my auntie in a burglary and nearly getting eaten by a dog? It was the Savannah way. No one did guilt-tripping better than an excluded Southern family member. Obviously excluded from what didn't matter.

"We still need to go to the savings and loan and find out about Cazy. We can do that tomorrow. Bet they still have some toasters."

KiKi folded her arms and tapped her foot. "That's nothing like sneaking into Dozer's office, and that's what you did if you're sending me emails from there at night."

"Rachelle Lerner's a caterer. She hated Scummy and doesn't care much for Mamma. I'm hoping Chantilly got a job with her, but just in case that falls through, we can order dinner and chat with her. She does a mean potpie."

"Potpie is no match for sneaking."

"We can talk to Delray Valentine, Scummy's campaign manager. I bet Valley will be mean as a snake and twice as rude when we ask him a bunch of irritating, nosy questions. That could be exciting."

"He sells insurance for crying out loud. Is there anything more boring than insurance?" KiKi let out a deep sigh. "All right, all right, I'll go to church. Pretty sad state of affairs when church is the most exiting thing on the list. I need to go anyway with all the half-truths I've been handing Putter lately. Think God will forgive me?"

"I think the question is will Uncle Putter if he finds out?"

THE CATHEDRAL OF ST. JOHN THE BAPTIST WAS across from Lafayette Square. It had twin spires because one just wasn't good enough, gorgeous marble columns, terrific stained-glass windows, and the baptismal font in the back where I was baptized. At Christmastime the place was decked out with a manger, greenery, and a huge red poinsettia tree.

For the next forty-five minutes I let my mind drift through church, thinking of how I should get here more often and I'd really appreciate any help God could spare in getting Mamma off the hook. I also told Him to watch out for Seymour 'cause he had a nasty side and could ruin the neighborhood.

"I don't see Marigold anywhere," KiKi said to me over the thundering pipe organ as we came out onto the steps, sunlight and a cloudless sky making it a perfect day in Savannah. "We know she was here because she did a reading. She didn't look real happy up there at the lectern."

"That's 'cause she had to pronounce Shadrach, Meshach, and Abednego. That's enough to distress anyone."

KiKi nodded to the side. "There's Detective Ross. Talk about someone down in the mouth; she looks plum miserable. Maybe we should go cheer her up?"

"Uh, she tossed you and Mamma in the slammer and has had me down at the police station more than once. I don't think cheer is a word she associates with the Summerside family."

KiKi tsked and made the sign of the cross. "We should at least try and console the poor girl, this being a church-going Sunday and all, and the sermon about helping out when needed. Besides, we haven't done anything this morning she can arrest us for." KiKi thought for a moment. "Have we?"

"Good morning," I said to Ross, KiKi offering a big smile. "You have the weekend off?" Idle chitchat with Ross felt really weird. Usually our conversations were Ross saying something like, *Dear God, it's you again,* and me responding with *I didn't do it, I swear.*

Startled, Ross looked around, probably searching for a dead body since KiKi and I were here. "I might have the rest of my life off with this new detective they brought in from Atlanta. He's trying to make me look bad." Ross opened her big purse and yanked out a glazed doughnut. She took a bite, eyes fogging over, grin and icing on her lips, a satisfied sigh escaping around a mouthful.

"Want one," she mumbled, holding her purse wide open to reveal six more doughnuts snuggled in right next to her gun. "They're from Cakery Bakery, of course. GracieAnn's doing a right fine job with the place these days." Ross brushed flecks of glaze from her blue suit. "I gotta go. GracieAnn said she'd have a fresh batch done by the time I got out of church. Chocolate with chocolate icing." Ross scampered down the steps.

"Is it just my imagination," KiKi wondered aloud, "or is her backside getting bigger? The seams on that there suit of hers are straining to keep the girl under wraps. Can't imagine how such a thing can happen in just a few days."

"It's the way of the doughnut." I knew from personal experience. *My name is Reagan, and I'm addicted to sprinkle doughnuts.* On more than one occasion I'd walked blocks out of my way not to pass Cakery Bakery and add unwanted poundage. "Looks like Ross is a stress eater," I said. "She's going to gain back all that weight she lost. Seems a pity."

"Except you got to admit she's a lot nicer with a doughnut in her mouth and five more in her purse. She didn't even try to arrest us." KiKi nodded toward Lafayette Square. "There's Marigold sitting on a bench staring at the ground. Looks like she could do with one of Ross's doughnuts."

"Are you all right?" I asked Marigold as KiKi and I parked beside her, the fountain in the middle of the square happily splashing from one tier to the next. "You don't look so good. Is there anything we can do to help?"

"You bet there is," Marigold said, fire in her eyes. "You can hand me a big old shotgun and stand back 'cause I'm going to put Butler Haber in the ground if it's the last thing I do." Marigold strangled her purse as if practicing for the event. "That jackass has done ruined our lives. I told him and told him not to do something stupid and get involved with Seymour, but did he listen? Heck no."

"Men never listen," KiKi offered. "Besides, Seymour's dead as a roach on the steps. We can all go toss rocks at his grave if it'll make you feel better."

"Only if we can put Money-Honey in that coffin right there beside him. Did you know she's taking over the construction company? Called Butler last night, the very night her husband is planted in the ground, mind you, to tell him it's going to be business as usual."

Time to go fishing. "What business?" I asked.

"When things were bad, Butler burned through our savings then cut lumber prices to attract business, but Seymour wanted more and more cuts. Honey is doing the same thing. We're doomed."

"So just refuse to sell to her."

"You'd think that would be the answer, except Butler says Seymour has him over a barrel. I'm done leaving things up to Butler. I'm taking the situation into my own hands and getting them done right."

"Like lighting candles at church?"

"Like going to see Odilia."

KiKi sucked air through clenched teeth, and we all three huddled closer together on the bench. In New Orleans such things were laughed and joked about and bought as souvenirs. In Savannah we knew better. Last year Buffy Codetta went to see Odilia, and three weeks later her abusive, rotten, fit-as-a-fiddle mother-in-law drove her brand new Lincoln right off the Savannah River bridge, and no one's seen hide nor hair of her or the Lincoln since.

"What did Odilia say?" KiKi asked, her voice just above a whisper.

"Drop the money in the jar on the table, put a basket of eggplants and eight colorful stones from the earth at Seymour's place of business, and come back tonight after midnight for more instructions."

Marigold opened her hand to eight rocks sitting in her palm. "I found these under the bench just now. Think they'll do?"

"This here is a piece of dirty glass," KiKi said, changing it out for a pinkish rock she found beside her. "That should work nicely."

Marigold dropped the stones in a white lace hanky then put them in her purse and snapped it closed. She tucked the purse tightly under her arm. "I best be getting to the grocery store before they're all out of eggplants and baskets. Got my eye on some pink lacy ribbon to make the basket look good. We got tough times here, lots of people needing eggplants and baskets and ribbons these days."

Marigold took off across the square, and KiKi waited a beat then said, "This has got something to do with you at Dozer's last night doesn't it? Butler has the lumberyard, Dozer's a contractor, and so is Seymour. What in the world did you find out?" She gave me the evil-auntie eye. "And I'm not budging from this here spot till you tell me what's going on with those three."

Here's the deal. I could lie and say I didn't find out anything at Dozer's, or I could make something up, but KiKi would know because I sucked at lying. She'd get all bent out of shape and be more ticked off than she already was, and she just might go off and snoop around on her own. God forbid! That's how she wound up on that fire escape the last time we played find-the-killer.

"I'm going to tell you what I know, which isn't much, and I have a lot of questions, and you can't go off half-cocked and get in trouble and—"

"Oh for crying in a bucket, you're worse than Congress. Will you just get to the point?"

"That attachment I sent to you is for Seymour Construction projects. That's it."

"You think I just fell off the cabbage truck? What's the rest?"

"There was also a manila folder in Dozer's desk with a picture of a stamp lumber yards use to grade wood along with articles on buildings with structural problems. Seymour buildings."

I pulled the copies from my purse and spread them across Old Yeller balanced on my lap. "This stamp says this wood is suitable for construction. The higher the number the lower the grade; spruce is nice for a Christmas tree but not so much for building. I don't know what the connection is, but there's something going on."

KiKi picked up the newspaper copies and studied them for a second. "I say we contemplate this tonight over a big pitcher of martinis, but right now we got other problems, like the Fox opens in ten minutes and you know your mamma's itching to redo that display in the front bay window."

"Oh Lordy, not the front window." I jumped up, and we hurried for the car. "Maybe we can head her off. You never warned me about the color issue, you know."

"Gloria and I shared a room for a while growing up," Auntie KiKi explained. "It was her chartreuse and plum phase. Who do you think talked her into being a judge?"

KiKi beeped open the Batmobile. "We can't be discussing any of this Dozer stuff in front of your mamma. It'll worry her to death if she thinks we're nosing around on her behalf."

I nodded in agreement and tried to figure out how to keep KiKi from the nosing part as well. The problem was, if there was another Mercedes occurrence and KiKi wasn't included, I'd wind up worm food in her rose garden. KiKi got in the driver's side, and Boone beat me to the handle on the passenger side. He put his arm across the opening, jaw set, eyes lit with fire, suggesting more Tony Soprano than Fabio.

"You got something against turning thirty-three?"

Chapter Ten

"I'M not in the mood for a lecture," I said to Boone, the breeze ruffling through the trees and messing my hair. Not that it looked great to begin with, but I did do the mousse and blow-dry regime in honor of church.

"Someone should chain you to the radiator and throw away the key. You're corrupting my cleaning lady."

"You don't have anything to clean, and we were taking a walk is all."

"Out by Delany Construction? One of the top scenic spots in Savannah for sure. You should have stayed on the street side of Dozer's fence. The man's real protective of his establishment."

"How do you know we didn't?"

"Dog inside, empty hot dog wrappers, recipe for meatloaf on the back of a Kroger receipt left behind and the checkout girl remembering exactly who she gave that recipe to. Dozer was mighty proud of himself last night at the Cemetery for tracking you down. Now you've pissed off Dozer and Archie Lee. Maybe you should think about taking a vacation."

Boone folded his arms and leaned against the car. "That guy in the suit who stopped you last night is the detective from Atlanta taking Ross's place. He was out doing a ride-along to get a feel for the city. He wanted to know who Ann Taylor was. He thinks you're cute."

I did the palms-up who-me gesture. "Ann Taylor?"

"That purse you lug around and the description of Mercedes don't leave much to the imagination. He wants to get to know you better, something about inverted turtle. We think you should go out with him. Keep him busy, give him something to do here in Savannah besides get in everyone's hair."

"We?"

"The Savannah police department. The guy's out for glory at your mamma's expense and is trying to make Ross and the department look inept in the process."

"So now I'm a decoy, a distraction?"

"For the greater good."

I studied Boone for a second, mulling over the Suit situation. "And there's the part that if I'm with the Suit I'm out of *your* hair. What happens when he finds out Ann Taylor is Gloria Summerside's daughter? Won't he be a little ticked off that he's been played?"

"Who's going to tell him? All I want to do is keep this guy busy while I nail the killer. As far as he's concerned it's a done deal. Your mamma did the deed, and he's not even looking at anyone else. He got a search warrant for Gloria's house and found a copy of *Pretty Poisonous Posies* and a hand shovel next to two shriveled-up foxglove plants in her garden shed. Like someone was digging in a hurry."

"That shed isn't locked, and Mamma would never leave her garden tools for days on end without cleaning up the mess, and she'd never own such a book. Bet they didn't find fingerprints on that book."

"They didn't find prints on anything, chalking it up to the garden gloves."

"A book would have fingerprints on it. Didn't it occur to that suited idiot if Mamma killed Seymour, she'd cover her tracks better than this? How stupid does this guy think a criminal judge is? He's got to see that the stuff in the shed is pretty thin evidence."

"He sees this as another nail in Gloria's coffin. Just keep him busy, will you? Entertain him. Charm him. Take him to dinner and tell him Savannah stories. Lie. I don't care what the heck you do with him, just do something. I have a few leads, but I need time without him sniffing around where he doesn't belong."

What leads? I wanted to know, and it wasn't going to happen. Boone looked at me for a second then trudged off. He stopped halfway down the block, paused, and came back. He ran his hand over his buzzed hair. "Forget it. Forget I said anything about meeting up with him. I don't want you messing with that guy."

"You think he's dangerous."

"No. Maybe." Boone tucked the strap of Old Yeller under the collar of my denim jacket and smoothed it down, his fingers warm at my throat, his eyes more soft than serious, "One More Night" playing in the back of my brain, slowly melting me into a big dish of oatmeal.

"He's an arrogant ass," Boone added, his voice without the edge. "I don't want you around that guy. I'll figure out something else to keep him occupied while he's here, but stay out of trouble for a while. I can't keep an eye on you and the suit, and find the killer, too."

"Let me help."

"Not going to happen, Blondie. Go sell some dresses and shoes."

Boone hustled off and I yelled after him, "I hate when you tell me to sell dresses and shoes."

He turned; the grin was back. "Really?"

I got in the car and slammed the door.

"What was that all about?" KiKi asked, edging out into the light Sunday traffic, a bank of dark clouds now crowding out the sun.

"Boone being Boone. He wanted me to make goo-goo eyes at some detective guy from Atlanta then said to forget it, that he'd take care of things all by himself. I swear I think the man's having some kind of mid-thirties breakdown; he doesn't know what the heck he wants. Do this, do that, don't do this, don't do that. I'm Mr. Wonderful, I can take care of everything by myself, and you can go sell dresses and shoes. He needs therapy or maybe a good swift kick in the rump for the dresses-and-shoes crack."

"He's a good lawyer, you know, and a good dancer."

The rest of my tirade died in my throat. "How do you know about the dancing? The kids tell you?" I puffed out a breath of exasperation. "The kids didn't have to tell you because every woman east of the Mississippi probably knows Boone's a good dancer in and out of the bedroom."

"Not exactly."

"Not exactly what?" I cut my gaze to KiKi, waiting for the rest of the story, but all I got from her was a sassy auntie smile as she turned into her driveway. At one time my dear auntie KiKi would have hog-tied Boone and thrown him in the Savannah River for the way he handled my divorce. Then he saved her bacon in the great fire escape caper and now she thought he was the second coming.

The front door of the Fox stood wide open, and BW rushed out, tail wagging, to meet us. Mamma stood on a stepladder in the bay window doing something with orange and lilac that would make Ralph Lauren weep.

"Thought I'd get a head start on the day," Mamma said, as KiKi and I came inside, a few customers filing in behind us, staring at the bay window in disbelief. Mamma rubbed her arms. "Better close the door; the weather's changing. Going to be colder today."

"We were at church," KiKi volunteered.

Mamma did a double take and nearly fell off the stool. "So that's what's brought on the change in the weather. Probably snow tomorrow."

KiKi retaliated with a sarcastic sibling eye roll and added, "Marigold was there. She said Honey is taking over Seymour Construction."

"Doesn't surprise me." Mamma put a lavender scarf to a Kelly jacket. "She'll do well; she has drive and ambition and . . ." Mamma looked around to see if anyone was listening, then added in a lower voice, "She's just as mean, ornery, and cantankerous as her husband."

I got the daily cash for the Fox out of the Reagan vault, also known as the rocky road container. I transferred the money to my Godiva chocolate box I kept at the counter.

Cheap, functional, and it smelled like dessert when I made a sale.

KiKi wrote up a sale for two customers at the counter, and three more customers came in the front door. Mamma hung up clothes from the dressing room. Business! I felt a little less panicked about the heating bills soon to be gracing my mailbox as Chantilly strolled in hand in hand with Pillsbury. Shoppers paused, Pillsbury's black leather jacket with dollar signs embroidered on the back, boots, and muscle-bound physique not those of the typical customer to frequent the Prissy Fox.

"I got that job with Rachelle Lerner," Chantilly said as the two came up to the checkout door. "Her shop is as cute as a button. It has a few tables for eating, but it's mostly catering and carryout. I'm already working. I dropped off quiches, sticky buns, and fruit salad to the First Baptist Church on Bull Street this morning and helped them get things organized for their brunch. Rachelle makes dynamite sticky buns, even better than my mamma's, but you can't be telling my mamma that. Problem is Rachelle's hurting for business, and I don't know why. Her menu is perfection."

Pillsbury drew Chantilly a little closer, the dopey, happy grin on the badass man of the hood a little startling. "This girl of mine is off the hook," he said in his deep baritone voice that sort of vibrated clear through the floorboards. "Scrambled eggs and French toast." Pillsbury kissed Chantilly on the cheek. "Babe."

"That means she's a good cook," I translated for KiKi then asked Chantilly, "Did you learn anything?"

"You bet. I'm a natural at mac and cheese, and you should see me whisk egg whites. Beat those suckers into shape in no time. I think I found my calling."

"I was thinking more along the lines of Rachelle doing you-know-what to you-know-who." I leaned across the checkout door. "Let me know if she mentions anything about a guy named Dozer or Butler Haber."

"Haber?" Pillsbury's brows drew tight together, his face hard, mean, scary, and back to badass. Not the kind of guy you want to meet up with all alone in an alley. Whatever Butler did he shouldn't have.

"Bad dude," Pillsbury added. "Big Joey helped fix up a house. Last week the woman fell through the steps and busted a hip. Had to vacate the premises; she's in a wheelchair. Haber thinks poor folk are stupid 'cause they don't live in some fancy digs. He gives them cheap wood for prime prices. Bad business that." Pillsbury shook his head. "Real bad business."

"Why do you think the wood's bad?" I asked Pillsbury. "Maybe it was something else. It could be the weather or even termites?"

He shook his head. "Wood don't rot like that in a few years unless something's wrong with it."

"What's going on?" Mamma asked, bringing a customer up to the counter to check out a dress and shoes. Mamma stopped dead when she saw Pillsbury. Oh boy, it was going to be one of those didn't-I-send-your-best-friend-to-prison confrontations, and things would get ugly fast.

"Well now, if you aren't the spitting image of Gerome Morehead," Mamma said to Pillsbury. "He used to do my taxes till he retired some years back and moved off to Arizona. He's a true wizard with numbers. Saved me a bundle, I can tell you that. I sure do miss him."

"He's my granddaddy." Pillsbury beamed. "Did he ever play his ukulele for you?"

"'Sweet Georgia Brown' was my favorite. Tell him I said hello, now, you hear?"

"Yes, ma'am, I sure will." Pillsbury took Mamma's small hand in his much larger one and gave her an ear-to-ear smile that warmed the heart. Mamma was the one woman who never ceased to amaze me.

KiKi was busy in the afternoon with a secret cha-cha lesson with the Danforths so they could show up the Reynolds at the next country club shindig. That was followed up by another secret cha-cha lesson with the Reynolds so they could show up the Danforths. It was the year of the great Savannah cha-cha wars.

Mamma and I were busy as ants at a picnic with customers and sales, and we locked up the Fox at five sharp. "I have dinner with the judges filling in for me," Mamma said. "I'll be back bright and early tomorrow morning."

I gave Mamma a big hug. "We're going to straighten this out, and you'll get your courtroom back, and then we'll give Archie Lee a run for his money."

She kissed me on the cheek. "I'm sure everything will be fine."

"Because you trust the system."

"Of course, and if I'm not alderman, worse things have happened." She glanced around the shop. "You have a nice business here. The displays were a little shoddy until I came along, but you've done well. You're going to need some help. Maybe I'll take early retirement and come lend a hand. I had fun today."

Mamma collected her purse, and I followed her out onto the porch. She headed for her black Caddy parked across the street. "Okay, God," I said while waving Mamma off as she drove down Gwinnett. "I did the church thing this morning, I was even nice to Ross and didn't take her doughnuts, and now you hit me with Mamma working at the Fox?" I rolled my eyes skyward. "Are you having a good time up there or what?"

I gave BW a potty break, cleaned up after him like a good doggie mommy, then grabbed my denim jacket from inside. The two of us headed for KiKi's, me looking forward to martinis, BW looking forward to handouts from the fridge. At my house food was pretty much the great unknown . . . do I have some or not? At KiKi's the fridge was Southern cooking at it's finest packed in Tupperware, and the golf ball cookie jar was always full of something chocolate.

BW and I went around the back of the house, letting ourselves in through the iron-rose gate that had graced the premises since before the Yankees came a callin'. I turned the doorknob to let myself in like I always did, except the door was locked.

"KiKi," I bellowed like a cranky five-year-old. I added a few knocks to the door for good measure. The only response I got was a big dose of worry sliding down my back. She wasn't home, and KiKi was looking forward to digging into the Seymour/Dozer/Butler quagmire as much as I was . . . maybe more. So where the heck was she?

I hustled to the garage. No car. "Maybe she had to run an errand," I explained to BW while trying to convince myself it was true. I know it's not logical to panic because your auntie isn't home to serve up a martini, but cutting KiKi out of the action, in this case the Dozer action, had consequences.

In my mind I was keeping her safe; in KiKi's mind it was *So she thinks I'm too old, does she; well, I'll show her.* I had a bad feeling this was one of those I'll-show-her situations.

The manila folder! I tore open Old Yeller to find no copies inside. Of course they weren't inside; that sneaky auntie had distracted me with visions of Mamma doing the display in the bay window and snatched the papers in my time of decorating distress. The missing copies of the articles and the picture of the lumber stamp coupled with Pillsbury's tales of Butler and the collapsed house told me where KiKi was. Well, I didn't know exactly where she was, but after letting myself into KiKi's house and dialing up the Chantilly/ Pillsbury duo for the address of the house where the floor collapsed, BW and I were hoofing it toward Blair Street at record speed.

Maybe KiKi had just left, I reassured myself. Maybe she was just poking around the abandoned house and had lost track of time. Maybe she was lying unconscious in a gutter. I walked faster.

Clouds of mist hugged church spires and treetops; a cold damp fog snaked at my ankles, BW looking as if he were walking on little tufts of smoky cotton. It was six and felt like midnight, only a few people out and about, darting to where they needed to be and staying put. Wind whipped through the trees, and I shivered as much from the chill as apprehension. We hung a right onto Heartridge then over to Blair, streetlights dim, few porch lights on, my footsteps and BW's nails on the sidewalk the only sounds, a boogie-man behind every bush. It was a jumpy kind of night.

KiKi's shiny navy Beemer sat at the curb completely out of place in the land of the dated. A few homes glowed from

within, but 214 Blair sat dark and deserted except for one
light deep inside, a new ramp for wheelchair access nearly
complete. BW and I started up the brick walk to the house,
BW giving me the *where the heck are you taking me* look.

"This place is a little creepy; can you butch it up a little?"
I said to BW. "It might come in handy."

I got out my flashlight but didn't turn it on. I didn't need
the neighbors calling the cops. Two encounters of the criminal kind between Mr. Suit and Ann Taylor would take a lot
of explaining, and right now I had a lot more questions than
answers. I followed the narrow driveway that circled around
to the back, looking in the deserted house windows as I
went, no movement anywhere. A wood deck extended from
the rear entrance, and something smelled strange, but I
couldn't put my finger on what it was. Where the heck was
KiKi?

A ruffling came from the tangle of trees and bushes that
butted up against the yard. I shined my light in that direction. KiKi was pushing and fighting her way out of the
growth looking like Lindsay Lohan on a bender. "Where in
the world have you been?" I fumed.

KiKi opened her purse to two eyes and a meow.

"You have a cat in a Gucci bag?" I put my hand in to pet
it, and it hissed. "A mean cat in a Gucci bag."

KiKi swiped her mangled hair from her dirty face and
tried to straighten her torn skirt.

"And you have scratches. That's bad from a stray. Maybe
we should get you to the ER."

"It's not from the cat; it's from climbing the tree. I was
thinking of naming him Guilt Trip. I was checking this
house just to see if it was tied in any way to the Dozer

copies, and the cat was living under the deck, and I scared him, and he ran off, and the dog next door chased him into the woods and up a tree, and all I could hear was this pitiful meow."

"You really climbed a tree?"

"These things happen."

"It was that help-others sermon, wasn't it? Does everyone else get into this much trouble after going to church on Sunday morning?"

"No one's fed us to the lions yet."

"It's not even seven; there's time." I put my arm around KiKi. "Let's get some tea."

"Forget tea, I have martinis chilling for us in the fridge."

"Amen." BW, KiKi, and I followed the flashlight down the drive to the front of the house. "Don't you smell that?" I asked KiKi.

"All I smell is cat pee in my purse. It costs twelve hundred dollars."

We crossed the deserted street to the Beemer, the fog giving the streetlights a soft golden haze. "You sure you want to keep that cat?" I asked.

"He's hungry."

"Twelve hundred dollars?"

"And sixty-three cents."

"That's a lot of dance classes. Next Sunday we should sleep in. For now you stay here while I go find us a box. Cat pee in the Beemer may not go over too well with Uncle Putter. He wasn't there for the sermon."

I handed KiKi BW's leash and started back across Blair, looking at the deserted house, trying to pinpoint that weird smell and—

Kaboom!

Fireballs blasted out the doors, windows, and roof. Bricks, wood, and God knows what else flew into the air; the impact slammed me backward, yellow flames and heat singing my skin as I landed hard on my butt, rattling the fillings in my teeth. Gasping for a breath, I glanced at KiKi to see if she was okay; the blaze reflected off her face, her eyes huge against the dark night. Two more pairs of eyes stared from under the Beemer . . . and three cars down a red '57 Chevy convertible sat at the curb.

Boone! What the heck? Pillsbury must have told him KiKi and I were here, and he feared for the neighborhood! But where was he now? This was my fault. If I wasn't here and KiKi wasn't here, Boone wouldn't be here . . . somewhere. God knows where! That cat wasn't the only one tagged Guilt Trip tonight. I cut my eyes back to the fire, orange and yellow flames devouring what was left of the walls, roof, and porch. I pushed myself up, then stumbled my way toward the blazing house.

The inferno lit up the night with thick black smoke billowing out every opening. I dodged a burning door in the middle of the street, jumped over a chunk of table, and prayed I didn't come across body parts. Oh, God, please no body parts. "Boone!"

My voice sounded muffled in my own head, the blast knocking out my hearing along with everything else. Flaming debris littered the sidewalk and the neighbors' yards. My jacket caught on fire till I smashed it out with the flat of my hand. "Boone!"

A wall of flames from a chunk of blown-out house blocked the driveway, keeping me from the backyard. Was Boone trapped there? Fire scorched pristine white clapboard, the flames coming closer and closer. Good Lord, a chunk of wall was falling right at me!

I screamed and was suddenly airborne, landing spread-eagle on my back in the grass, staring up at sparks soaring into the sky. Walker Boone landed on top of me, all hundred-and-whatever superb pounds squashing me into the ground. Fire crashed down next to us, shaking the ground, with flames and heat everywhere. I could feel Boone's heart pounding against my chest, his hot breath on my right ear, his rough stubble on my cheek, my hips firm against his . . . oh boy.

It had been a long, long, over two-years-long, time since I'd been in this particular position, and never in a million years did I ever think it would be with Walker Boone!

Chapter Eleven

B OONE pushed himself up, grabbed my arm, and propelled me through the flames to the sidewalk.

"What the hell are you doing?" Boone whispered. I was
100 percent sure it wasn't a whisper at all, but my nonwork-
ing ears made it sound that way. It was probably more like
a million-decibel roar. I tried to tell Boone I couldn't hear,
but the man was on such a rant I decided against pushing the
point. Least this way he could get it all out of his system and
I didn't have to listen to it, or at least I listened at a decreased
volume.

"I was looking for you," I explained when I could finally
squeeze in a word.

Boone said something, but it was lost in the blast of sirens
from fire engines, two police cruisers, and two ambulances
outfitted with enough strobe lights to be seen from outer
space. Firefighters stretched hoses and hooked them up to

hydrants, and a cop made his way over to Boone to ask if anyone was in the house.

Everyone knew Boone with him having one foot in the law enforcement camp, one foot in the hood from days of yore, and his behind in half the female beds in the city . . . or so the kudzu vine reported. I took the opportunity to back away into the night, fading into the crowd of neighbors pouring out of houses and gathering in the street.

"We should get out of here now while everyone's busy," I said to KiKi as I pulled up beside her, BW wiggling out from under the car. "We'll have to get the Beemer later. It's hemmed in by all this equipment."

"Was that Boone I saw you with?" KiKi asked. "He saved your sweet Southern behind when that there wall collapsed. Maybe you should bake him a cake, or buying him a cake might be better."

"Hey, I can cook."

"Of course you can, dear." She held up Old Yeller. "That explosion blew it right off your arm, not a scratch on it. We should tell the army about this here purse."

I straightened KiKi's hair to calm down the *finger in the socket* look she had going on. "We just act normal, like we belong to the neighborhood," I said. "We don't need the police asking why we were at the house." I took in KiKi's tree-climbing attire and looked down at my ripped denim jacket, filthy khakis, glued-together shoes caked with soot and burned, and spotted Mr. Suit getting out of a cruiser.

"We need to get out of here now; that guy with the cops is bad news. I met up with him at Dozer's."

KiKi pointed to her purse. "We can't leave without my cat."

"He's not your cat."

That got me the *sad auntie* look, which is the one thing even worse than the *ticked off auntie* look. "If I hadn't climbed that tree," KiKi said with a hitch in her voice, "I might have been in that house. God works in mysterious ways. He sent us to church."

"Meaning you were supposed to follow the cat?"

"Meaning I'm supposed to give him a home."

There was no arguing with the God theory. I took off what was left of my jacket and shimmied under the Beemer, dragging my jacket with me. I reassured myself this would just take a minute and that I really didn't hate confined spaces as much as I thought I did.

Rocks, leaves, and other street flotsam ground into my elbows and forearms. I knocked my head on the undercarriage and came face-to-whiskers with the cat from hell. "You should know it's been a bad day and I'm not in a good mood and I hate, hate, hate being under here."

He hissed. I hissed back, flipped my jacket over his head, and tied the arms together, making for a bag full of snarling, screeching, scratching feline. I started to back out and caught sight of shoes, not black police uniform shoes or firefighter boots, but Sperry Top-Sider loafers from the Macy's catalog, the obvious choice of young, obnoxious up-and-coming Southern detectives everywhere.

I curled my feet under the car to stay hidden, beads of sweat slithering down my back. I had no idea what Suit said to KiKi but trusted the queen of half truths and story spinning to save the day and somehow explain away her appearance, a BMW on this street, and a cat howling his head off under the car, and that she'd do it fast. The Top-Siders walked away, and I forced myself to count to ten then shimmied out dragging Hellion with me. I peeked over the car hood to make sure Suit wasn't hanging around and caught site of Boone still chatting with the cops, his hand tucked behind his back and favoring one leg. Neighbors crowded closer, a WSAV news van with enough antennae to reach Mars pulling up.

"I told that detective I was out for a walk looking for my cat," KiKi said, a bit of my hearing returning. She held out her arms. "I sure look the part, don't you think? Now where is my little precious?"

I didn't think KiKi was referring to me, so I dumped Hellion in her purse and shook my jacket to dislodge any cat vermin lurking inside. I took BW's leash, and the four of us headed off. The street was congested with onlookers, and more were coming by the minute, all of them far more interested in a good old house explosion than two grungy women walking a dog and a meowing purse.

Twenty minutes later I had KiKi settled in her favorite chair with a martini and Hellion sequestered in the garage with a blanket, water in a china bowl, and fried chicken deboned and diced into bite-size pieces. Saving KiKi had perks. I promised KiKi we'd pack the little bundle of joy off to the vet tomorrow to get rid of the ticks and fleas before granting permanent inside residency.

"How are you going to explain this cat to Uncle Putter?" I asked KiKi before heading out the door to reclaim the Beemer.

KiKi took a contemplative sip of martini and munched an Oreo, the perfect combination to chase away the woes of the day. "The way this here house operates is that Putter lives in the world of *Golf Digest*, where are my clubs, when's dinner, and I have surgery at ten. With a little luck he'll think we've had a cat all along. It's either that, or I'll tell him he's the one who brought the cat home and it must have slipped his mind."

"Think it'll work?"

"It's how I got the Gucci." She nibbled her bottom lip and gave me a hard look. "Honey, when you pick up the car, it might be a right fine idea to avoid the cops; you sort of look like a witness to the occurrence. They could be wondering why you were there."

"The clothes are a dead giveaway, huh?"

"That and you don't have eyebrows."

BW and I headed off to get the car. I burrowed into my shredded jacket wondering if I could duct tape the thing back together. I was a great believer in the wonders of duct tape. The closer we got to Blair Street, the slower BW walked. He came to a dead standstill right in the middle of the sidewalk, staring straight ahead at the bank of strobe lights. "Bad memories? I'm with you on that one."

More than likely the Beemer was still hemmed in by emergency equipment, blown-up houses being a big deal and all. As much as I wanted to get KiKi's nice car back in her driveway tonight, it wasn't going to happen right now. Instead of heading for home, my guilty conscience got the best of me, and I headed in the other direction and turned onto East Charlton. BW perked right up, his head held higher now and tail wagging.

This was one of our favorite walks, with live oaks so big they formed a canopy of green across the entire street and roots so strong and old they pushed up brick sidewalks making them uneven, memorable, Savannah. The houses here dated back to the 1850s and weren't just places to live, they were members of the family, the guardians keeping those inside safe and warm and protected, and they had done it oh so beautifully for all these many years.

We passed Troup Square, and BW got his usual drink from the doggie fountain there, then Lafayette Square and Madison Square with the illuminated statue of Sergeant William Jasper, noted soldier of the Siege of Savannah right in the middle. The trivia I knew as a Southern history major was frightening. Across the street stood the home of Walker Boone, and BW pulled me in that direction with all his might.

Since Boone could have gotten turned into pixie dust tonight because of me, I owed him an explanation. Besides, if I didn't come to him now, he'd come to me tomorrow, and I didn't want that hanging over my head all night. There was also the niggling fact that Boone didn't look so good when talking to the police, and his jumping on top of me had a lot to do with saving me from a wall of fire and nothing to do with his hormones.

Boone's house was a pristine Federalist that did Savannah proud but was pretty much unfurnished just like Mercedes said. I had made a beer run to his fridge once and got a firsthand look. I took the steps to the raised entrance and rapped the brass pineapple doorknocker, the knocker of all Southern homes worth two hoots. No answer. I tried again with the same result.

I started to leave, tugged on the leash for BW to come along, but he didn't budge. Poor doggie was fast asleep, sprawled out across Boone's welcome mat, snoring like an oncoming freight train. Not having the heart to get him up after the night from the damned, I sat on the porch beside him, gazing across to the lovely lit square. I snuggled up close to keep warm, tension fading away, a bit of peace at last.

"Drink this."

I was jostled awake, a cup of something hot and steamy shoved into my hand.

"Maybe it'll make your eyebrows grow back."

I blinked a few times, trying to figure out where the heck I was. "KiKi?"

"Not exactly," Boone said, dropping down beside me. He opened a white pastry bag, pulled out a sprinkle doughnut, tore off a piece, my mouth watering in anticipation, and fed it to BW.

"Why are you here?" he asked. "You look like something the cat dragged in." He gave a sniff. "And you smell like it, too."

I grabbed a handful of jacket and took a whiff. Maybe Febreze and duct tape. I sipped some coffee to get my brain working and clear away the fog. "I didn't have anything to do with that house blowing up. I think there might have been a gas leak inside."

"Along with a hefty dousing of gasoline."

I stopped the coffee halfway to my mouth. "This was on purpose?"

"Neighbors said there was a light on inside the house. Remove the glass from the bulb, turn on the gas, and the exposed filament is the perfect igniter."

Boone pulled another doughnut from the bag and took a big bite. "What did you find at Dozer's that connects to the house on Blair?" he asked around the crumbs. "You were at both places when you had no business being at either, and I don't believe in coincidence."

Boone had a cut across his forehead, and both hands were blistered and scraped raw. I didn't know what part was from just being near the blast and what part was from that blazing wall and Boone being between it and me. Either way he was at that house because KiKi and I were there. I owed him. I hated when that happened. "How about I buy you a new jacket and we call the night even."

"How about you tell me why I almost got blown to hell and back."

"What if I bake you a cake?"

"I've already had one near-death experience." The little lines at Boone's eyes crinkled with a laugh, and I socked his arm. Love didn't make the world go round, guilt did.

"I'm not all that sure what's going on," I said to Boone.

"But you have a hunch."

"Yeah, I have a hunch." I settled back against the door and grabbed a chunk of doughnut. I took a bite, trying to put the pieces together. "Seymour was underbidding Dozer on contracts, and yet Seymour lived large, handing in low bids and still making money. The question is how, and I think Dozer wondered the same thing. In Dozer's office I found newspaper clippings of buildings with structural problems all from Seymour projects. Then today Pillsbury came to the Fox with Chantilly and said something about a friend who repaired a house with bad wood he bought from Butler Haber and the house falling apart. That makes two building problems in two days. I don't believe in coincidence either."

Boone licked icing and sprinkles off his thumb, his

forehead furrowed in thought. "And Seymour's dead, and now this house is suddenly blasted off the face of the earth. Nothing's going to put that house back together, and dead men don't talk. Another two for two. Someone's trying real hard to hide something."

I split a piece of doughnut with BW. "Dozer had a picture of lumber with the Haber Lumber stamp tucked in with the newspaper clippings. My guess is Haber was selling inferior lumber to Seymour at cheap prices so he could turn in low bids. Haber marked it good grade, but it wasn't. Now that things are falling apart, Seymour must have suspected what Haber did."

"Haber kills Seymour to keep him quiet. Somehow Pillsbury's bro got the bad lumber by mistake to make the repairs on the house, so Haber had to get rid of the evidence. With Seymour's murder stirring things up, Haber blew the house."

Boone finished off his coffee as I stared at him bug-eyed. "You know about this?"

"You're not the only one trying to find the killer, remember? Seymour made enemies, and these are two super-size ones. Dozer knocked off Seymour because Seymour ruined his business, or maybe Haber did the deed because Seymour was on to him."

I set down my cup. "The thing is, I can't see either Dozer or Haber using poison. They'd arrange for a building accident. Seymour gets run over by a backhoe, squashed by a load of lumber if they were into irony. Construction is loaded with accidents waiting to happen."

Boone and I both eyed the last doughnut sitting alone in the bag, a devilish half smile on Boone's face. "About my jacket . . ."

I always came out on the short end of guilt.

"The thing about the poison," Boone said after devouring the last sprinkle, "is that it dumps the blame on your mom. A construction accident makes Dozer and Haber look a lot guiltier." Boone leaned back against his door, looking content till he cut his eyes my way. "Who else you got?"

"Who else *you* got?"

"I don't have anything firmed up yet."

"You expect me to believe that? You're not telling me because you want me out of the picture. I sit here and spill my guts about Dozer and Haber maybe killing Seymour, and you give me nothing?"

"Hey, I chipped in coffee and doughnuts. You spilled your guts because you were feeling guilty. Don't you feel better now?"

"No." Yes. "Are . . . are you okay? You were sort of limping." I touched the cut on his head, my fingers sticky with dried blood. I suddenly felt sick, and it had nothing to do with too many carbs and too much sugar in my stomach. "Maybe you should go to the hospital and have someone take a look."

"I'm not the one without eyebrows."

I had to say the next words or I wouldn't be able to sleep tonight. "Thank you."

"For . . . ?"

Oh for crying in a bucket! "You're going to make me say it, aren't you? The falling wall, the fire, flames cooking us alive, you jumping on top of me." A blush inched up my neck at the last part.

"Seemed like a good idea at the time." A spark of

devilment lit Boone's eyes. He was messing with me, and we both knew it.

"I'm out of here," I said and levered myself off the porch floor.

Boone didn't budge. "I can drive you."

"I have to get KiKi's car, and you dropping me off with the cops still around will raise eyebrows."

"But not yours." Boon stood. He fiddled with a strand of my hair for a beat. "I know you're trying to save your mom and nothing I can do is going to stop you, but people don't blow up houses because they're bored on a Sunday night with nothing else to do. You get in the killer's way, and he'll get rid of you just like the house and Seymour."

He fastened my jacket, two buttons falling off in his hand. He stuck them in his pocket. "Got another coat?"

"I like this one. It has memories."

"Some better than others. Watch your back, Reagan."

I headed for Blair. Boone never called me Reagan, Blondie maybe and sometimes shop girl if he really wanted to tick me off, but not Reagan. I glanced over my shoulder, the night feeling a little spooky. I walked faster. Maybe I should scrape some money together for a phone, except there was that water bill sitting on the kitchen counter and the soon-to-arrive heating bills.

BW and I rounded the corner onto Blair, rivulets of dirty water snaking down the street, the acrid smell of soaked wood saturating the air. Smoke curled from the pile of dank rubble. A fire truck, two police cruisers, and a few pockets of kibitzers kept watch. I charged up the Beemer, and BW and I headed for home.

When I pulled into KiKi's drive, the lights were off in her kitchen, meaning KiKi was in for the night. I beeped the car locked and took the keys with me for KiKi to pick up tomorrow. I checked on Hellion, aimed my flashlight through the garage windowpane, capturing him snuggled up all cute and sweet on his blanket. He yawned, pried open one eye, flipped me the bird, then went back to sleep. A perfect ending to a perfect day.

Clouds made for a moonless night, the street midnight quiet, the dining room light in Cherry House shining through the bay window out onto the porch, the silhouette of a man suddenly right smack in front of me. He smelled of beer and cigarettes, and he threw a hotdog wrapper at my feet.

"Stay out of my business if you know what's good for you." Dozer gave me a hard shove, sending me stumbling back against the porch railing, rattling the whole structure. BW in true BW fashion went after the hotdog wrapper.

Was I scared? Heck yeah, but I was also fed up with mean cats, nearly getting blown to smithereens, ugly displays in my very own shop, my favorite jacket ruined, one measly doughnut, and all of it getting me absolutely nowhere. "So," I said, angry and tired winning out over chicken. "Why'd you kill Seymour? Revenge? Fed up with losing contracts? Bored?"

Dozer scoffed. "Shows how little you know about anything. I didn't kill Seymour, and if you come on my property again, you'll be pushing up daisies with that bastard out at Bonaventure Cemetery, and I can dance on both your graves."

"Honey Seymour's taking over Seymour Construction, and it's going to be business as usual. That's what she told Butler Haber."

An evil smile played at Dozer's lips. "I can keep Honey Seymour in line and Haber, too."

"By telling everyone Seymour knew about the lumber switch all along? No one will believe it. Seymour wouldn't do something so stupid that would have his construction projects falling apart in a few years."

"All I have to do is plant the seed that Seymour was cutting corners. That along with the building problems cropping up in the papers these days and Seymour Construction takes a tumble."

Before I knew what was happening, Dozer grabbed my arms, lifting me off the porch. My bulging eyes now level with his raging with anger, his hot beer breath on my face. "I'm winning the next contract that comes out and the one after that and the one after that. Honey Seymour is not getting in my way if she knows what's good for her and that company she's running, because I'll take her down. Butler Haber is giving me the deal of a lifetime on lumber, good lumber. I'm going to make a killing this time, and you're going to keep your big mouth shut." He shook me like a ragdoll. "Got it, sweet cakes?"

Dozer let me go, and I slid onto the porch, my back against the railings. He stormed down the steps and headed for his red pickup, hit the gas, and roared down the street, the noise deafening in the dead quiet.

I sat on the floor, my legs rubbery and my heart thudding so hard it jarred my head. BW contentedly licked the hot dog wrapper.

Dozer was clearly over the edge. After years of getting dumped on he finally had the upper hand and loved it. The problem was I knew why Dozer Delany was sitting in the catbird seat, and that made me a big, fat walking liability to him and Butler Haber not to mention Archie Lee and Popeye. When I made enemies, I did it big.

I finally wobbled inside and locked the door behind me. I wedged a chair I got on consignment under the kitchen doorknob like they do in the movies. I bunched the "Elect Gloria Summerside" signs around the chair in case anyone got through; the racket of them hitting the floor would act like a cheap alarm system. I flipped on every light in the house, making the place look like High Mass at St. John's. I picked up the baseball bat Hollis forgot to pack when he moved out. BW moseyed upstairs to take advantage of the bed all to himself, and I sat on the steps keeping watch over my humble abode.

I didn't think Dozer would come back tonight, but there was Butler Haber to consider, and by now he knew I was nosing around the house on Blair. Boone was right in that this was about more than winning an election, and the Summerside girls were right in the thick of it.

A BANGING ON THE FRONT DOOR JARRED ME AWAKE, sunlight streaming in through the bay window. I peeled myself off the steps, my neck stiff and pains in my knees and back. I opened the door to, "What in heaven's name is going on over here? Your back door is wedged shut tighter than a lid on a honey jar and . . . Sweet Jesus in heaven and Lord have mercy. You look worse than when you left my house last night, and frankly I didn't think that was possible. And you're still in the same clothes, what's left of them. What's with the bat?"

KiKi stepped inside. "And you've got all the lights blazing. At this rate Georgia Power is going to start sending you flowers."

"Have you checked Twitter this morning?"

"Good Lord, now what?"

Chapter Twelve

"I've been thinking," I said to Auntie KiKi, both of us standing in the hall by the checkout door. "Maybe you should visit Uncle Putter at that fancy golf course in Augusta. You could do a spa getaway. Just think of it: sea wraps, mud baths, Klaus the massage guy. Bet Klaus is really yummy. Bet he has hands like velvet."

"You really think I'd run off to a spa while my sister and niece are neck-deep in doo-doo? What kind of Southern woman would do such a thing? Besides, Fanny Harper says there's nothing at those spa places besides steamed fish, celery and carrot sticks, and grass tea. Have you ever had grass tea? She says it tastes like someone cut their lawn and threw it in water, and they charge you fifteen dollars a cup for the stuff. If I'm paying fifteen dollars for a drink, it's going to have *martini* somewhere in the title."

KiKi sat at the dining room table and pulled me down

in the chair next to hers. She shoved the scarf, purse, and jewelry display out of the way then folded her hands together all prim and proper and leaned close like she meant business. "Okay, spill it."

It was one of those situations where I could lie and soft-pedal what was going on, but with four badass dudes snapping at my heels, one could easily go after KiKi, and she needed to be prepared.

"The explosion at the house last night wasn't an accident," I told KiKi. "I think Butler Haber was trying to cover up that bad wood situation Pillsbury mentioned when he was here at the Fox. I think maybe Haber could have killed Seymour because he was using the same stuff, didn't know it, then threatened to expose Haber. The Blair house was further proof of what was going on, so Haber blew it up."

KiKi flopped back in her chair. "Well, I do declare. Butler Haber is a no-good rotten swindler. Who would have thought? No wonder Marigold was having a conniption and hurrying off to see Odilia. I guess that means we add Butler to our I-polished-off-Seymour list along with that Dozer person."

I took KiKi's hands in mine. "These are mean guys. You got to be careful, promise me. Lock your doors. Maybe you should get one of those alarm systems in your house."

"Heavenly days. I'd never remember those code numbers, and I'd wind up setting the alarm off and driving the neighbors crazy with the racket. Besides, I have Putter's nine iron right behind the back door, and Putter Vanderpool does maintain a right proper Southern home if you get my meaning."

Translation: Uncle Putter had enough firepower stashed

away to arm a small country, and his wife knew how to use it.

"You know," KiKi said. "You got all these bad guys wanting to kill Seymour, but we never did figure out why Rachelle Lerner had it in for the man. Big bad guys and poison doesn't feel right to me. We know Rachelle didn't like Gloria because she sent darling sonny boy up the river, but what did Seymour ever do to her? Maybe we should have a chat and find out."

"And pick up some sticky buns."

KiKi's eyes twinkled. "I'm hungry as a working mule. It's still early, and with a little luck those sticky buns will be right out of the oven and just waiting for us. It's Monday; we could stroll into Cuisine by Rachelle for coffee before you open the Fox." KiKi gave me the *critical auntie* stare. "But we can't go anywhere with you looking the way you do."

"The missing eyebrows and clothes are a bit much, huh?"

"And your hair."

"Hair? This is the first I'm hearing about hair."

"I figured there's just so much unpleasantness a body can deal with at one time, and the no-eyebrows thing sort of took precedence. Bet you'll look right smart with one of those pixie cuts. Some aloe on your face might be in order, too."

I touched what used to be a curl by my cheek, realizing it felt a little crispy. KiKi gently peeled a flake of skin from my nose. "Think of it as having a sunburn in November."

I stifled a sob.

"If you use a bottle or two of conditioner, I just bet it'll flatten out that kink. You might have to cut off a few burnt ends here and there, but short hair is in, right? Tell you what.

I'll take my little Precious to the vet and stop back for you in half an hour. I just ordered him a satin bed off Amazon this morning and some toys. I figure since I'm having his jets cooled, this will make up for it."

Personally, I didn't think there was a male in all of Christendom who thought a satin bed and toys made up for having the family jewels deleted. At least my hair would grow back.

KiKi left, and I headed upstairs. I sucked in a deep breath, clenched my fists, glanced in the mirror, and screamed.

Twenty minutes later I ran out to the Beemer idling at the curb and took shotgun. "How's the cat?" I asked KiKi.

"His meow will be two octaves higher from here on out, but he'll be better off for it. Nice hat. Looks like you fell asleep in the sun and you got a really ticked-off chicken sitting on your head."

"It's an Angry Birds hat. I took it in on consignment two days ago, it's all I had, and it looks a million times better than what's underneath. None of the stores are open yet, but I'll get something else later on. Maybe one of those bucket hats would work." My voice cracked, another crying jag threatening. I pointed out the windshield. "Just drive."

KiKi put the Beemer in gear, and we motored off toward Cuisine by Rachelle, located near City Market, the hub of Savannah tourist action.

"I know you're in distress," KiKi said to me, "and I hate to add to it, but have you given any thought to what you're going to tell your mamma?"

"Mamma," I said on a whisper, my stomach cramping. That's what happens when you are absolutely positive things can't get worse. They do!

"She'll know about the explosion," KiKi continued. "One

look at you and she'll put it all together. She'll want to know what's going on and have a fit that you're poking around and nearly getting blown up."

KiKi stopped for a light and tuned to me. I gave her a sly grin and wiggled my brows . . . well, what would have been my brows if I had any. KiKi stared back for a beat then held up her hands as if warding off a charging bull. "No way. Uh-uh. You wouldn't do that to your favorite little ol' auntie."

"You're not old, and you're my only auntie, and it's your turn. You take Mamma this week. Keep her busy, have her help you with dance lessons."

"Holy mother of God!" KiKi's eyes bugged. She put her hands back on the wheel, and we moved through the light. "You think your displays are bad; Gloria Summerside can't dance for beans. Not one lick of rhythm in her whole body. Miracle the woman can walk upright."

"You can have her help out with the teens, offer some free introductory lessons at the senior centers."

"Like those people don't have enough afflictions in their lives already."

"It's your turn."

KiKi turned onto Saint Julian, her eyes steady, lips pressed together. "Fine. You get till Friday, and then I'm sending her back to the Prissy Fox. I can set up a few things at the kindergarten classes and day cares. Those little kids don't have so far to fall to the ground. She can teach the chicken dance and the Hokey Pokey."

"I really think you should let her have a crack at the teen class. Bet Linton Parish would simply love dancing with a judge."

"Linton give you a hard time?"

"Linton Paris is a letch with pimples."

City Market was just gearing up for business at nine A.M. with Lolly's Trolley and other tour trolleys lining up to collect early bird tourists and propel them around our fair city. The carriage drivers hitched up horses, smoke curled into the air from the stone ovens over at Vinnie Van Go-Go's, and Cazy Ledbetter hustled off the trolley and booked it hard down the sidewalk right past us.

"Did you see that?" I asked KiKi as she took a left onto Barnard. "It was Cazy Ledbetter dressed in a karate outfit, and he had on a black belt."

"Guess he needs something to hold up his pants so they don't slide off his bony behind."

"Not that kind of black belt, but the one as in hi-yah tick me off and you die. Pull over."

KiKi tucked into the curb. "Cazy? Sounds more like Chuck Norris."

"I saw Lolly's Trolley back at City Market. Lolly was driving, and Cazy got off. I thought Cazy Ledbetter was this mild-mannered, harmless guy who wouldn't hurt a flea, but then we had this discussion about Seymour, and he went a little ballistic and nearly drove his trolley right into a pole. I think there's another side of Cazy, the crazy-Cazy side."

"You really think Cazy Ledbetter has it in him to knock off Seymour? It's a mighty big stretch from whacking boards and doing some fancy kicks to out-and-out murder."

"He told me how Lolly followed Mamma and the bottle of honey bourbon to Seymour's. He knew what was going on, and he really hated Seymour. We should follow him. Maybe he just wears the outfit to feel important." I chewed my bottom lip. "I suppose we could just ask Cazy where he was when Scummy was murdered."

That got me the *evil eye* stare. "These here people have been friends of your mamma's for as long as we've all been on this earth. You can't just out and out accuse them of murder, and if your mamma found out we did such a thing, she'd blow a gasket. We'll just snoop around and see where it takes us. Now let's get a move on."

KiKi joined me on the sidewalk, and I said, "We need to blend in so Cazy doesn't see us following. If he is the killer, we don't need him thinking we're on to him."

"Unmannerly?"

"Unhealthy."

KiKi's eyes rolled up. "That blend-in part's gonna be a tough one with a red chicken on your head." Before I could stop her, KiKi whipped off the hat, her eyes rounding to half the size of her face. She gulped and pulled the hat back in place. "Right, we'll blend in. We can do this." She took my hand and pulled me down Jefferson.

"There," KiKi whispered, nodding up ahead to a dingy gray clapboard storefront with a Ken's Karate Klub sign in the window and a picture of two dudes kicking at each other. "That's got to be it, and I got us a plan."

"It involves me, doesn't it? You've got that look. I'm the guinea pig."

"I got a good use for that there hair of yours. The Lord provides." Before I could ask about the Lord providing what, KiKi ducked into the Klub, a bunch of Japanese sounding words echoing out from a back room.

"She needs lessons," KiKi said to a guy behind the

counter as she ripped the hat right off my head. "Look what somebody did to her. She needs to learn how to kick butt so this doesn't happen again."

. "Holy crap, who did this to you?" The guy was young, dressed in a white karate outfit tied in front with an orange belt of thick material.

"She needs to be one of those black belt people," KiKi explained.

Orange belt guy gave a patronizing smile. "That takes years and years of practice."

"Can a black belt really whip someone's behind if they have a mind to?" KiKi asked.

"Karate is all about discipline and respect and honor."

"So if someone dishonors and disrespects you, then what?" KiKi asked.

"Then you can whip his butt." Orange Belt pointed to a room off the side, and I caught sight of Cazy looking mean and determined and kicking the beejeebers out of some imaginary guy in front of him.

"You need to be real fit," Orange Belt said. He pointed to a shelf of white plastic bottles off to the side. "We recommend taking vitamins to keep your body strong and healthy. Karate is very demanding if you do it right. We set the dosage. Take too many, and you'll get sick as a dog. You learn a lot of things when you take karate. The good stuff to put in your body and the bad stuff to stay away from."

I picked up a book titled *When Enough Is Too Much* with a picture of a bunch of pills on the cover. I cut my eyes to Cazy to make sure he hadn't spotted KiKi or me. If he was the killer, I didn't need Mr. Black Belt visiting me in the middle of the night like Dozer did, thank you very much.

"When would you like to start?" Orange Belt shoved a clipboard with papers attached in my direction and studied my hair. "If someone did that to me, I'd have it in for them big-time."

"We'll think about it," KiKi said, both of us inching back toward the door as Cazy headed into the hallway. "Maybe we'll just get a dog."

I followed KiKi outside, and we hurried down the sidewalk. We ducked into an alley in case Cazy caught a glimpse of us and wanted to check things out. "See?" KiKi said. "That hair of yours is a good thing. Got us some great information, and from what I can tell Cazy is not the mild-mannered trolley driver all the time. He's like Clark Kent without the phone booth. He puts on another outfit and changes into someone else."

"You think he could have killed Seymour?"

"He's on medication for his nerves, and he knows something about pills with being in karate for years. We know he was plenty ticked off at Seymour for treating him badly for a long time. Now that I think about it, you were right in wanting me to open that account at the savings and loan. Just because somebody is into karate and taking vitamins doesn't mean they're into murder. We need another opinion, and the people at the savings and loan saw what happened and how Cazy reacted. I can go this morning."

I pulled off my hat. "Remember me, the scarecrow? Mamma can't see me like this. You have to take her today."

"We'll get the Abbott sisters to mind the Fox with Gloria, and you can go to the beauty parlor and get your hair done."

"How am I going to explain this at a beauty parlor?" I yanked at a chunk of hair.

KiKi pulled out her iPhone. "Mercedes is probably at Eternal Slumber right this minute and can work you in and give you a good deal."

"Wait a minute. You want me to go to a funeral home to have my hair done?"

"Mercedes is used to people in car wrecks and fires and probably even explosions. You're right up her alley."

"I feel so much better now."

"Think of it this way, you won't be scaring anyone to death 'cause the deed's already been done." KiKi punched in some numbers. "I'll call Mercedes and get the Abbott sisters on over to the Fox. This will work out fine and dandy."

"Tell the sisters the spare key's under the flower pot in the back."

"Honey, everybody knows the spare key's under the flower pot."

Rachelle's place was two blocks down the other way on Jefferson with *Cuisine by Rachelle* stenciled in pumpkin orange script across the front window along with a display of Thanksgiving brunch and all the trimmings. Anyone could put on a nice spread these days and not lift a finger except to punch in Cuisine by Rachelle's phone number.

"Why hi there. Nice seeing you again," Rachelle greeted KiKi and I when we walked in the door to the aroma of things baking and simmering. Rachelle had on a blue apron and matching cap perched in a nest of salt-and-pepper hair. The shop had a low counter for checking out and a glass case with an array of quiches, pies, rolls, and sticky buns. Beat shelves of white plastic vitamin bottles all to heck. Three tables occupied the narrow space up front, the real action of catering and take-out in the back.

Rachelle eyed my head. "My nephew has a hat like that; it matches his bicycle."

"My friend, Chantilly, said you have great sticky buns," KiKi said, her eyes glued to the glass case. "Lord be praised, you put pecans in them." A little drop of drool pooled at the corner of KiKi's mouth.

"You know Chantilly?" Rachelle beamed. "She's a real jewel, I tell you. Never seen anyone take to cooking like that girl has. She's making a delivery right now, and that there boyfriend of hers is something else."

KiKi and I exchanged looks, both of us wondering if this was a good something else or a bad something else. With Pillsbury it could go either way. "You know," I said, "Pillsbury might look a little rough, but he's—"

"Sent by the Lord above to save me!" Rachelle belted out in song like a member of the choir and clasping her hands to her bosom. "He has business meetings on Wednesday mornings and Friday lunches, and he wants me and Chantilly to cater them both. Pillsbury says he needs the tax write-off. Now that's the kind of businessman I need in my life. That whoreson bastard Seymour wanted a 40 percent discount on everything. All I could do for that kind of money was serve up bologna and cheese and pass it off as some kind of delicacy. People know better, and it would have ruined my reputation. I told that sorry excuse for a man no way, and he went and spread the word my food was terrible and I cheated him, and I lost a lot of business. I even brought him and his campaign workers sticky buns and quiche as a peace offering, but the man just laughed at me and told me to get lost."

Rachelle's face reddened, and she pounded her fist on the

counter, KiKi and I jumping about a foot off the floor. "If anyone deserves to rot in hell for all eternity, it's Kip Seymour."

Rachelle readjusted her hat, smoothed her apron, her face morphing back into a big customer-friendly smile. "Now what can I get for you ladies today?"

Ten minutes later KiKi and I sat in the Beemer, a bag of sticky buns between us. "You know," I said, thinking about the buns. "The day Scummy bit the dust, or more accurately, the carpet, sticky buns were at his headquarters. I ate one. They were amazing. Rachelle must have been there. If she saw the bourbon bottle and heard the fight with Mamma, spiking the bottle would have been easy. She'd get her revenge on Mamma, and Scummy would be out of her life. We should talk to Delray Valentine and see if he remembers seeing Rachelle."

KiKi glanced down at the white pastry bag emitting smells from heaven and beyond. "Do you think Rachelle recognized you as Gloria's daughter?"

"With this hat and face?"

KiKi sighed, made a sad whiny sound, sniffed, then powered down the window and tossed the delicious bag into a garbage can at the curb. "Just in case."

THE ETERNAL SLUMBER WAS WHITE CLAPBOARD with black shutters and had a widow's-walk on the roof that seemed more than appropriate. Back in the day, when married to Hollis and with a little money to spare—or at least thinking I did—I went to Jan at the Cutting Crew to get my hair done. Jan was fantastic. Mercedes was fantastic too and free, in honor of the great escape at Dozers. The problem with Mercedes was that a die job had a whole new meaning.

I took the driveway to the right wondering if the hats and wigs from Cher-on-the-run that I had stashed in the bushes were still there. A green Flora's Flowers van pulled up to the big double doors under the portico. Two guys hauled in a spray of really pretty yellow roses, a wreath on a stand, and a palm probably to replace the one KiKi dumped on Scummy.

KiKi said to enter through the red door, so I continued on to what looked like the service entrance. "Mercedes?" I whispered when I closed the heavy door behind me, the silence creepy as all get out. I followed the thick, padded gray carpet to another hall, then another, the only sound my heart thumping in my head. I should have swiped one of the sticky buns KiKi bought and dropped crumbs. "Mercedes?"

"Psst. Over here," she whispered behind me. At least I hoped it was Mercedes. If I turned around to some shadowy figure, I was out of here . . . if I could figure where *out* was.

Mercedes waved to me from a doorway, and I hurried over and stopped dead. "What's it like in there?"

"Just finished up doing Tarsey Goodall, ninety-seven, hair like a goat. She's on her way to the Serene Pastures room as we speak, viewing at five. I'm sitting here customer free for an hour. Lovell Graham comes in at eleven."

Mercedes yanked me into a room with a tile floor, a gurney on one side, a table with a ton of cosmetic and hair styling stuff, a sink, and two chairs. "I don't want to get caught working on a customer," Mercedes said. "The owners won't like it. What's the story that goes with the face and chicken hat? KiKi said you were in a desperate way." Mercedes gave me a hard look. "I think it was an understatement."

"Hear about that explosion over on Blair?"

"Guess you're lucky to be here in the upright position." She pulled off my hat and sucked in a breath. "Bet you always wanted to be Tinkerbell when you were a kid."

"How about Lara Croft in *Tomb Raider*."

"That there is Tinkerbell hair." Mercedes froze. "Uh-oh, someone's coming."

"I don't hear a thing."

"You don't hear anything around here; you just feel the vibes. Quick, get on that there gurney, don't breathe, act dead."

Mercedes put her hand over my mouth, which was probably a good thing since I started to scream. "I need this job," Mercedes whispered. She stuffed the chicken hat in my pocket, grabbed Old Yeller, flipped me onto the gurney like a sack of potatoes, and tossed a sheet over me.

Chapter Thirteen

I STARED up at the sheet, trying to breathe as little as possible so as not to make it go up and down, a dead giveaway the person underneath wasn't . . . dead.

"Tarsey Goodall's makeup is too green. We got new lighting in the Serene Pastures room, and it's throwing everything off," a man's voice said. "Can you add some beige to tone it down a little?"

"I'll get right on it," Mercedes said as if it was just another day at the office.

"What's this over here?" the man asked, his voice coming closer.

"Sent here by mistake." Mercedes was cool as a cucumber; I on the other hand had sweat prickles collecting on every indent of my body.

"One of those independent contractors," Mercedes went on. "They deliver to that new budget funeral home out by the mall, Heavenly Slumber. They must have gotten the two of us confused. I called the contractor, and they're sending a transport to pick her up now. Should be here any minute."

I could feel the guy standing over me. My heart was pounding so hard it had to be shaking the whole room. I closed my eyes, held my breath, and prayed like mad. *Don't pull back the sheet! Don't pull back the sheet! Don't pull back the sheet!*

He pulled back the sheet!

"Good God, what happened to this one?"

"Hear about that explosion over on Blair? I think this was part of it."

Mercedes flipped the sheet back over me. "She's really a mess. Don't envy the person trying to pretty her up. Let me get my makeup kit, and you can show me what needs to be done to Tarsey."

I heard footsteps retreating, then nothing, counted three Mississippis and puffed out a lungful of air. I peeked from under the sheet into the empty room, then slid off the gurney. Old Yeller was by Mercedes's jacket, looking as if it belonged to her . . . yeah, like Mercedes would own a pleather purse. I checked the hallway for whatever roamed around these parts and tiptoed off down the hall as fast as I could tiptoe. I took a turn then another and another ,and wound up at what had to be the Serene Pastures room because Mercedes was there with a guy. She saw me, tripped, and dropped a tube of something right in the casket.

I backed down the hall, took the next one to the right, and wound up in an office area. A man sat behind the desk with Delray Valentine across from him. If either looked this way, I was dead meat. Did I really just think that? I ducked behind an antique cabinet.

"A plant on the head," Valley groused. "I thought you all did a better job than that, or we would have gone somewhere else."

"Eternal Slumber is extremely sorry for the situation," desk guy said. "We are an exemplary funeral home in every way, but we have no control over the mentally unbalanced who come in to pay their respects. We gave you a discount on the bill and trust that will make amends to Mrs. Seymour. Personally I'm deeply sorry Mr. Seymour will not be our new alderman. He was a wonderful man, and now it looks as if that barkeep of all people will fill the position."

"You never know with politics what's going to happen next," Valley said, a lilt in his voice. "Things change when you least expect them to. Mark my words, Archie Lee isn't a shoo-in by any stretch."

I heard papers shuffle and Valley say, "Now I have an appointment in Beaufort that I must keep, so I best be on my way."

I waited a few beats, giving Valley time to leave, then glanced around the edge of the cabinet to the man at the desk. He looked as dumbfounded as I felt after the conversation. Scummy was dead, Mamma accused of the murder, and Archie Lee the only soldier left standing. How could Archie Lee not be a shoo-in?

Desk guy got up and went into anther room, and I crept past his office to the front door and out onto the porch. I sucked in deep breaths of formaldehyde-free air and soaked in the sunlight. I was so done with funeral homes! I didn't care if it was KiKi or Mamma or whoever. The next dead friend or family member would have to get along in this place without me.

I bought a bucket hat at a shop on Broughton. The checkout gal took one look at my hair and gave me a pity discount, the best thing that had happened to me all morning. I got a double scoop of Old Black Magic ice cream at Leopold's to celebrate life and decided if Mamma asked about my appearance, I'd tell her I fell asleep under the sunlamp like I did when I was fourteen and that my curling iron malfunctioned and cooked my hair. She probably wouldn't buy it, but it's all I could come up with after a morning of sleuthing and playing dead.

When I got to the Fox, the door was wide open, the nice sunny morning drifting inside. The Abbott sisters were holding court, talking about the explosion on Blair and how could such a terrible thing happen. They all stared at me when I came inside, exchanged wide-eyed looks, then fell instantly mute, everyone scurrying back to business. A hat can hide just so much.

The Abbott sisters said Mamma was helping KiKi with dance classes, then Elsie and AnnieFritz hurried off to get rested up for the Tarsey Goodall viewing at five. With Tarsey being rather antiquated, there wouldn't be many mourners, and the sisters felt morally obligated to put in extra weeping and wailing to make up for it.

Business was good, and by noon I'd opened two new accounts and mentally paid my water bill. I had cleared out the dressing room and started to hang clothes back where they belonged when KiKi hurried in from the kitchen carrying a box and stopped right in the middle of the hall. "Where's the new do?"

I pulled her behind the checkout door and dropped my voice. "We got interrupted. You should know that if you die, I'm planting you under that pink rosebush in your garden. I'm swearing off funeral homes."

KiKi plopped the box on the door and grinned. "I got you a toaster, and we need to move Crazy Cazy to the top of the suspect list. The man's a nut job." KiKi sidled up close. "Seymour pushed him and pushed him for special favors or threatened to steer clients to get loans elsewhere. The girl I talked to at the savings and loan said Seymour demanded cases of wine and vacations and expensive dinners. Cazy was the loan officer. His job depended on getting loans, but it was costing him a ton, and he snapped."

"That's just like what Rachelle Lerner said this morning. Seymour wanted kickbacks for throwing business her way, and she couldn't make any money. She refused, and he nearly ruined her business. I bet it was the same thing with Haber. Seymour wanted a discount on lumber, and Haber switched the lumber stamps and sold the cheap lumber for good. He had to or go belly-up with the building business already in the toilet."

KiKi cut her eyes out the window toward her house. "Your mamma's finishing up with the Benders' cha-cha lesson. I tell you there's going to be some cha-cha smackdown at Sweet Marsh Country Club. Next we're off to the kindergarten class for the Hokey Pokey."

KiKi darted for the back door, and a woman in faded brown slacks and a pilled sweater, her arms loaded with clothes, stumbled in the front door. "I want to sell these. They don't fit me anymore, same for my . . . husband."

"Sure," I said. "These are nice items, really nice. Some a little older and there's spots on this skirt."

I'd seen the skirt before, cream with black stitching at the hemline, probably in the Nordstrom's catalog. "It's really expensive. I know a great dry cleaner. I can get the spots out and sell it. It'll make some nice money for you." *And for me* I added to myself. "Everyone can use some extra cash, right?"

The woman blushed. "You can say that again. I got these out of the Goodwill bag that the lady I work for was going to give away of all things. She said I could have them," the woman rushed on. "I got this here skirt with the stains right out of the trash, if you can believe it. Why would she throw a skirt like this away? I didn't have time to get them cleaned. You can do it, right? It's an expensive skirt. I can use a little extra money. That woman pays me next to nothing and always has me working overtime for free."

I handed the woman the account form and explained about the fifty-fifty split once the items sold. She nodded, signed my clothing log that stated I'd taken twenty-five items from her today, then hustled out the door. I put the skirt under the counter along with a few other things that needed dry cleaning.

A customer in a taupe cashmere sweater hurried over to the checkout door, her hands shaking, eyes glazed. "Holy saints above, I do declare these are some mighty fine things that woman has to sell. I spied them right off when she came in the door. I've got an eye for retail."

Cashmere girl pawed through the pile on the counter and

pulled out a Burberry coat. "How much for this? It's worn. Look right there on the sleeve. Can you make me a good deal? I gotta have this here coat."

I quoted cashmere girl a price more than what I had made all morning. She forked over her credit card without batting an eye and skipped out the door. I studied the other items on the counter. All the woman's clothes were expensive, like Saks expensive, older but still in great shape. The man's tux was Italian, and it was new. I always had nice things at the Fox, but his was high-roller nice, put me in the black nice.

"Is that an Hermes bag," a consigner in tight jeans and swanky boots asked, running up to the counter. "How much? I gotta have this bag."

"That's an Hermes belt. I want that belt," a customer in a black-and-white flowered scarf said, holding up the belt, swanky boots yanking it right out of her hand.

"Hey, that was mine." Scarf gal gave swanky boots a hard shove and two ladies walking by caught the scent of designer mania and charged up the walk.

"I want this dress," claimed one of the street gals, holding up a mango Tory Burch sheath, a glazed look in her eyes.

"Like heck, I saw it first," second street gal snarled, nostrils flaring as she grabbed a handful of mango material. She swung her handbag full circle, knocking first street gal upside the head, sending her to the floor. First street gal grabbed second gal's leg, tripping her, and another woman rushed up the sidewalk, grabbed the dress away from both of them, tossed a wad of money at me, and ran out as three more women ran in from God knows where. One snapped up a cream coat, the other snatching it out of her hands while lunging for a blue sequined evening gown at the bottom of the pile.

"But I haven't even priced anything yet," I yelled into the din, not making one bit of difference, as women tore into the clothes. A tour bus drove by, five women jumping off before it stopped, heading full tilt for my door, hot on the scent of a big sale. A woman in a maroon suede jacket snatched up a Saint John's navy skirt, another ripping it out of her hands running around the shop, three customers in hot pursuit. BW cowered behind me, and I backed to the wall.

Sirens wailed and a cruiser screeched to a stop at the curb in front of the Fox. A uniformed officer and Mr. Suit hustled up the walk, Suit taking one look at me and grinning. "Hey, Ann Taylor, we meet again. What's with the hat?"

"Who you calling Ann Taylor?" Swanky boots asked, staggering to her feet, the obvious winner in the great dress struggle. She tossed her head, flipping straggly hair out of her face as she pitched her credit card on the checkout door. "That there is Reagan Summerside who owns this shop, and this dress is mine, and no one's taking it from me. I don't care who they are!" She had the stance of a Georgia Bulldog linebacker.

Suit's smile wobbled, the realization that he'd been had registering, cop face sliding into place and making me wish I were back under the sheet at the funeral home. Suit stepped over a tangle of shoppers on the floor to get to me. "What's going on, and I'm not just talking clothes. What were you doing out at Delany Construction, and who the heck are you?"

And twenty minutes later I was sitting at the Bull Street police station in a grungy blue interrogation room with bars at the windows. The last two times I'd frequented this establishment I had been hauled into the putrid green room with bars at the window. That I knew the layout of the police station underlined the present state of my life.

This time the problem stemmed from me giving false information to a policeman. Seems that's a big no-no in Savannah, and then there was the part about inciting a riot in my own shop. Lord knows how Suit came up with that one. The upside of all this was that I'd made a killing off the designer clothes fiasco; the downside was Walker Boone stood outside the grungy blue room this very minute talking to a cop and laughing his behind off.

"How do you do it?" Boone asked as he came and took the seat across from me. "Dead and arrested all in one day?"

"You talked to Mercedes."

"She feels bad about the hair." The cuts and scrapes on Boone's hands were red and angry along with another nasty cut on his face that I hadn't noticed last night. "Least they let you keep the hat," he said to me.

"I told them I had lice and if I took off my hat, the little critters would jump off everywhere and infest the place."

Boone stretched his long legs out in front and settled back in the chair. He wore a blue button-down dress shirt not buttoned down and no tie. As far as I knew, Boone didn't own a tie. "You're enjoying this, aren't you?" I said to him.

"I enjoy knowing where the heck you are for a few minutes, and I'm willing to bet the rest of the city feels the same way."

"I think this thing with Suit is all about him getting even with me for not being Ann Taylor and me actually being Mamma's daughter. Any woman knows that having a shoving match over a designer clothes sale is sport and that a riot around here is what happens at the Pirate House when they run out of she-crab soup."

"Why do you call him Suit?"

"He wears one, and he never told me his name, not that I care."

Boone cocked one eyebrow. "You will care. Sit tight, Blondie. Try not to blow anything up while I'm gone." Boone strode out of the room, and I suddenly felt really alone. What if I did get arrested, or what if something even worse happened to me? The way things were going both were definite possibilities and even heading toward certainty. If Mamma took over raising BW, she'd never let him have a hot dog or sleep with her in bed. She was much too healthy minded to tolerate preservatives and red food dye. Oh, she'd take BW because she felt obligated, and she'd tend to him as best she could, but she wouldn't like it, and BW would not be happy.

Boone strolled back in and sat down. "Well, it seems—"

"Will you take Bruce Willis if something happens to me?" I blurted. "Mamma's great and all, but she's not really a dog person, and KiKi has the cat from hell, and I don't want BW subjected to that. You got to let him sleep with you in your bed, not just by your bed on the cold floor, and you have to give him a hot dog every day, just one no matter how much he whines, and let him chase rabbits in the morning. It's a game; he just chases. Will you take him?" I felt a tear slide down my cheek and splat onto the scarred metal table, but I didn't care. I needed to straighten things out.

"And don't sell Cherry House to just anyone," I added after a good sniff. "If you let Hollis have it, I swear I'll haunt you forever and put a pox on your sex life." I had no idea where the last part came from, but considering I was talking to the hound of Savannah, I felt it carried weight. Another tear smacked the table.

Boone sat perfectly still, not moving a muscle. He leaned across the table, his jaw set, and eyes serious. "You've had a bad day is all and—"

"Promise me. Cross your heart and pinky swear." I held up my right pinky. "Do it."

Boone traced a cross over his heart and took my pinky with his. "I promise."

"And you won't forget."

"I won't forget."

I swiped the backs of my hands across my teary face and runny nose, sat up straight, and tried to gain some composure after making arrangements for my untimely demise. "Okay, we got that out of the way. What were you going to say when you came in?"

"That you're a free woman. Mr. Suit never identified himself to you or stated he was a detective, so the Ann Taylor thing is off the table because he's the one who asked you your name. As for the riot over at the Fox, no one saw anything; that's the story your customers are dishing out, and they are sticking to it, though you should know there's a list of phone numbers taped to the top of your Godiva candy box if clothes like that come in again."

I braced my hands on the table and levered myself across, my face an inch from Boone's. "You let me blubber on and on about BW and Cherry House, and you knew I was getting out of here?"

"You didn't give me much chance to jump in, Blondie."

"Don't you Blondie me."

Boone did a Cheshire cat grin.

"You're despicable, you know that."

"Do you want to get out of here or hang around and call me names?"

Boone had the top down and heat humming as we turned onto Bull Street. Bull was Savannah's scenic route circling five of the major squares. If getting somewhere fast was that important, you needed to move to New York and take the subway. The late afternoon sun hugged the horizon, casting long shadows across the city. Off in the distance St. John's rang out six o'clock. Seeing the city in a convertible was intimate; you were part of the scene. There was no chunk of metal to insulate you from what was happening around you, like Mr. Red packing up the palm roses and hats he made right there in the square and had sold to tourists for going on nearly twenty years now or the lights on in Scummy's campaign headquarters where Delray Valentine was headed in the front door, his arms piled high with boxes.

Okay, this was the second time today I'd run into Delray Valentine, and I'd probably only seen the man a handful of times my whole life. Earlier today he was at Eternal Slumber, and now he was going into Scummy's campaign headquarters. Why the headquarters at six o'clock at night? Something was going on.

"What am I keeping you from?" I said to Boone. "My guess is Auntie KiKi called you, and I know you didn't get all spiffed up to come rescue me at the police station. Hot date?"

"A meeting."

"Something to do with Scummy's murder, and you're not telling me, no doubt."

"Why don't you—"

"If you say go sell hats and dresses, I swear I'll beat you about the neck and shoulders."

A half smile tipped the corner of his mouth. "I was going to say have a long bubble bath and some tea. You've had a tough day."

"You are so lying."

"Sounded pretty good even to me." Boone stopped, letting a band of merry tourists cross over to Wright Square, and I got out of the car. "What are you doing?" Boone asked me.

"Walking home so you can get to your meeting."

"Reagan?"

"I'm walking," I said, backing away from the car with a little swagger I couldn't resist. "Just walking."

"Now who's lying?" he called after me, the car behind giving a toot for him to move on.

"It was my turn," I yelled back, fading into the crowd at the square.

I watched the Chevy's taillights fade down Bull, then doubled back to Scummy's campaign headquarters, where a Lexus was parked out front. Money-Honey? She could be cleaning things out, and Valley helping her made sense. I strolled by, doing the woman-in-a-hat-minding-her-business routine and cut my eyes inside the headquarters. Money-Honey was there all right, looking ticked off, flapping her arms up and down, and yelling at someone. It was life as usual in the campaign world, nothing else, and I was here on a wild-goose chase.

I walked back in the other direction, catching a glimpse of the old red London phone booth that stood outside Six

Pence Pub. A little splurge on onion soup and shepherds' pie was just what I needed after a really crappy day, I thought as the door to Scummy's campaign headquarters flew open and poodle-pin girl darted out. She collided into me full force, both of us crashing against Money-Honey's perfect iridescent white Lexus.

"I'm so sorry," poodle girl stammered, tears streaming down her face.

"Are you okay?"

"I'm not a slut," she sobbed into my shoulder.

"Of course you're not," soothed mamma-bear Reagan.

"We were in love," poodle girl choked. "He was going to leave her and run away with me to Cancun. I was there on spring break. I told Kippy he'd love it in Cancun. We'd be happy, open up a T-shirt store right there on the beach, and make love under the stars."

Kippy?

Poodle girl looked up at me with big watery eyes. "That witch said Kippy had others, and I should tell everyone what a fornicating bastard he was," she blubbered. "But that's a lie! Kippy loved me, just me, only me. He gave me a cute poodle pin, and I gave it back to him. I wanted Kippy to have it with him in heaven. How will I get along without the love of my life for ever and ever?" she sobbed louder.

Kippy and poodle girl together was interesting. That Honey and Valley knew about Kippy and poodle girl was the icing on the cake and motive for murder. If it got out that Kippy was messing with the help, he'd never get elected, and maybe knocking him off was the only way out. So why did Honey want poodle girl to tell all now?

I put my arm around poodle girl as she choked back more

tears, and I led her toward Six Pence. "You will survive, I promise. There are Kippy's everywhere, and you can do much better than a Kippy. Let's get you something to eat." And a copy of *Married Men Don't Buy the Cow When the Milk's Free* . . . especially when the old milk has money.

Chapter Fourteen

AFTER I fortified poodle girl with caffeine, soup, and a box of tissues, I walked her to her sorority house then turned for home. It seemed like a year since Suit had hauled me off to the police station. Tired to the bone, I finally got to Cherry House and trudged up the sidewalk to the porch, footsteps sounding behind me. At last count I was on Archie Lee's, Dozer's, Butler Haber's, and Suit's black list. Crazy Cazy and his black belt were unpredictable as the weather, and Boone . . . only the Lord himself knew what was going on with Boone and me.

I gripped Old Yeller in both hands, spun around, and nearly took out Mercedes right there in my own front yard.

"Whoa, girlfriend." Mercedes held up her hands in surrender. "I come in peace. Nice hat."

"So everyone keeps telling me. Did you have to let Boone know about me being dead under the sheet?"

A big, toothy grin broke across Mercedes's face, and she perched her ample weight on one foot. "Something that funny's for sharing, and Mr. Boone needs cheering up these days. He's trying mighty hard to find that killer and not having much luck as best I can tell. My previous employment gave me special insight into the male half of the population."

Mercedes held up her big pink bag. "I felt right bad about not getting a chance to fix your hair and all. You just give me an hour now, and you'll be a new woman." She pulled off my hat. "Okay, two hours."

Mercedes followed me inside, BW all excited I was back to home and hearth. I'd like to think his dancing and whining was because he missed me, but truth be told his internal clock had chimed out hot dog time and he needed me to open the fridge. I gave BW a backyard break and told him I'd bequeathed him to Boone with proper eating and sleeping instructions. When we went back inside, Mercedes had moved Mamma's election posters to one side of the kitchen and set a chair in the middle. Garbage bags were spread over the floor, and hair paraphernalia sat out on the counter.

"Put your head in the sink and let's shampoo you up and get started," she said to me. "I'm the Rembrandt of hair." She nodded to something bushy lying on the counter.

"Bugs!"

"Eyebrows. Superglue's a wonderful thing. You look like a bowling ball in a hat, so anything's got to be an improvement, right?"

I stuck my head in the kitchen sink, and Mercedes turned on the water. "What are you doing tonight?" I asked around suds floating over my face.

"Fixing it so you quit scaring the daylights out of people.

How do you expect to get Mr. Boone interested if you look scary?"

"I don't care if Mr. Boone's interested." Mercedes rinsed and wrapped my head in a towel, and I sat in the chair. "Did . . . did he say anything about me?"

"Uh-huh. Thought you weren't interested." I heard the snip, snip of the scissors, pieces of scorched hair falling onto the bags.

"Just curious."

"Honey, every woman in Savannah's just curious about that man. The thing is he's one of those quiet types, so you never know what's going on with him. He's sort of like his grandma if I remember right, God rest her soul."

Grandma? That got my attention. "How'd he wind up a lawyer?"

"Same way Big Joey is *The Man,* Pillsbury watches the Benjamins, I'm the dead-hair diva, and you got a shop. You do what you got to do to survive in this here world, and right now if you intend to survive a little longer, you should be a brunette. You need to forget blonde hair and being all flashy. Draws too much attention to your sorry, unfortunate self. I got a plan: we'll give you a low-profile image and try and prolong your life expectancy, which's looking right poor at the moment. You need to fade into the woodwork for a while."

"Yeah, but do I have to look like the woodwork."

Mercedes's answer was to slather brown goop on my head. "So, how about we take my hair out for a test drive after we finish up here?"

"Now you're talking. I'm down for martinis at Jen's and Friends."

"What about being down for breaking and entering into Seymour's campaign headquarters? I need a lookout."

Mercedes puffed out a big sigh. "Girl, do you ever just have fun?"

"I have fun, lots of fun. I'm a real fun girl. I eat sprinkle doughnuts . . . and stuff." There was no stuff, but I had to add something to the doughnuts. "Here's the thing. When I was visiting with you this morning at the Slumber, Seymour's campaign manager was paying the funeral bill. He said the campaign wasn't over, that Archie Lee as alderman wasn't a slam dunk. I'm not great at math, but there's only one candidate left; the other two are down for the count. What do you think the guy meant?"

"I think he was just shooting off his mouth like they do in politics. They make up junk to feel important. Kip Seymour sure liked to feel important, I can tell you that. You couldn't swing a dead cat around this city without hitting one of his campaign posters. That man thought he was the cat's meow."

"Well, Mr. Meow was diddling the cute chickie volunteers, and his wife and campaign manager knew about it, and they both told one cute chickie to spread the word. Why would they want that information out there?"

"Well, now you got yourself two questions without answers. Maybe there is something going on with that election. I suppose a little night stroll on the way to Jen's and Friends can't hurt anything."

It was ten when Mercedes, BW, and I headed out the door. I fastened the one remaining button on my jacket, and Mercedes pulled up the collar on her purple coat. "We could have taken my car, you know."

"You mean the inconspicuous pink Caddy? If Suit picks me up again, I'm toast."

We took Habersham and cut across Oglethorpe, the Cemetery just ahead lit with floodlights, red, white, and blue banners flying, "God Bless America" blaring from a speaker. Popeye handed out bags of boiled peanuts and pamphlets to late-night passersby, telling everyone, "Come to Liberty Square tomorrow at six o'clock for the rally to support our next great alderman, Archie Lee."

"We should head 'cross the street to the other side," Mercedes said, pulling on my sleeve, a little chunk coming off in her hand. "You need to keep with the low profile and stay away from anything to do with elections, especially Archie Lee and elections."

Mercedes started to the other side, but I didn't follow, slowing my steps. "He's handing out boiled peanuts," I said to Mercedes. "How about I walk real quick. Maybe he won't recognize me and will just hand me the peanuts. I have short dark hair now. Bet my own mamma wouldn't recognize me."

"It's not your mamma I'm worried about."

BW and I picked up the pace with Mercedes at my side grumbling about me not having the good sense God gave little green apples. We blended into the back of a line of people. Popeye smiled, and then his smile faded when he got to me. "You're like a bad penny; you just keep coming back."

"I have brown hair and glued-on eyebrows, and you still recognize me?"

"That ugly purse."

I held Old Yeller tight. "It's a great purse."

"And here we go," Mercedes said on her second deep sigh of the night.

"You better stay away from this here rally if you know what's good for you," Popeye said to me. "Archie Lee is going to win this election and be the best alderman ever, a heck of a lot better than your snooty-ass mamma would be."

I was all ready to walk away, I truly was, but then he had to go and bad-mouth my mamma. I poked him in his big barrel chest. "I wouldn't go counting my chickens before they're hatched, if I were you. Word on the street is there's something going on, something real big with the election. Maybe Archie Lee's going to get disqualified, didn't fill the paperwork out right; you never know what can crop up in an election."

"Oh, sweet Jesus." Mercedes closed her eyes as Popeye's voice dropped to a growl deep in his chest.

"I'm warning you, you better not do anything to mess this up for Archie Lee. He says he has everything under control, and you better not interfere. Got it?"

"Yep, we got it loud and clear," Mercedes said, grabbing my arm, tugging me along. "We need to go."

"Listen to Ms. Chubalini there," Popeye sneered. "Archie Lee said I needed to be nice to people, but no one's around right now, so I don't gotta be nice to you and pork chop in purple. You aren't voting for Archie Lee, so you can go pound salt."

Mercedes stopped dead, her eyes thin slits, little puffs of smoke curling from her nostrils. Could be from the chill in the air, but I didn't think so.

"Who you calling 'Chubalini'?" Mercedes said with a curled lip and a snarl. "Pork chop?"

"Uh, maybe you should apologize," I said to Popeye,

meaning it for his own good. "She has connections at Eternal Slumber. Dead is her thing."

"Can't be her thing. There's no coffin big enough to hold her." Popeye laughed, and Mercedes connected with a left hook, sending Popeye stumbling backward, tripping into the tub of nuts, knocking over the speaker, breaking the spotlight, and tearing down the banners, all of them landing across his prone body bedecked in discarded peanut shells.

I pulled Mercedes along behind me. "The cops are going to be here any minute, and I do not need cops."

I hustled us across the street to Colonial Cemetery, which was surrounded by a wrought iron fence and high brick wall, except for a broken section by the magnolia tree that I knew about as a haunted Savannah guide. I shoved Mercedes through the opening, tugged in BW, and squashed myself behind them as sirens and cruisers zipped by.

"Archie Lee's going to give us up to the cops, and Suit's going to find me and have me arrested and hauled off to jail, and Mamma will have a cow, and Boone will laugh his behind off . . . again."

Mercedes grinned. "You really think that big-mouth piece of crap barkeep is going to say he was decked by a woman?" Mercedes let out a full-body laugh and took my hand, dragging me out into the open. "He'll make up some story about tripping or duking it out with another guy, something that has nothing to do with a woman getting the drop on him like I did. Lordy, child, we are free as a bird. Now let's get to that headquarters and finish up our business so we can be moving on to the martini portion of the night's activities."

We rounded the corner onto Bull, the headquarters just ahead, the street pretty much deserted. "You and BW stand out front, and I'll duck down the alley," I said to Mercedes. "Knock on the window if someone's coming, and don't give BW any peanuts. He'll have gas all night and we live together."

"It's after ten." Mercedes scanned the street. "Who you expecting to show up at a campaign headquarters at this hour?"

"See this hair?" I pulled at a tuft. "See this jacket." I held up a ragged sleeve. "Unexpected is my life."

"That's from when you had the blonde-hair curse."

Mercedes and BW continued on, and I headed around back. The windows were above eye level, a light in one; the other in Scummy's office was dark. Black garbage bags lined the side of the building along with a can overflowing with smelly gross stuff. Using a piece of jacket, I dragged the can under the dark window, pulled myself up, and pushed up against the glass. The can wobbled then flipped over backward, taking me with it.

The window flew up, Mercedes and BW sticking their heads out. "What in all that's holy are you doing out there?" Mercedes whispered down to me, sprawled on my back gasping.

"Getting a concussion. What are you doing in there?"

"Key under the front mat. BW and I needed a drink. Lordy, you stink something fierce, and you're covered in garbage."

"Is it moving?"

"Bugs in the summertime; fall is more mouse and rat season."

I jumped up doing a quick rodent check while swiping off pizza sauce, half an eggroll, some orange rinds, and a piece of doughnut. How could someone throw away a doughnut? "Meet me at the door."

Mercedes's nose crinkled. "Do I have to?" She fought back a gag then closed the window.

I kicked the garbage back into the can, picked up a black garbage bag to toss in, Kip Seymour campaign flyers falling out through the hole in the bottom. The other bags were stuffed with pamphlets, buttons, and those cardboard stand-ups of Scummy. Kip Seymour was dead and buried in more ways than one. I craned my head around the corner of the building then slunk my way to the door, Mercedes letting me inside.

"You still have noodles in your hair," Mercedes said. "Lo mein. Stinking lo mein." She plucked them out and tossed them into a garbage can. "So now what are we looking for?"

"Nothing." I held up a campaign button, Kippy smiling back at us. "Seymour's wife and Delray Valentine, the campaign manager, were here earlier. They must have spent the day clearing the place out." I waved my hand over the empty tables and cabinets. "Everything from Seymour's campaign is in garbage bags out back. I thought there was something going on with the campaign because I wanted it that way, not because it's so."

Mercedes folded her arms and wagged her brows. "I've seen this Honey Seymour on TV a few times. She's always dressed in some fancy clothes with perfect hair and nails. Trust me, Honey baby is no cleaning lady. If she was here, it was for a reason, and the reason is all about her rich-witch self. I guarantee it. Give me that there flashlight you carry around and let's take a look-see."

I handed off the light, and BW and I followed Mercedes down the hall. "This is Seymour's office," I told Mercedes when we got to the closed door. "It's where KiKi and I found the body."

"Lucky you." Mercedes turned the knob, and we went in, the light picking out Scummy's desk piled with boxes. I pried off a lid to more campaign buttons, but this time Kippy wasn't the one smiling back, but Honey Seymour in all her bleached white teeth and hair glory. "Holy freaking tomatoes!"

"Okay, now we're getting somewhere." Mercedes opened another box to find "Vote for Honey Seymour" flyers. "Honey Seymour's taking her husband's place in this upcoming election. No wonder she wanted the word to get out he was doing the wham-bam with the cuties. She's going after the pity vote, the poor wifey angle, when she announces her candidacy, and from the looks of all this stuff she's gonna be doing that announcing right soon."

My eyes met Mercedes's across the pile of boxes, my heart skipping a beat. "Do you think she and Valentine had this planned all along . . . the murder, framing Mamma, running for alderman? If Seymour's philandering had gotten out before the election, he never would have won, and all that money and effort they had invested would have been for nothing."

"So just get rid of the donkey's butt. Heck, that's what I'd do," Mercedes said. "We need to find the bill for all this stuff. If Honey ordered from the printers before Seymour died, then it goes to premeditated murder and shows that your mamma could have been framed."

Mercedes held the flashlight over the desk so we could both see. She rifled through the boxes, and I rooted through a drawer that had escaped the big Scummy campaign clean out. There were "Vote for Kip Seymour" pens, pencils, note-pads, mints, sticks of yellow Juicy Fruit gum, and matching aspirin scattered about for those headaches on the go. Guess running for office wasn't all fun and giggles.

"Here it is," Mercedes said, holding the sheet of paper under the light. "The order was placed the day after Sey-mour croaked, not before." Mercedes hunched her shoulders. "I thought we had her. I really did. Don't you get yourself all down in the mouth now, you hear. This doesn't mean Honey didn't have it all planned out right from the start. She has motive out the ying-yang; we just don't have proof yet."

"The problem is we have lots of people with a lot of motives for wanting Seymour dead, but not one shred of proof anywhere."

Mercedes locked the front door, and I replaced the key under the mat. I couldn't smell myself anymore, but that Mercedes walked two steps behind and BW stretched his leash as far out in front as possible proved I was plenty ripe. The blonde-hair curse had morphed itself into the brunette curse. Having had enough of encounters of the rotten kind at the Cemetery, we detoured onto Abercorn to head home that way.

A trip to Jen's and Friends was definitely out in my pres-ent state of grossness, so Mercedes ducked into Pinky Mas-ters, the bar for cheap PBR and lovers of Tabasco popcorn. The beer she could do without, the popcorn not so much. BW and I waited outside, wanting nothing more than to get home . . . especially since Dozer the Delightful was walking right toward us. Would this day ever end?

"Well, well, just who I was looking for," Dozer said to me, his mouth curled in an ugly sneer. "If it isn't the blight of Savannah with ratty hair out walking her doggie. I left something for you on your porch. A little reminder of who's in charge now."

"Just like you left something in that bourbon bottle for Kip Seymour? Was that a big reminder of who's in charge now?"

Dozer grabbed my arm. "You stink, you know that."

"Right back atcha."

His fingers tightened, digging into my muscle. "One of these days you're going to get what's coming to you, and I hope I'm around to see it." Dozer let go and walked off, a sinister laugh trailing behind him. I was tired of being manhandled and threatened, and falling into garbage.

"You okay?" Mercedes asked, coming out the door. "That man has a mean streak a mile wide. I wouldn't put anything past him."

"Thanks for fixing my hair and going with me tonight," I said to Mercedes when we finally got to the steps at Cherry House, the light in the bay window never looking better. "It's been a rotten day."

"But hey, it's looking better. There's a package by your front door; it's even got one of those sticky bows. Bet it's a present. See, this is what happens when you have brown hair instead of that blonde stuff: good things start to happen. Sometimes it just takes a while to settle in." Before I could stop her, Mercedes picked up the box and handed it to me.

"Go on, open it."

I took the package, *Boom* scribbled right there on the front of the brown paper wrapping. It was just too much.

Dots danced in front of my eyes, the world started to spin, and I couldn't breathe, followed by a clanking in my head, then everything went dark, and I sank to the floor in a big heap.

Chapter Fifteen

"**W**HAT in the world happened to you?" Mercedes said, lifting my head, my eyes still not focusing and BW licking my face.

I grabbed the package and threw it as hard as I could out into the yard. "Duck!"

"What duck? I don't see a duck. Why are you trying to hit a duck of all things?"

"Not the quack-quack duck, the we're-all-gonna-die duck. Duck!" I grabbed Mercedes with one arm, BW in the other, and held them tight against me. I had no idea how that would help the situation, but it felt right. I cut my eyes to Mercedes, her cheek pressed tight to mine, eyes big as saucers.

"I think you done lost your mind."

"It's a bomb. *Boom* was written right there on top. Dozer said he'd get me, and this is it."

Mercedes wiggled free, retrieved the package from the

yard, and trudged back to the porch. I was too tired to protest. If the darn thing blew, I'd croak quick, and the day
would finally be over. Amen!

Mercedes sat the box between us and pointed to each
letter on the front. "B-o-o-n-e not B-o-o-m." She kissed me
on the forehead. "We'll get the remedial reading teacher
here in the morning. Right now just open the package."

My fingers were still shaking as I fumbled with the paper.
"Bet it's a tracking collar."

"For Bruce Willis?"

"Not exactly." I pulled off the lid. "It's a jean jacket."

"Oh, and it's a nice one. Soft, already broken in." Mercedes handed me the card.

"To new memories," I read aloud.

Mercedes cocked her left brow. "So, what kind of memories are we talking about here?"

"Not those kind of memories."

"Uh-huh, that's why you're blushing like a school girl.
See, it's that brown-hair karma starting to do its magic."

I WOKE LYING FLAT ON MY BACK, STARING UP AT THE
ceiling, my baseball bat at my side after the night of Dozer
and the boom package. BW was sprawled across my chest.
I think he was in protection mode after the day from hell. I
glanced at the denim jacket on the dresser. What did this
mean? Anything? Nothing? Boone was embarrassed to be
seen with me?

It meant that my old jacket was falling apart and I was
looking a little beat-up these days, period. A denim jacket
was not like a dozen long-stemmed roses for Pete's sake. I

was overthinking this. Sometimes a jacket's just a jacket like a dance is just a dance.

It was almost ten, and I had a shop to open. I peeled BW off my prone body, covered him with a blanket, and started for the bathroom. When Hollis the Horrible and I moved into Cherry House five years ago, the whole place needed big-time work. Hollis didn't know a saw from a hammer, leaving the rehabbing to me and a copy of *Home Improvement for Dummies*. The first thing I tackled was turning the putrid, rusty, cracked, flaking bathroom into something new in celery green and cream. I still had the scars to prove it.

"Nice hair," KiKi said, coming in the front door just as I opened up. "You got that Harry Potter with a sunburn look going on. Kind of cute."

"I was thinking more Anne Hathaway."

"Why now I do declare, you are absolutely right, except you're better looking," KiKi lied as any good auntie would. She handed me a cup of coffee. "Your Mamma's off teaching Zumba Gold at the senior center. Don't go worrying yourself into a state. It's a sitting-down kind of class. I think everyone's safe."

KiKi dropped a newspaper clipping on the checkout door. "This was nailed to the side of your porch. Something about Delany Construction building an addition to the firehouse. What do you have to do with that?"

"It's a little present from Dozer, a warning for me to stay out of his business."

"You get some mighty strange presents."

"More than you can imagine."

Two customers walked in, and KiKi came around the checkout door to where I stood. She dropped her voice. "I have news, really juicy news. You're-going-to-love-it kind of news."

"I have juicy news, too."

"Bet my news is juicier than yours."

When it came to dishing the dirt, Auntie KiKi was the queen bee. "Guess who's taking their husband's place in the alderman election?" KiKi mouthed *Money-Honey*. "It's all over Twitter. *Good Morning Savannah* says she's having a big rally at Johnson Square at five, and it's leaked she's announcing her candidacy from there. She's following it up with a private party at her house for contributors. What do you make of that?"

I eyed the customers and gave KiKi the *not now* look. KiKi drummed her fingers on the door, impatiently shifting her weight from one foot to the other, the customers leaving without buying a thing. When the door closed, KiKi blurted, "We need to get ourselves to Honey's rally."

"Don't even think about it." I added a lot of stern to my voice. "Someone will recognize us, and it will be a disaster, and Mamma will look guiltier than ever for us being there. Besides, I need to keep the Fox open for business. This is my busiest time of year, and I should make enough money to take me through January and February when no one buys anything."

"We can go just for a little while; this rally is important. The killer will be there, you know that. With Honey taking over Seymour Construction, Dozer's going to show up, and Butler Haber will be there and Archie Lee, all three prime murder suspects. Archie Lee has a rally just three squares over, so the fur's bound to be flying. We'll dress up in disguises."

"Because that worked out so well for us before."

"We'll stay in the background where we can see everything and no one will pay any attention to us. We'll do the blend-in thing."

"Somehow we always get attention, the wrong kind of attention, and all that's going to go on at that rally is a bunch of blah, blah, blah about how Honey's going to save Savannah from wrack and ruin. What we need is solid proof somebody spiked that bourbon."

"Party pooper."

I gave Kiki a hard look. "Uncle Putter won't appreciate your picture on the front page of the paper surrounded by the riot squad. Promise me you won't go on your own."

"Fine, I promise. But I'm not happy about it. I better go save the Zumba seniors from two-left-feet Gloria."

KiKi hurried out the door as Lolly's Trolley pulled up to the curb, Lolly sprinting up my walk. "I need a nice dress and maybe some jewelry," Lolly said as she came in behind another customer.

"A funeral?" I wasn't sure Savannah could survive another red-dress-at-the-coffin encounter. The occurrence headlined the kudzu vine for two days straight.

"Heavenly days, no. I've had my fill of funeral homes for a while. My darling Cazy's doing a martial arts demonstration at the Weston tomorrow, and I want to look presentable and—Sweet Jesus have mercy." Lolly stood dead still staring at me. "What in the name of heaven and earth happened to your hair and face?"

"Sun lamp and curling iron malfunction," I said as if it were the gospel truth. "You know," I said, hurrying to change the subject and do a little fishing along the way, "I never pictured Cazy as being a martial arts kind of guy. Is he any good at it?"

I led Lolly over to a jewelry display on the dining room table, and she held up a pair of sparkly earrings. "He's really good, black belt and everything. Last week he was splitting boards with his head for the Daughters of the Confederacy luncheon at Sweet Marsh Country Club and got interviewed by that blonde leggy gal on TV."

Lolly picked up a bracelet. " 'Course the whole thing got cut because it was the same day Scumbucket Seymour croaked and all the news was about him. But I got to tell you the best part of the day was when your mamma decked Scummy right there on the sidewalk. Wish I did the deed myself. I was so tickled I did a happy dance right in the middle of Bull Street then got my nails done at Jan's Cutting Crew to celebrate the occasion. Blushing Cherry will always bring back fond memories."

"Sorry I missed you dancing."

"Honey, you had your hands full with hustling Gloria off in that there Caddy and getting her out of harm's way like you did. But it is a pity you missed it; it went something like this." She put down the earring and bracelet, and right there between the racks of blouses and sweaters Lolly Ledbetter did a pretty fair tap dance that would have made KiKi proud. I applauded along with two other customers, Lolly taking a little bow.

I put Lolly, three dresses, and a taupe suit in the changing room. As I checked out the next customer, it occurred to me that I was two for two in the suspect department. Not only couldn't Cazy have killed Scummy because he was out at

Sweet Marsh doing the head-bashing thing for the Daughters, but Lolly had her fingers in the soaking bowl at Jan's. That was good in that I liked Lolly and Cazy, and didn't want them to be murderers, but it also gave me two less suspects in getting Mamma off the hook.

"What are you frowning about," Chantilly asked, coming in through the kitchen, a takeout bag from Cuisine by Rachelle in her hand. She made it do a little dance in the air. "Bet this will cheer you up and . . . Holy mother in heaven! Blair Street?"

"The moral of the story is don't get close to exploding houses."

"You look like Harry Potter."

"I'm going with Anne Hathaway."

"Why'd you go brunette?"

"Word has it they live longer."

"Worth a try."

I peeked in the bag and tried not to salivate.

"It's Honey's Hazelnut Cake and some mac and cheese with toasted bread crumbs on top that I bet you'll love. Guess who's catering an event tonight at Honey Seymour's house?" Chantilly batted her eyes and twitched her hips. "Rachelle and I've been working since last night to get things ready, even hired two temp people to help out. I talked Rachelle into taking the job even though we'll lose money. It's good advertising, and we need the business. How would you like free lunch like this for a week?"

I arched my eyes over the bag. "You got my attention."

"We need help, we're desperate, and we can't afford to hire anyone else for the event. I was going to have you wear a wig since you're Gloria's daughter and all, but no one's going to recognize you now, especially in a white blouse and black slacks like the rest of the staff. Just don't carry your purse—it's a dead giveaway. You can stay in the kitchen, set things up, and no one will know you're around."

Serving little hot dogs to Savannah's snooty rich was not in my top-ten list of things to do in life but this was a great chance to poke around. Money-Honey and Valley had a litany of *whys* to knock off Scummy, but I was clueless on the *how* part and needed something concrete to connect them to the deed. Mamma was running out of time, and I had no idea if Boone was making any progress at all. "I'm in."

"Really?" Chantilly gave me a big hug. "We'll need you at five to help set up. That's when Honey's rally starts and we'll be ready when they all come back there."

I told KiKi I was keeping the Fox open late, even used it as a reason not to attend Honey's rally, and now I was closing early and going to Honey's house? If KiKi found out, it would be hissy part two around here. "I'll be there," I said to Chantilly. Somehow.

Customers tapered off around four-thirty, shoppers heading home to dinner and family, and when the Beemer pulled into the driveway, I still hadn't come up with a reason why I was closing early. Keeping the motor running, KiKi and Mamma got out of the car and trotted over to the Fox.

"We just wanted you to know we're going out to dinner and won't be back for a few hours," Mamma said, KiKi nodding enthusiastically beside her.

"That's a terrific idea. Where?"

"Where?" Mamma repeated, not even mentioning my new do and toasted face. This must be some dinner. She looked back at KiKi, eyes wide.

"Vic's," KiKi said as Mamma blurted, "Maxwell's."

"You haven't made up your mind?"

"That's it," KiKi said in a rush as she grabbed Mamma's arm and hurried her toward the door. "Haven't decided, either is great, love Maxwell's crab cakes and Vic's salads, but we'll be gone for a few hours, and we're just fine and dandy, and don't wait up or whatever."

Mamma gave me a toothy grin and a little finger wave, KiKi slammed the door, and I heaved a sigh of relief. Mamma and KiKi were dining out and wouldn't even notice the Fox closing up; all that worry on my part for nothing. I watched out the bay window till the Beemer turned onto Lincoln, then told the two remaining customers I was closing and would hold their selections till tomorrow and give them a discount for the inconvenience. *Discount* was music to any consignment shopper's ears.

I gave BW his daily hot dog then changed into black slacks, a white blouse, and my glued shoes. I could probably afford better ones that came in on consignment, but these were comfortable; with a stand-up job, comfort trumped glue.

I hurried off to Charlton Street, Money-Honey's humble abode being the William Battersby House, an incredible Greek Revival with lovely gardens built way before the days of AC. The house had long verandas stretching south to north catching the ocean breezes drifting in from Tybee Island. A white van with *Cuisine by Rachelle* scripted across the sides stood by the back entrance, doors flung wide open.

"Lord be praised, you made it," Chantilly said, thrusting a tray of cucumber sandwiches my way and hoisting up a huge bowl of Vidalia onion salad. "Rachelle's putting the crawdad stew into the chafing dishes, and I'll finish up the shrimp and grits, then cut servings of Granny Jackie's peach cobbler and put them on the buffet. It got rave reviews from the Daughters of the Confederacy at their last luncheon. Wait till you see this dining room," Chantilly added as we headed inside. "Chandelier from Italy and silk oriental rugs and—"

"Wait," I said getting in front of her. "Rachelle served at the Daughter's luncheon out at Sweet Marsh?"

"The country club said they'd try her out to do their desserts; their pastry chef up and left, so now we're getting business from them. I make a mean lemon meringue pie. The gig was great for Rachelle's business and—"

"That was the day and time Scummy got knocked off. If Rachelle was out at Sweet Marsh serving the Daughters, she wasn't lacing Scummy's honey bourbon."

Chantilly bit her bottom lip. "I never thought of that. So Rachelle's off the hook, and I got myself a job permanent. I was mighty worried she'd be getting hauled off to jail. Seymour was definitely not one of her favorite people, and doing him in was not out of the realm of possibility. Anyone who can whip meringues the way that woman does has definite hostile tendencies."

A slow grin spread across Chantilly's face. "This is mighty wonderful news, I have to tell you. My Pillsbury will be tickled pink all the way to his toes that I'm still a cook."

A mental image of Pillsbury tickled pink boggled the mind, but right now we had work to do. Chantilly used her behind to hold the door for me, and I scooted past and into the kitchen. "Drop this off, then set out boiled peanuts and pralines," she said. "We need to look real Southern, and then go set out the glasses for champagne. The servers will pass the drinks, and you can help us keep bowls and platters filled. Well-fed, inebriated guests write fatter campaign checks." She gave me a critical once-over. "Just stay out of view. We don't need any Gloria Summerside drama."

A parade of delivery people carried in vases and baskets of fall flowers, and the valet guys set up a key system so guests didn't have to hunt for parking places. I found the wood-paneled parlor, a fire crackling in the hearth, the bar ready for action. I pulled rented fluted glasses from boxes, set them on the silver trays, then started opening bottles chilling in tubs of ice. My first attempt at champagne popping took out an ugly ceramic bird on the mantel, the second cork nailed a painting of something modern so the dent blended in, but by the third bottle I was a pro.

"That campaign manager just called," Chantilly said in a rush, her hair frizzed out as if she had just stepped off a rollercoaster. "They're running a few minutes late; seems there was some kind of problem at the rally, two men causing a scene. They had to call the cops, and no one wanted to leave and miss the action and how are we to keep everything warm and it not get dried out. Mercy!"

Chantilly shoved a little cordless vacuum my way. "Walk around and make sure everything looks good. If things aren't perfect, Honey won't pay us."

I didn't know who the men at the park were, but thank you very much, this was just the break I needed. Chantilly hurried off to check the dining room, and I sucked up stray leaves and dirt that had been tracked in along with peanut shells that had missed the bowls. I worked my way toward the curved staircase, the second floor being the best bet for unearthing incriminating evidence that indicated Money-Honey's campaign was planned and much more than a sudden whim.

I scooted a maroon and gold upholstered chair away from the wall to hide the vacuum till I got back downstairs, except a reed basket was already there. It held colorful pink lacy ribbons tied around a chunk of wood, two eggplants, and a bottle of white rum. Marigold and round two with Odilia? Pink lacy ribbon and all. Knowing better than to ever come between a basket of offerings and the powers that be, I scooted the chair back in place and hid the vacuum behind a curtain.

Three guest bedrooms occupied one side of the upstairs hall, the master on the other side. A cherry antique desk sat in the corner, a Tiffany lamp casting shades of greens and gold across the white carpet. I pulled out the top drawer of the desk to find legal pads and what looked like Honey's campaign speech on how Scummy should be here tonight at this rally with you all and how he was taken from us by a desperate, no-account, scheming, unscrupulous woman with no sense of decency.

Wow, good thing I talked KiKi out of going to that rally. She would have had a hissy fit right there on the podium when she heard these things about Mamma, and I would have been right behind her.

The clothes in Honey's closet were Chanel, Saint John's, Hermes, and other high-price names, everything in perfect I-have-a-maid order. Jackets hung on one side, skirts on the other, then blouses and suits, with shoes in see-through marked plastic boxes. I stopped and went back to the jackets, to the cream one with black stitching. It was the jacket Honey wore when she and Scummy harassed Mamma the day he died. The matching skirt to the suit was the very one the woman had brought to the Fox to sell. The woman was

Honey's maid, and the cream skirt with the spots belonged to Honey. But why did Honey throw away the matching skirt?

A series of car doors slammed outside, guests arriving, valet taking over. I did a quick rummage through the dressers, then the nightstands with floral lamps perched on top. One nightstand had reading glasses, a copy of *Winning Elections for Dummies*, and a king-size bottle of aspirin. The other nightstand was empty, obviously Scummy's, and everything of his gone. This was not the house of a distraught mourning widow who had difficulty moving on. Money-Honey had left Scummy in the dust three days ago when she buried his sorry behind out there at Bonaventure.

Creaking came from the hallway, high heels clicking across the hardwood floor. I hunkered down beside the bed and scooted under, expensive shoes coming my way. That I hated little closed-in, cramped-tight places where there wasn't enough oxygen and the whole place could collapse in on me at any time did not add to the joy of my current situation.

Breathe I ordered myself, perspiration slithering down the sides of my face. *Think of a happy place.* A scream inched up my throat.

Honey sat at the edge of the bed, the backs of her shoes inches from my face. She clicked on the nightstand lamp then kicked off her beige heels, nearly hitting me in the face with the spiked end. Her purse tumbled off the bed onto the floor right in front of me, a pen, comb, and a no-lid prescription bottle of digoxin for Kip Seymour right in front of my nose. Money-Honey muttered something very unladylike, scooped up the things, then padded over to the bathroom.

The door closed behind her, and I shimmied from under the bed. I gulped in massive amounts of oxygen, my gaze landing on the no-lid prescription bottle Honey had sat on the nightstand.

It was Scummy's all right. Why would Honey have Scummy's prescription bottle when she didn't even have a tie or sock or shirt of his lying around? A little yellow pill lay on the carpet by the nightstand, probably a straggler from the bottle. It was just like the yellow pills in Scummy's desk at the headquarters with writing on the top, numbers and letters. Prescription. I hadn't paid attention in the dim light at the headquarters, but here in the bright light of the lamp it was obvious these weren't aspirin. I slipped the pill in my pocket and crept out into the hall. It was too crowded to get the vacuum so I headed straight for the kitchen.

Chantilly flung a plate of something puffed at me. "Where have you been? Put these in the dining room right away. They're all a bunch of vultures out there. You'd think they hadn't eaten in a month, and they're gobbling up everything in sight. Keep your head down and no one will pay any attention to who you are, and they won't even care as long as you're bringing them food. Go!"

The rest of the night was a blur of shrimp things, crab things, puffed this and that, and various chunks of meat on little wood skewers. Personally I preferred SpaghettiOs surprise on the front porch with BW. Lord knows the company was better. By midnight the food was eaten, the moochers gone, and campaign checks written.

Money-Honey stood in the kitchen doorway, probably as close to a kitchen as the woman ever got since she found money. "You," she said, pointing a bony finger at Rachelle and holding out a cream-colored skirt in her other hand. "Put club soda on this right away. Some moron dribbled whiskey, and the cleaners will have a dickens of a time even if I tell them what it is. I've already lost one Chanel suit to whiskey, and I'm not losing another. These skirts don't grow on trees; they're expensive. I'm going to bed and this place better be spic-and-span in the morning or I'm not paying a dime."

Rachelle waited till Money-Honey left and folded her arms. "First we had Mr. Jackass and now Mrs. Jackass. Neither one worth a hoot if you ask me; I think that there Archie Lee guy is the best of the lot."

"I can take care of the skirt for you," I said to Rachelle, snatching it from her hand and hurrying off to the parlor and the bar for club soda. The stains on the skirt were little brown dribbles, and I'd seen them before on the Chanel skirt the maid brought into the Fox to sell. Whiskey stains? Honey just said so herself. I wouldn't have connected the two if Money-Honey hadn't just mentioned it.

The thing was, she didn't try and save the skirt the maid had brought in. The maid said she found it in the trash. Why didn't Honey take it to the cleaners? And what was with Scummy's empty prescription bottle in her purse without a lid, the scattered pills in Scummy's desk drawer, and the complete absence of Scummy at home and at the headquarters?

Scummy was dead, Mamma framed for the murder, and no one happier about it all than Money-Honey Seymour. How did she make this happen and why?

Chapter Sixteen

"Look, dog," I said to BW as he licked my face at seven thirty in the morning, "I didn't get to bed till two A.M. That's not much sleep even in dog time, and I need to teach you how to use a toothbrush and mouthwash."

In reply BW sat on my chest, flattening out what little attributes I had and making it impossible to go back to sleep. I scooted out from under seventy pounds of loving doggie, stumbled downstairs, and opened the door for BW, then stopped. I wasn't alone . . . again. Slowly I turned around to Mamma, Auntie KiKi, and Boone sitting at my dining room table with a big plate of sprinkle doughnuts.

"Holy mother of God, who died?"

"Oh, honey," Mamma said, getting up and patting me on the back. "No one died. My, what a nice Tweety Bird night-shirt you have on."

"It's from the Goodwill over on Broughton and has a

chocolate stain down the front, and why are Boone and both of you here in my house at this hour?" I sucked in a quick breath and looked at Mamma. "They're going to put you back in jail?"

"I'm protection," Boone offered, picking up a doughnut.

"From the cops?"

"From you." Boone handed me a cup of coffee. "Drink this, all of it; you're going to need it." He took a big bite of doughnut to hide the smile pulling at his lips. It wasn't a gee-isn't-this-a-nice-day kind of smile but more of a *You are so screwed* smile.

"It wasn't our fault at all," KiKi said matter-of-factly. "Anyone would have done the very same thing in our shoes. You would have done the same thing. We were provoked. It was that Money-Honey person and all those lies that made us do it."

"I needed to set the record straight," Mamma chimed in. "So we did, both of us together. We just couldn't sit still and do nothing, now could we? How would I ever get a fair trial in this town or get a decent table over there at the Pink House if I just let things slide?"

"What things slide? Where?" My brain started to churn. What was that Chantilly had said last night about a disturbance? The police being called in? "Holy crap, you both went to that rally!"

"We went right up to that podium they had set up to tell the truth to everyone who was there," KiKi said, chin held high. "How dare that woman accuse Gloria of murder right out there in a public place? But then some know-it-all called the police before Gloria could make a statement."

"I remembered the alleys that we ducked down to keep

away from the press, then we got to Walker's house and sort of hid out till the cops went away. He drove us home but said we needed to tell you everything before you found out on your own, that you might be a bit upset. He brought you doughnuts, isn't that right nice of him? But I don't see how you can be upset, honey. We didn't take any chances at being recognized; we wore disguises, good ones."

Auntie KiKi held up a fedora and a leather jacket. "We were so badass."

Boone handed me a doughnut. "Sort of like drag in reverse."

"I don't believe this."

Auntie KiKi folded her arms. "We needed evidence to get Gloria off the hook, and we knew the killer would be there. Archie Lee was having a rally over on Liberty Square, and we intended to head over there next. We wanted to have a look-see for ourselves as to who was acting suspicious."

"*You* were acting suspicious by being there! You . . . you . . . you're both grounded! For a week! Go to your rooms!"

"Honey," Mamma started, a spark of amusement in her eyes. "You can't—"

"Watch me." I gave KiKi my best *ready to throw a fit* look and pointed to her house. "If I see you out of Rose Gate, I'm telling Uncle Putter exactly who dumped the plant on Scummy's head over there at Eternal Slumber and just how he wound up with the cat from hell living in his house."

I glared at Mamma. "If you leave your place, I'm moving back in, bringing BW, and contaminating your fridge with hot dogs. I'll let BW sleep on the bed, and I'm making SpaghettiOs surprise for dinner every night."

Mamma's jaw dropped, and KiKi's eyes bugged. I jabbed my hands to my hips. "Now both of you go . . . but leave the doughnuts."

Mamma snatched up her purse. "But—"

"Hot dogs? SpaghettiOs surprise?"

"I was just going to say you might want to fetch a robe, dear. You got yourself all in a tizzy and are showing off some things best left to the male imagination, if you get my drift." Mamma nodded at my front, two little points protruding under Tweety's big black eyes. Mamma followed KiKi out the door, BW scampered back inside, and I grabbed a navy jacket from the rack, Boone averting his gaze.

A part of me commended his gentlemanliness, another part thinking *Hey, what's wrong with the girls*? A little on the skimpy side but a ten on the perky scale.

"You grounded badass one and two, got eyebrows, and fixed your hair. What's this city going to do for entertainment now?" Boone said, dragging me back to the situation.

I took a big gulp of coffee. "How did the police not know it was Mamma and KiKi at the rally?"

"Ross was over at Cakery Bakery loading up on fats and sugars for the night and took the call. She said it was hard to give chase when doubled over with laughter. I told her we were onto something and would let her in on it if she conveniently got lost and couldn't identify her two suspects." Boone leaned back in the chair. "*Are* you onto something? I gave sanctuary to fugitives; it's your turn."

"It's always my turn. There was a basket of eggplant, ribbons, and rum over at the Seymour house hidden behind a chair. Last time I talked to Marigold, Odilia had her dropping offerings at Seymour's business; my guess is this is the

second round since Honey's taking over the business."
Savannah was one of the few places on the face of the earth
where you could make a statement like that and it would
make perfect sense.

"Butler and Marigold Haber had no use for Scummy and
felt pretty much the same about his wife. I think there's bad
blood there, and the decorated basket proves things have not
improved."

"Ross needs more than eggplant, ribbons, and rum," Boone
said. "And what in heaven's name were you doing at Honey
Seymour's? Being Gloria Summerside's daughter puts you on
Honey's hit list big-time."

"I was helping Chantilly with a catering gig. With my
brown hair Chantilly said no one would recognize me.
Besides she promised me free lunch for a week."

"And it gave you a chance to case the joint. Find anything?"

"Champagne corks are lethal." I took a sip of coffee, the
gift of caffeine jumpstarting my brain. "Doesn't it seem a
little strange to you that Honey Seymour is so ready, willing,
and able to take her husband's place? I know everyone thinks
it's because she's overwrought after Scummy's death and
honoring his memory, but in her house there's no sign the
guy ever existed. Takes moving on to a whole new level."

"And you think she did him in because he was messing
with the help and she got fed up. She knew he was going to
lose the election, so she took matters into her own hands
and got rid of him."

"You knew about all this?"

"Like I said, I did some legal work for Kip a few years
back. He was fooling around then, and I can't imagine that

marrying Honey would change him. Honey and everyone else in the city tuned into social media knew Gloria was coming to the campaign headquarters with the honey bourbon to try and smooth things over. It was easy for Honey to spike it and frame Gloria, or maybe Delray Valentine did the deed."

Boone thought for second. "My guess is they were both in on it. They were in and out of that office, and they both had a lot to lose if the election went south. It sure as heck is easier to substitute the grieving widow who suffered through a cheating husband than defend the rotten, no-good cheating husband. But there's no proof that I can find that ties Honey and Valley to killing Seymour. Even ordering Honey's campaign paraphernalia was done after Seymour died."

I sat up straight. "You broke into his headquarters to check the invoice, too?"

"I checked with Francie over at Spanish Moss Printers for the order dates." Boone shoved his hands in his jeans pockets. "What else do you have for Ross. We got to get something to her quick. She's keeping Cakery Bakery on double shifts and should be the size of a house by Thanksgiving at this rate."

"There were digoxin pills lying loose in Scummy's desk at his campaign headquarters and an empty prescription bottle for the pills in Honey's purse with no lid. Why the pills one place, the bottle another, and the lid somewhere else? Like someone was in a hurry to clean up?"

"What else?"

"I landed in a garbage can and hid under a bed to get that information, so show a little appreciation, and how do you know there's an *else*?"

"Your fake brows are squished together in one long

shaggy line. Either you're thinking, or you're coming down with some disease."

"There's this skirt. One of Honey's maids brought it to me to sell at the Fox, but it has spots on it, and I can't sell it this way. The thing is it was the skirt to the suit Honey wore the day Seymour was knocked off. I recognized it because Honey and Scummy came to Mamma's headquarters to harass her that day, too. Honey kept the jacket; I saw it in her closet when I was there."

Boone let out a long weary sigh, but I ignored it and went on. "Here's the thing, Honey didn't send the skirt to the cleaners to try and save it. She just tossed it in the garbage like a rag."

Boone hunched his shoulders. "It's just a skirt, and Honey has money. So she threw out a skirt, no big deal. She gets rid of a lot of things."

"Let me tell you about the rich. The reason they have money is because they hold on to it. This is a five-hundred-dollar skirt, maybe more. I think the stains were whiskey stains because Honey admitted she'd ruined two skirts that way, and the spots on the first skirt were dead-on to the ones on the second. The second skirt was going to the cleaners." I held out my hands. "Why didn't she take the first one? What was different about it? Why throw out a Chanel skirt?"

Boone stared straight ahead, gazing off into nothingness, lips thin, jaw set, little gray cells churning behind dark eyes. "Or what's the difference between the whiskey stains on the first skirt and the whiskey stains on the second?" Boone offered. "If Honey did spike the bourbon that killed Kip and she spilled some of the liquor, she'd want to get rid of the skirt and any trace of what was on it that could be linked back to her. Best to just toss it out."

"Except the maid came along and saw dollar signs."

"Okay, we got Kip playing bedroom bingo, and Honey and Valley seeing their work going up in smoke and then turning it all around with a sympathetic candidate who's man did her wrong. Framing Gloria gets her out of the way, and Archie Lee's not going to win against Honey. Ross should take a look at those spots. The police can analyze material and residue. Where's this skirt the maid brought to sell?"

"It's expensive."

"Right, got the memo."

"So I sort of took it to the dry cleaners to get the spots out."

Chapter Seventeen

BOONE pushed open the door to Soap Box Cleaners with me right behind him, the little bell tinkling our arrival, my fingers crossed the skirt was untouched by dry-cleaning chemicals.

"Don't get yourself all bent out of shape, now ya hear?" came Mary Kay's voice from the back, carrying over the hum of machines and ringing phones. "I'm dancing as fast as I can, and I'll be with you in a flash."

"Well now, Reagan honey, what can I do for you and . . ." Mary Kay's gaze shifted from me and landed solidly on Boone. "And thank you, Lord, you done remembered my address and sent me Walker Boone to start my day right. How you doing this morning, handsome?"

Mary Kay was fiftysomething or maybe sixtysomething, the preservation of dry-cleaning fumes in the air making it hard to tell. She was skinny as a broom handle with red hair ironed and double starched to poker straight. She'd been behind the counter at the Soap Box for as long as I could remember, the little dish of lollypops for kids always full, with a red one on top.

"Any luck finding Seymour's killer and getting Gloria off the hot seat?" Mary Kay asked Boone. "Word has it you're her attorney. Guess it's your turn to pay her back for helping you get in law school and all."

"That she did," Boone said, a genuine smile on his face as my jaw dropped to the floor. Law school? What law school? Mamma?

Boone said to Mary Kay, "We're here about a skirt that Reagan dropped off. Cream colored, expensive, spots down the front. Maybe you haven't cleaned it yet?"

Mary Kay snorted. "I went and cleaned that there skirt the very day it came in here. For a second I thought it was one of Honey Seymour's pieces. She has a pricey suit just like it. I am sorry as can be, but I couldn't get the stains out for diddly," Mary Kay said to me. "I tried everything under the sun and then some. Usually I have pretty decent luck with setting stuff to rights, but this skirt was the devil. I couldn't put my finger on exactly what the spots were. Seems to me they were liquor and sticky like and something else that just wouldn't budge. I'll get it for you."

Mary Kay hit the button for the carousel thing that brought the clothes forward. She plucked off the plastic-bagged skirt and handed it to me. "Sorry about that, Sugar. No charge. Come see me next time you have a problem, and I'll do better for you."

She gazed longingly at Boone. "And you, Mr. Gorgeous,

can come pay me a little old visit any time that suits you, now, you hear?"

Boone followed me outside, then I turned in front of him, making him stop. "What is going on?"

"At this rate probably not much. After dry cleaning fluid hit that spot, I'd say we're toast on Ross finding if there was foxglove dissolved in the honey bourbon spilled down the front and—"

"Not that. Mamma? Law school?"

"It was either that or juvie."

"That's your answer to everything, and you don't go to law school as a juvie. Try again."

Boone gave a resigned shrug. "My time in a courtroom hasn't always been as a lawyer. Guillotine Gloria said she saw more of me than most of the attorneys in this city and was tired of me taking up their time. Said I could go to jail for three years or go to law school for three years and that she'd pay the freight."

Boone held up the skirt. "I'm taking this to Ross. Maybe there's some new procedure I don't know about, and even if there's not, the possibility of Honey being involved in the murder is still there."

Boone started off, and I grabbed his arm. "Mamma never said anything to me about you and going to jail."

"Maybe because it was none of your business."

"But . . . but I'm her daughter, and she didn't offer to send me to law school."

Boone's eyes danced. "Blondie, you could never keep your mouth shut long enough to be a lawyer and besides"— devilment replaced dancing as he turned and strolled off toward the Chevy—"she likes me better."

Gotcha. I walked right into that one with my eyes wide open because Mamma and Boone had secrets and I was feeling left out. There was more going on with Boone than days in the hood and days as a legal eagle. Making that jump took some doing, and Mamma seemed to be involved. That was a feather in Mamma's cap. That Boone did the jumping but kept a foot and friends in both camps was a feather in his cap. I didn't have any feathers. I had a dog and a slightly falling-down house.

"Wait," I yelled at Boone, catching up with him and the skirt by the Chevy, passersby crowding us to the edge of the sidewalk. "What now?" I asked. "The spots are not going to help us nail the one or possibly two who we thought it was going to nail. What do we do next, and don't give me the go sell a dress routine?"

"I have work at the office, and you should check on Bonnie and Clyde."

"You're going to powwow with Ross and leave me out like you always do."

"I'll tell you if something important comes up."

"After it's over and done with."

"Yeah, but I will tell you."

BY THREE THE FOX WAS A HUBBUB OF ACTIVITY. With the sun offering up an unusually warm November afternoon, I had the front door wide open. Marigold strolled inside, her face pulled into angry lines.

"In my humble opinion the only thing eggplants are good or is making an eggplant Parmesan casserole," Marigold said as she drew up to the checkout door while I wrote up a sale for a tan Michael Kors purse for another customer.

"You look ready to pull all your hair out by the roots," I said.

"Butler says things are worse than ever. How can they be worse? I thought we passed worse six months ago, and yet here we are. Things were supposed to be turning around." Marigold held up a white cotton bag. "I just picked this up from Odilia; it's round three in the setting things to rights ritual. What do you think?"

I took a step back and the Michael Kors customer sucked in a quick breath, snatched up her purse without even waiting for change, and raced out the door. One mention of Odilia and a strange white bag had that effect. "Is there a snake in there?" I asked, every hair on my body standing straight on end. Snakes outside were one thing; snakes in my house were a whole new ballgame.

"Lord have mercy, no. I don't do snakes, no matter how bad things get around here." Marigold undid the swath of material that tied the bag closed, then reached in and pulled out a rattle of sorts made from a dried gourd. "I've got a drum in there, too. I'm supposed to beat and shake at sunset at the lumberyard right as the sun fades and before the crescent moon rises, meaning it's got to be tonight because there's a crescent moon and not a full one. It's the perfect time to call in the good ways for business and shut out the bad ways, or so Odilia tells me. Personally, I got serious doubts about there being any good left or if any of this will work, but I got to try something now, don't I? I'm flat out of options and money, and I'm afraid Butler's going to do something stupid, even more stupid than he's done in the past, and that's going some."

Marigold retied the bag and handed it across the checkout door. "Watch this while I look around. Odilia said not to let these things out of my sight. She said it would be best to wear a white cotton dress to do my rattling and drum beating in. Actually, she said it would be best if I did it in my birthday suit." Marigold pinched the bridge of her nose. "How do I get into these messes?"

Marigold scurried off, and I put the bag in a safe corner behind the checkout, not wanting any harm to come to it on my watch. I wasn't real clear on the practices of Odilia, but there was Buffy Codetta and the Savannah River bridge occurrence to consider.

I cleared out the dressing room and hung things back where they belonged. BW meandered inside, a fedora on his head, little holes cut through for his ears, and a black tie around his neck with a note attached. "You look like part of the Ratpack," I told BW. "Frank Sinatra with a tail." The note read . . . *Like Cher says, snap out of it.*

I looked to the front door and saw Auntie KiKi poking her head around the edge. She gave a little finger wave and held up her iPhone, making it do a little air dance. Something was up. I was really tired of things being up. Whatever happened to down and boring? "You're grounded, remember?"

"Five hours is all the grounded I can manage and the same for your mamma."

KiKi pulled up beside me by the rack of little black dresses. "Gloria says she's done with politics and maybe even being a judge. She's home with her computer, high-speed Internet, and time on her hands. Her last text said she was signing up for a fashion design class over there at the community college so she can help you out here in the shop."

KiKi put her arm around me. "She thinks you should paint the entrance hall persimmon orange and we should wear matching shirts with little polka dot bowties. And there's something on Twitter you need to see."

"I've already seen cats playing the piano."

"Take a look at this." KiKi held up her iPhone. "Archie Lee was on *Good Morning Savannah*, and he's done invited Honey to the Cemetery for a happy hour of apple pie and politics this afternoon. It's an antimudslinging get-together with Money-Honey and Archie Lee. Archie Lee's saying that now with your mamma out of the picture it's better for everyone because she was the one who caused all of the problems by running a dirty campaign. Do you believe this bunk? This is just another black eye for Gloria. I swear I could wring all their necks and do it gladly."

"Let me see that," Marigold said, snagging the phone right out of KiKi's hand. "My phone's dead as a brick. Why can't these things just recharge themselves? Lord have mercy, look at this right there on Twitter."

Marigold read the little screen, her face getting redder by the minute, eyes on fire. "This is so much bull honkey." Marigold stamped her foot. "Seymour was the guttersnipe who ran all those nasty ads, not Gloria, not a one. Fact is, that's how Gloria got accused of murder in the first place; she was trying to make nicey-nice with the jackass over a bottle of honey bourbon, and look where it got her, in a mess of trouble and all for nothing."

Marigold flung a white dress on the counter and yanked out her wallet. "I bet this is all Honey's idea. Well, she's not going to get away with it. I can promise you that. She was as much a part of sewer politics as her husband. I'm willing to bet most of it was her idea. If they all want a fight, we can give them a fight. I still have my connections with the press and TV stations, and I'm going over there right now and set things to rights. Gloria may be accused of murder, but she is not going to be accused of running a mudslinging campaign when she did no such thing. Enough's enough."

Marigold poked herself in the chest with her index finger. "That was my campaign too, you know." She grabbed the dress before I could put it in a bag and stormed out the door and down the sidewalk to her car.

"That there is one royally ticked-off female," KiKi said. "I hope she has some good luck with the press, but I doubt if she will."

Luck! The drum! The rattle! I snatched up the white cotton bag from the corner and tore after Marigold just as her little Civic squealed away from the curb and tore down Gwinnett, leaving me looking after her waving the bag in the air hoping she'd see it in her rearview mirror. No such luck.

I hated that Marigold wasn't going to shake and drum at sundown because she was off trying to help Mamma. Marigold had her own set of problems to deal with these days. Maybe I could meet her at the lumberyard at sunset. She was in such a tizzy over Mamma being unjustly accused of running a dirty campaign she probably wouldn't realize she'd left the white cotton bag with me. It wouldn't dawn on her till she got all the way out to the lumberyard. KiKi could hold down the Fox, and I could borrow the Beemer and meet Marigold with the loot. That might work.

I turned to go back inside and bumped right into Valley, the manager for the new-and-improved Seymour-for-alderman campaign. Usually Delray Valentine was your mild-mannered insurance salesman in his gray JC Penney's suit, no-iron blue shirt, and unpolished worn shoes. Today he had on the same sort of clothes, but there was no hint of the mild-mannered element anywhere.

"I know it was your aunt and mamma at Honey's rally last night causing all that uproar," he said in a barely controlled voice. "You may have that Detective Ross in your hip pocket, but things are changing here in Savannah, and if you know what's good for your battleaxe aunt and stick-up-her-behind mother, you'll keep them away from the get-together we're having at the Cemetery between Archie Lee and Honey. This is important; the election's in one week, and those two better not mess it up for us."

"You're not a very nice man, are you?"

"You have no idea what I'm capable of," he snarled. "Nothing will give me more pleasure than getting your mother and aunt locked up, and from what I hear the new detective in town would like to put your interfering behind in the cell right beside them. I have this election in the bag, we're way ahead in the polls, and I'm getting backers and raising money, and you and your lunatic family aren't getting in my way."

My way? Interesting. "I didn't realize *you* were running for election, Mr. Valentine. Tell me, what's in it for you? I'm guessing plenty or you wouldn't have sunk all your time and effort into this campaign then poisoned your own candidate with that foxglove in the honey bourbon concoction. Why was that, to get him out of the way so Honey could step in and take his place? Sounds like a plan to me."

Something mean and dark and scary sparked in Valley's eyes, his hands fisting at his sides. "You're so desperate you'll say anything," he snarled. "Your mamma killed Kip; everyone knows that."

"Do they? You and Honey are the ones benefitting from his death. Tell me, what does Honey get, the fame and notoriety and social standing, and you . . . you get some fat municipal insurance policies for all your hard work? Sounds like a lot of money and a lot of motive to me."

"Prove it."

"I'm getting closer all the time. You'd be surprised just how close."

"You're lying."

"That's what you think." I threw in a sassy smile for good measure.

Rage hardened his dark eyes and pinched the corners of his mouth. "You better stay out of my way and quit stirring up trouble if you know what's good for you. Accidents happen all the time, take it from an insurance man, and your mother has a better chance with a jury getting her off than she does with me. I've got a failing business on my hands and a year of my life in this here campaign. I wasn't about to let Kip take it down the tubes, and I'm not letting you."

"So you did kill him."

"Didn't have to; someone did it for me, sort of. Insurance covers more than homes and cars; there's life insurance. I know a lot more about dying than you think I do. Keep it in mind. You get in the way, and you'll be sorry. One way or another I swear you'll regret it."

Valley got back in his old Honda and rattled off as Auntie KiKi charged out of Cherry House, baseball bat in hand. "I was with a customer and just now looked out the door. What's going on with Valley? Never seen him that way before, not that he's one of my favorite people, but I've never seen him in Darth Vader mode."

"I accused him of killing Scummy."

"Well, that will do it. You sure do have a way with words."

"He said someone beat him to knocking off Scummy, and my guess is that someone was Honey. Except Valley used the words 'sort of' when talking about the murder. How would he know what was going on with killing Scummy unless he was directly involved?"

KiKi looked like a kid at Christmas. "We should go to that there apple-pie-and-politics meeting."

I gave KiKi a look that would cut straight through solid steel.

"Or not. What's with the white bag?"

"Marigold forgot it when she was here. It's an Odilia thing, round three to help turn her luck around. Can I use the Batmobile?"

The Christmas kid look was back in spades. "Why heavenly days, yes. I'd be plum tickled to watch the Fox for you. My pleasure."

Uh-oh. Just because I pooh-poohed the apple pie meeting didn't mean KiKi wouldn't go anyway with Mamma right beside her in God knows what kind of a disguise this time around. And there was Valley's threat to consider.

"Why don't you come with me?" I said to KiKi. "And Mamma, too."

I got the pouty look with sad-auntie eyes. "You don't trust us."

As far as I can throw you is what I thought, but to keep

the peace I offered up, "We'll all be together, and I'll lock up the Fox early. When was the last time we visited a lumberyard together?"

"You've done lost your marbles."

"You were the one who fumed and fussed when I didn't take you to Dozer's place of wood, big equipment, and snarling dog. Well, now I'm making up for it, and we can help Marigold drum and rattle her way to a better life."

I pulled the gourd out of the bag. "See, this is straight from Odilia. It'll be an adventure, and we'll bring good luck to Marigold. We owe her for all that she's done for Mamma with the campaign."

"What in the world did Valley say to you when he was out here? Nothing good, I can tell that much. Something's sure got you in a tizzy if you're packing us off to who-knows-where for drumming and shaking dried vegetables."

"Valley knows it was you and Mamma out there at the rally last night. He thinks the three of us are nothing but trouble and out to ruin Honey's campaign. He might try and deter our enthusiasm."

"Like cause bodily harm to you, me, or your mamma?"

"I think it's crossed his mind."

"I'll bring the bat."

Chapter Eighteen

"I'M not so sure Marigold knows how to drum," Mamma said from the front seat of the Beemer as Auntie KiKi drove out Old River Road. BW and I occupied the backseat, the white cotton bag between us. With the threat of mayhem in the air I wasn't about to leave BW behind. Uncle Putter was spending the night in Beaufort to take part in a charity golf outing, so he was out of harm's way, and KiKi considered bringing Precious/Hellion, but I convinced her the cat would be fine. In truth, no one with an ounce of sense would get near that ornery critter.

"If I remember correctly," Mamma went on with the sun hovering right at the edge of the Savannah River making it all shimmery, "Marigold flunked band back in high school. In desperation and because her daddy donated the uniforms, they finally gave her that little triangle thing to ding at the appropriate time. But I have to say no one strutted her stuff better than Marigold, and I think that had a lot to do with why Butler Haber went and married her."

"Musical talent probably isn't as important as the four of us making enough racket at sunset that the powers that be will take notice," I said. "Or maybe they'll all just have a good laugh and turn Marigold's luck around for her."

KiKi slowed at the next turn and pulled into the far edge of a gravel parking lot beside the weathered red and white Haber Lumber LLC sign. Red-roofed open-air buildings stood in a row with lumber stacked inside along with fork-lifts tucked away for the night. The last two buildings nearest to us had tracks that brought the logs to the behemoth saws for cutting. Long trucks for hauling were parked behind; Butler's aging Buick and a beat-up Ford pickup were parked by the A-frame house on the other side of the lot that probably served as the office; there were lights on inside. A chain-link fence surrounded the premises, the gates wide open and no sign of another Killer the dog.

"I don't see Marigold's blue Civic," KiKi said.

"I tried to call to tell her we had Odilia's bag out here with us," Mamma added. "But I didn't get an answer. Maybe we should drive around back of the warehouses to the river. She could be there. A setting sun over the water sounds like a good place to do whatever we're doing. And we best do it right fast or the sun's going to be beyond setting."

Wheels crunched over stones as the Beemer slowly circled the warehouses and trucks to keep out of sight. We didn't need Butler in on the action to be sure. KiKi killed the engine, and we piled out of the car, staring across the calm and serene river now reflecting golds, grays, and blues of sunset.

"Well, Marigold's not down here either," Mamma said.

"But I'm thinking we can go ahead and do this Odilia thing for Marigold on our own. How hard can it be? She's been a good friend for a lot of years. We're here anyway, why not? Hand me that there drum. KiKi, you man the gourd, and Reagan can walk BW; we'll have a nice little procession going, probably have more of an impact than just one person anyway. I think we should chant something. Spiritual rituals are always accompanied by a nice chant."

KiKi folded her arms and tilted her head. "Now I ask you, do we look like or have we ever sounded like a contingent of the Mormon Tabernacle Choir?"

"Fine," Mamma huffed. "Then we'll do a song, a little old tune we all know, and hurry up and think of something; the sun is dropping like a rock."

"'I Got You Babe,'" KiKi volunteered. "That's Cher's favorite and mine. I always sing it to Putter when he has a bad golf game. He thinks I'm cute."

"What about Johnny Cash's 'Folsom Prison Blues'?" Mamma said. "I consider it my theme song; I hum it on the way to work sometimes. Sort of sets the mood for the day."

"What about 'Happy Birthday'?" That got me the *you've got to be kidding* look. "'Jingle Bells'?"

Mamma sighed.

"The Oscar Meyer Wiener song," I announced in triumph. "Everybody knows the Oscar Meyer Wiener song. Even BW can bark along. It brings down the house at Wet Willies every Friday night."

"Sweet Jesus, we're going to beseech the wisdom and graces of the spirits on high with a song about extruded processed meat? It'll be a miracle if this place doesn't burn down around us."

Mamma faced KiKi, her eyes narrow and menacing. "One word of this on that Facebook page of yours or one little old tweet and I'll hunt you down, sister dear."

Mamma followed KiKi. BW and I brought up the rear, all of us making noise, BW doing the doggie howl. Calling it singing was a real stretch, and I couldn't remember a time when I'd been so darn glad to be out in the middle of freaking nowhere with no one around to witness the spectacle. We kept going till the sun dropped behind the horizon, casting the earth and water in shades of deep gray.

Mamma zipped up her jacket. "What do you think?" she asked the three of us huddled together as she put the drum and rattle back in the bag and fastened it with the cloth.

"I think I need a double martini, three olives," KiKi said. "And maybe a little girl's room."

"Now? Here?" Mamma passed her hand over her eyes.

"I can't help it," KiKi huffed. "All that singing and carrying on like we did got things stirred up. It's the way of the world."

I pointed to the edge of the river, the crescent moon peeking out from behind the clouds. "You'll have to use the bushes." We all rummaged around in our purses for tissues and hand sanitizer.

"It's getting dark, and it's cold as a well digger's behind out here," Mamma said, heading to the car. "Hurry it up, will you?"

"You think I don't know it's cold," KiKi grumped as she stomped off for the riverbank. "And it's not just the well digger's behind that's going to be cold."

Another car pulled into the front lot, tires spitting gravel, headlights cutting a swath across the buildings.

"Is that Marigold finally getting herself here?" KiKi asked. "She's a little late to be any use. What is that girl thinking?"

"Will you just take care of business so we can all be on our merry way," Mamma hissed, shooing KiKi off like a pesky fly.

"It's a Lexus," I said, keeping my voice low and watching through the open building. "It's Money-Honey's; I recognize the iridescent white paint job. What in the world is she doing out here at Haber's Lumber at this time of night?"

"It's just six thirty," Mamma said. "She's probably buying lumber for Seymour construction. She is taking over the business, after all."

"Maybe," I said, but doubted that was the issue. More like something to do with the Haber Lumber/Seymour Construction debacle if Money-Honey felt she had to be here in person. Butler opened the office door, his silhouette and another guy's backlit by the lights inside. Valley got out of the passenger side of the Lexus, and Butler came his way. This was so not about buying lumber for the construction company.

"I'm going to see if I can get close enough to hear what they're saying. You stay with KiKi." I put down the white bag and handed BW's leash to Mamma. I did the finger-across-the-lips *shhh* thing, ignored her shaking her head in fierce disagreement, and crept off toward warehouse number one.

The scent of fresh-cut wood hung heavy in the air, sawdust covered the ground, towers of lumber loomed high on either side. The world hovered between pearl gray and night black. I got close enough to see what was going on but couldn't hear what Butler and Money-Honey said; both were ticked as can be. Butler yelled something at Valley about wood, Valley yelled something back, then Butler punched him, knocking him down, and the other guy in the office pulled up beside Butler looking defensive. My guess was he was an employee as he and Butler had on the same yellow polo shirts.

Money-Honey and Valley got back in her Lexus, tearing out of the lot spewing gravel at Butler, and Butler hurled a fistful of rocks at the retreating Lexus. He and his friend turned, and Butler stormed back inside, slamming the door behind them, the sound echoing into the stillness.

"Good heavens, what was that all about?" KiKi asked when I climbed in the car beside BW.

"I couldn't hear," I said, fastening my seatbelt. "But there's obviously something going on. There's a lot of hostility between Honey and Butler, and now Valley's involved because of the election."

"Why are they so upset with each other nowadays?" Mamma wanted to know. "They all grew up together and used to be friends, being they were in the same sort of business." KiKi used just the low beam parking lights to maneuver through the lumberyard and edge her way around the trucks and not draw attention. Only Butler's car sat in the lot now.

"Butler Haber was selling poor quality wood to Seymour Construction," I told Mamma, praying she wouldn't ask how I knew such things. When we got on the highway, KiKi turned on her headlights and hit the gas.

"Now Seymour Construction buildings are falling down; it's been in all the papers," I continued. "My guess is Money-Honey is blackmailing Butler or she'll spill the beans that he sold the wood, and Butler's threatening to say that Seymour knew about the poor quality lumber all along and was out to make a buck."

"And it doesn't even matter if it's true or not," Mamma said, the Batmobile powering us silently through the night. "Any hint of something not quite right will kill Honey's chances at election and her business, just like getting accused of murder ruined my chances. That's certainly a stroke of bad luck for Honey, especially if it's not true."

I settled into the cushy comfort of expensive leather and personal temperature control as Mamma asked Auntie KiKi if she had heard about Cousin Samuel's gallbladder surgery. When KiKi said he wanted to have the thing preserved in formaldehyde and kept in the pantry so he could be buried with all his body parts when the time came, I figured I'd had my fill of crazy for one day and let the conversation wash over me. My eyes started to close, BW's head snuggled in my lap, and a little voice in my brain yelled, *wake up, stupid!*

But I didn't want to wake up. I was tired to the bone and wanted to sleep, and I to let myself drift off and . . .

I bolted upright. I frantically searched the backseat. "Where's the white bag?" I asked KiKi and Mamma, and if BW answered, that would be okay, too. "Did either of you put Odilia's white bag in the trunk? I set it down when I went after Money-Honey and Butler."

Mamma and KiKi exchanged wide-eyed looks.

"We've got to go back," I said. "Hopefully Butler is still there and hasn't locked the fence for the night. If we lose that bag . . ." I didn't have to finish the sentence, all of us thinking of Buffy Codetta's mother-in-law.

KiKi jerked the wheel and made a U-turn right in the middle of the road, tires squealing, BW sliding into my lap.

KiKi floored the Beemer, all the bunches of horsepower sitting under the hood coming to life at once with enough G-force to send us back to the future.

The Beemer purred along at breakneck speed, taking bends with the greatest of ease. KiKi passed a pickup, then an eighteen-wheeler like they were standing still. We took the next turn, then the next; there was a glow of yellow and orange up ahead . . . oh Lord, right up ahead . . . fire arching high into the dark sky behind the Haber Lumber LLC sign.

KiKi tore into the gravel parking lot, coming to a skidding stop. Frozen in terror the four of us stared at the scene in front of us.

"Holy Lord above, how did this happen?" Mamma grabbed her cell and punched in 911, and KiKi and I scrambled out of the Beemer. I closed BW safely inside, the intense heat taking my breath away.

The fire roared angry and mean from the sides and end of the first warehouse. The only thing not ablaze there was the metal roof. Mamma pulled up beside me, the three of us horrified as flames trailed across the ground following the path of sawdust like a hound on the scent, the second warehouse suddenly igniting like a match tossed on gasoline.

"Ohmygod!" KiKi shrieked, the three of us taking a step back.

"Butler?" My eyes cut to his old Buick parked in the same place by the A-frame, lights still on inside and the door wide open. "I don't see him. He's probably trying to put the fire out. He might be hurt or trapped," I said to Mamma and KiKi. "Stay here and don't move."

I took off before parental protectiveness became an issue, then glanced back to see Mamma and KiKi heading for the far warehouse. I stopped in my tracks. What in the world were they doing? Going for the bag of course!

"No!" I yelled after the dynamic duo, fearing for their lives. Neither paid one bit of attention. Did parents ever listen to their kids? Then again did kids ever listen to their parents?

"Butler!" It occurred to me that this was the second time in less than a week that I'd been hunting for someone in a fire. The last time it was at the house on Blair Street, and I was looking for Boone. Before all this the only outside fires I'd ever encountered were of the s'mores variety. Why was all this happening? Why now?

"Butler!" The first warehouse was a towering inferno. If Butler was in there, he didn't stand a chance. I did a mental fingers-crossed he was trying to save the second warehouse and was holed up there or maybe trying to save one of the forklifts. Why didn't he call 911? If he did call, they would have been here by now. Fire soared up the sides, consuming masses of wood, the heat cooking my skin, but there was no sign of Butler. I ran for the third warehouse, a ribbon of fire curling across the ground in that direction.

I stopped and took off my denim jacket and beat at the line of threatening flames. I hoped I could help just a little bit till the fire trucks came, maybe keep the fire from spreading to the next warehouse. I felt the heat coming near again but this time from behind.

I swirled around to lumber already ablaze in the third warehouse. Creaking and moaning filled the air, the sound coming from the first warehouse. The whole structure swayed, then the metal roof collapsed down onto the flames with a massive *whoomf*, sparks and smoke shooting out the sides.

Butler Haber could very well have been in that warehouse trying to put out the fire and wound up getting trapped. How could this happen to him? Why?

I cut my gaze back to the car. Where were KiKi and Mamma? They should have the bag by now. The car door was wide open, and Odilia's white bag was stashed safely inside.

But where were Mamma and KiKi? Where was BW?

Chapter Nineteen

SIRENS sounded in the distance, red and white lights blasting through the black night. Common sense said to stay put and let the pros handle things, but with a missing mother, auntie, and BFF, common sense was out the window. Where could they be? Why didn't they stay in the car? I wanted to cry, I wanted to scream, I wanted it to be two weeks ago when life was normal and my biggest concern was whether to have a second doughnut, and everyone I loved was safe and sound.

I ran full-out to where we left the bag down by the river because I had to start looking somewhere. The fire hadn't spread to the trucks and two cutting sheds, and maybe with the firefighters here they'd be spared. I came around the last log-hauling semi and crashed right into Mamma and KiKi.

"We're looking for BW," Mamma panted, her face lit with terror. "We opened the car door to put in the bag, and he bolted out; my guess is he's looking for you.

Think, Reagan, think! "Go tell the firemen that we can't find Butler or BW. And then you two stay by the car, and we'll meet up. Promise me, please. Don't move. BW's scared; he'll come to me. I'll be careful," I added in a rush, knowing that would be the very next thing to come out of Mamma's mouth.

I gave them each a hard shove to get them moving, watched them head for the fire trucks, then I headed down to the river. It's where we'd parked the car before and maybe where BW would go looking for me. I could feel the fire on my back and neck, seeping into my scalp. The flames burned hotter by the second.

"BW? Come here, baby," I yelled because I had to do something but doubted I could be heard over the roar of the fire.

"BW, I have hot dogs," I lied, my voice more of a sob than a yell this time. I headed toward the worst of the fire, smoke now pouring out of the buildings in roiling black clouds. I spotted the tie from the white cotton bag on the ground. It must have come undone when Mamma and KiKi grabbed it. I stashed it in my jean jacket pocket and looked up at BW staring right at me through the smoke. He blinked and took a few steps, then stumbled and collapsed to the ground.

"BW!" I sank down beside him coughing and choking, my eyes watering as much from the smoke as fear.

"Wake up, come on, boy. Wake up!" I gagged, each breath becoming more impossible, ash clogging my lungs. He was suffocating. I was suffocating. I slid my arms under BW and somehow lifted all seventy pounds of pup right off the ground. Coughing and sputtering, I staggered around the corner of the warehouse heading for the strobe lights in the front; the air was so dense the lights were the only things I could see.

A fireman drew up beside me. He said something that didn't register in my fogged brain and tried to take BW from my arms, but I couldn't let go. The fireman ran ahead and then came back with a red canister tucked under his arm, a plastic cone thing attached that looked like a funnel. He slipped the funnel over BW's snout, and miracle of miracles, BW opened his eyes. He looked at me, and he smiled.

IT WAS GOING ON TWO A.M. AS I SAT HUDDLED UNDER a blanket on Mamma's front porch with BW asleep in my lap. I had the baseball bat in hand, and Mamma and KiKi were asleep inside. We figured it was a night we needed to be together and circle the wagons, strength and security in numbers just like the days of the pioneers. A red Chevy pulled to the curb, and Walker Boone got out. He swung wide the white picket gate that squeaked same as it did twenty years ago, and he sauntered up the brick walk. He sat down beside me and petted BW.

"Hot date?" I asked, glad for the distraction from fire and pandemonium even if it was Boone's love life.

"Meeting with a client out on Tybee."

"Is that what they're calling it these days."

"Not that kind of meeting." And from the hard set of Boone's jaw and the steely look in his eyes, he wasn't lying. "You don't look so good, Blondie," he said.

He cut his eyes to me, a half smile on his face. "Don't you think sitting out here at two A.M. with your dog is carrying this grounding your mother thing a little too far?" He leaned closer. "You smell like smoke."

"You smell like diesel fuel and Gray's swamp."

"Like I said, I was out at Tybee. What's with you and eau de barbecue?"

"Mamma, KiKi, and I went to shake and drum up good luck for Marigold out at Haber Lumber, and then KiKi had to pee in the bushes, and we forgot the drum and rattle, and they belong to Odilia, so we had to go back, and by the time we got to the lumberyard, the place was on fire, a whole lot of fire. We couldn't find Butler, and then Mamma and KiKi went looking for BW because he went looking for me and . . ." My voice cracked; I couldn't go on. Telling the tale was like living the hell all over again.

Boone got up and went to his car and rummaged around inside for a minute. When he came back, he passed me a silver flask. "Dr. Boone's magic elixir."

I took a swig, whatever was inside burning my throat and stomach, and realigning my scattered brain cells.

"I bet the Savannah fire department is taking up a collection as we speak to send you on a nice, long vacation someplace far away," Boone said to me. "This makes you a double whammy in the fire category."

"And Scummy's dead and Delray Valentine stopped by to warn me to keep Mamma and KiKi away from Honey and his election or else. And of course there's Dozer. I know way too much of his business to suit him, so he's not happy with me, and Archie Lee is just a pain in the butt on general principle."

Boone took a swig of his elixir then gave me the long, slow stare. "That's why you're out here? Standing guard with a baseball bat?"

"I swing a pretty mean baseball bat."

"Did you see anyone out at the fire?"

"I couldn't find Butler, and I really searched for him, and

so did the firemen. It doesn't look good, and his car was there and . . ."

"What?"

"And Honey and Valley were there at the lumberyard, too. I forgot about that because it happened before the fire and I was a mess over nearly losing BW. Honey, Valley, and Butler had words; Butler decked Valley, then he and Honey left, and then we left. None of them saw us because we were around back of the warehouses; we went down by the river to do our drumming and shaking, and we waited till the coast was clear before bugging out."

"These days Honey, Valley, and Butler aren't a let's-meet-for-drinks kind of group; sounds like part of the lumber-switch situation. Butler could trash Honey's campaign if he had a mind to, and blackmail is a good motive for murder. Valley and Honey could have doubled back after you left to get rid of Butler like they got rid of Kip. If you saw Honey's car, she could have very well seen KiKi's and known they needed to wait till you left to do their thing."

"There was an employee there, too. They just waited till he left then killed Butler and tossed him in the fire?"

"One match and a little accelerant and a lumberyard is history. Not that many years ago Money-Honey was serving me beers at the Red Lion over on MLK and living in the projects. The woman's got street smarts and knows how to survive. She took on Kip to up her social standing. When that backfired, she got rid of him. If she felt threatened by Butler, she'd get rid of him, too."

"What about Dozer? He was furious Butler and Scummy nearly drove him out of business, except now he had a deal with Butler to get cheap lumber so he could win the contracts. But what if Butler reneged on the deal? Dozer would go after him big-time, like burn him out."

I took another swig from the flask and passed it back to Boone. He took a drink then said, "You saw Honey and Valley, the election is days away, and they can't afford the scandal. If it looks like a duck and quacks like a duck."

Boone gave BW a final pet then eased him off my lap. Boone took my hand and pulled me to my feet. "You need to take our dog inside and get some sleep."

"You really do look terrible." I kissed him on the cheek and had no idea why. Adam Levine wasn't even playing in the background. It was probably the aftereffects of Dr. Boone's magic elixir. That's it, had to be. Why else?

Boone's dark stubble felt rough and sexy against my lips, his breath slow and steady and warm as it curled around my neck and down my spine. His hands circled my back, resting easy, and truth be told, being here with Walker Boone was the best, the safest, I'd felt all day, probably all week.

"What was that for?" Boone asked, his voice as smooth and rich as the excellent bourbon in the flask, his eyes black and mysterious with a spark of heat deep inside.

"It seemed like a good idea. Take care of yourself, Walker Boone." Then I eased out of his embrace, opened the door, went inside my mother's house with our dog, and dunked my head under the kitchen faucet to cool off.

BY THE TIME I CRAWLED OUT OF THE SHOWER EARLY the next morning, the aroma of coffee and something delicious baking had swirled its way up the steps to the second floor of Mamma's house along with the homey chatter of family. I found an old green warm-up suit from high school tucked away in what used to be my room, which was now a guest bedroom done up in yellow and white thanks to some lovely decorator no doubt. I could sort of squeeze into the pants because they had an elastic waist, and as long as I didn't pig out on the baking goodies downstairs, I'd be fine. Since my upper endowments hadn't increased with age, the zip-up top wasn't too bad of a fit.

"Well, goodness me," Mamma said as I came into the kitchen, the table set for three, BW enjoying a plate—a china plate if you please--of scrambled eggs and neatly cut-up pieces of hot dog that Mamma must have just bought this morning. Mamma was a good doggie mamma.

"You look like you're still on the soccer team." She handed me a strip of bacon, knowing I'd sneak one anyway.

"I sucked at soccer." Proven by the fact that my warm-up suit was in pretty bad shape; I wore it a lot sitting on the bench.

"Just like your days in high school," Mamma added.

"Even down to kissing your beau right there on the front porch," KiKi chimed in over the edge of her coffee cup, a glint in her eyes.

There were times when I thought I missed being a kid and being clucked over and taken care of and not having the responsibility of a shop, a big old house, and a dog. Next time I paid my electric bill and outrageous mortgage, I'd kiss the checks and happily send them out the door. "Do you two miss anything?"

"Not when it counts." KiKi chuckled. "Nice of Mr. Boone to stop by and see how you're doing even if it is the middle of the night."

"I was out getting some air, is all," I said, feeling as if

there was more high school going on in this kitchen than just my warm-up suit.

I turned to Mamma. "Do you know if something's bothering Boone? He looked upset, and Boone never looks upset. Usually he's just, you know, Boone the Unreadable, smug and conceited with a superior smirk thrown in from time to time. Arrogant, he does arrogant really well, especially if he's cleaning my clock in a divorce; you can take my word for that. He said he was out at Tybee, and from the look on his face he wasn't thrilled about it."

"He has a house out there. Maybe there was a problem with the electric or plumbing or something. You know how beach houses can be."

"Maybe," I said but wasn't convinced. Something was up, and it had Boone on edge. Walker Boone was never on edge. Mamma poured the coffee, and KiKi dished up the eggs and biscuits. It was a morning of cholesterol be damned and bring on the comfort food.

"Is there anything in the news about the fire," I ventured around a mouthful, knowing we'd have to talk about this sooner or later.

Mamma and KiKi exchanged looks, and KiKi said, "I couldn't even bring myself to tweet about it, but last I heard they did find Butler's body. The police seem to think he was trying to put out the fire in the second warehouse and got overwhelmed by the smoke."

But I looked there, and I didn't see him. Even called his name. Maybe by then it was too late, and he'd already collapsed. I should have gone in, dragged him out. Why didn't I go in?

"I'm going to check on Marigold as soon as we finish up

here," Mamma said, breaking into my internal tirade of guilt. "I haven't talked to her, but she must be terribly upset. She and Butler had problems, and now this had to happen, that poor woman. So much for bringing her any good luck with the drumming and rattling we did."

KiKi bit into a strip of bacon. "I think we need to get those things in that there bag back to Odilia right quick before anything else happens around here. They're still out there in my car parked on the street where we left it. I wasn't about to bring it into this here house."

Mamma took a sip of coffee. "I'd take the bag, but I have an appointment over at the community college this morning. I'm thinking about taking some classes."

"You should teach classes there." I added a lot of enthusiasm to my voice and used the opportunity to steer the conversation away from last night. We'd had enough of last night. "Bet you'd love to teach law. You'd be a fantastic teacher with all your experiences, and you'd have a ton of stories to tell."

"I think I want to try something else." Mamma took a forkful of eggs. "Something more creative for a change, something with color. Doesn't that sound like fun?"

"As a barrel of monkeys." I was fighting a losing battle on the creative-class idea and on returning the bag. No one wanted to do that, and I was sure KiKi had a ready excuse tucked away.

"I'll take the bag back to Odilia before I open the Fox," I volunteered. "And if I don't show up by noon, come looking for me."

"I have a dance lesson with Bernard Thayer at nine," KiKi said on an exasperated sigh while slathering a biscuit with honey. "And I need to get cleaned up. I used to think Bernard was the bane of my dancing existence till this group of teenagers came into my life. They've got him beat by a mile, I can tell you that. See if Odilia has any suggestions as to how to get them to pay attention to me and learn how to dance just a wee bit before the cotillion. They're going to make me look bad. No one will ever take lessons from me again. Maybe there's some special music or some incense?"

"Maybe a taser."

We helped Mamma clean up and get things neat as a pin. Mamma was a neat-pin kind of woman. I studied her and Auntie KiKi and Bruce Willis, a huge wave of thankfulness that we were still here in this kitchen sucking air pouring over me. "We need a group hug," I blurted.

"Honey," KiKi said in her best auntie voice. "This isn't California; we're Republicans. We're more a kiss-on-the-forehead-you'll-be-fine-as-a-fiddle kind of family, then we just move on with life."

I folded my arms across my too tight green warm-up suit and held my ground.

"Sweet Jesus." Mamma sighed as we put our arms around each other, BW in the middle. "First we're singing about hot dogs, and now we're hugging. I better not be getting a pair of those Birkenstock ugly shoes for my next birthday, or there'll be hell to pay around here, I can promise you that."

KiKi pulled into her driveway, and we agreed that home never looked so good. I got out of the car and snagged Odilia's white bag from the trunk. When I closed the lid, KiKi was staring at me across the back fender, arms crossed, and tapping her foot. The tapping foot meant something was going on.

"You went and did it on purpose, didn't you?" she said.

"Which purpose are we talking about?"

"The syrupy stuff? The group hug? Odilia's not going to be happy that Marigold isn't returning the bag herself. If your ears fall off and teeth fall out, I'll feel guilty as can be, and I've had enough of that with nearly losing BW last night."

She puffed out a resigned breath. "Give me ten minutes to grab a shower and call Bernard to move his lesson to later and I'll go with you. If both of us have Lord only knows what befall us, at least we'll be in it together."

"You just want to see if Odilia has some potion for your teenagers."

"There is that."

I put the bag on the porch, left BW outside in the backyard to do his doggie thing, and did a quick change. I turned on my old Maytag and dropped in the smelly clothes from the fire. I held up my jean jacket wondering what to do.

"You really think you can wash that thing?" KiKi said, pulling up next to me. "It's held together with a few threads and a prayer now."

"It survived the explosion and the fire, and I even used it to try and beat out flames at the lumberyard. This jacket has good karma, and karma counts for plenty. Maybe I should just wear it dirty and smelly, Febreze it and hang it in the sun, and take my chances that it'll be okay."

"It won't be okay. It's smelly and needs soap, lots of soap. What's this?" KiKi asked pulling a piece of material from the pocket.

"I picked it up at the fire behind the warehouses when looking for BW. There was smoke in my eyes, and I thought it was the tie for the Odilia bag that we left behind, and I didn't want anything else to happen to it for all our sakes; we had enough problems at the moment."

"The tie is still on the bag. This is a scarf," KiKi said, turning it over in her hand. "Silk. It's expensive, really expensive. Honey Seymour expensive. What was it doing behind the warehouses? It wasn't there when we did our chanting and drumming, I can tell you that. We would have spotted it."

"When Honey and Valley arrived at the lumberyard, they drove in the front lot by the office. They stayed there, and then they left. So how did the scarf get to where I picked it up in the back? Money-Honey isn't the only person in Savannah with expensive clothes," I said to KiKi.

"But she was the only one at the lumberyard last night."

Chapter Twenty

"Yep," Mary Kay said to me and KiKi as we all three studied the cream silk scarf over Danish and espresso from Cakery Bakery that KiKi and I brought along. The dry cleaning machines churned rhythmically in the background, the humid warm air inside the Soap Box reminding me of August in Savannah instead of a chilly November morning.

"I do believe this here is Honey Seymour's scarf that goes to one of her suits that I've done up for her. See?" Mary Kay pointed to the edges. "That ruffled tan piping is the reason I can tell. She's got a suit just like that. How did you get it?"

"Found it in a parking lot," I chimed in, then changed the subject away from any more questions to the obvious topic of the day. "Guess you heard about the fire."

"Heard you two were out there at the lumberyard when it happened," Mary Kay said around a mouthful of pineapple pastry. "Lordy, what a mess. Least poor old Butler was dead before he got turned into a crispy critter. Guess that's something to be thankful for."

"How did you know about Butler?" I asked, the guilt of not finding him riding me hard.

"Detective Ross comes in here right early almost every day to get her suits cleaned. Seems they always have a smear of glaze or powdered sugar. I keep a doughnut or two on hand, kind of gets her in a chatty mood, and I find out what's what around here. She said Butler was whacked in the back of the head. Best the police can tell he was dragged into the warehouse from someplace else and stashed behind a pile of lumber. If you all hadn't come along and dialed up 911, the whole place would have been totaled."

Mary Kay started in on the cherry Danish and glanced down at the white cotton bag by my feet. "Since you're not dropping off laundry and you've got that bag, I'm willing to bet you're heading off to Odilia's. I have to say that woman scares the daylights right out of me."

"Think it would help if I brought her a Danish?" I asked.

"I think it would help if you two dropped that bag on her porch and ran like the devil himself is after you, 'cause he just might be."

KiKi and I left the Soap Box all casual like then stopped at the corner. "Well I'll be," KiKi whispered. "The scarf is you-know-who's. She and her partner in crime did the deed sure as I'm standing here. We saw them, there was an argument, then we left, and they came back. Scummy was in her way and he's worm food, and now Butler. It fits together like a big old puzzle."

"But we have no real proof we can take to Ross," I said. "She needs something concrete. She knows we don't have

any use for Honey; we could have found the scarf anywhere." I held up the white bag. "Let's get rid of this thing.
Maybe our luck will change if it's out of our lives. It sure
didn't do Marigold any good."

To walk off the Danish we left the Beemer parked at the
Soap Box and cut across Oglethorpe. Odilia's house had no
street number; it didn't need it. It was tucked in an alleyway
behind the Sorrel Weed House, one of the most haunted places
in Savannah, and just walking by the place gave me the willies.
The place was constantly on the market, people thinking
ghosts don't exist then finding out otherwise real quick.

Odilia's house was a small white frame with quaint blue
shutters and porch, a wild variety of plants in the compact
front yard, and various fruits and vegetables on the porch.

The fruits and veggies weren't because Odilia had good
eating habits but were offerings to whatever from whomever.
As a kid, I thought if you touched an offering, you'd shrivel
up and die; as an adult, I was absolutely sure that would
happen.

We stepped over the candy and pennies there for prosper-
ity and the apples for good health and healing. I knocked,
then knocked again. Shuffling came from inside, and Odilia
opened the door. She was wearing a white floral dress, and
her head was wrapped in a yellow turban. "You lent this to
Marigold," KiKi said, a little shake in her voice. "And we're
returning it. Her husband was—"

"Murdered," Odilia said in a gruff tone, her piercing
black eyes watching us close. "*Bad to you and bad to me,
bad comes back in groups of three.*"

"Amen," I said out of habit, getting a shin kick from
KiKi.

Odilia started to close the door then stopped. "Did Marigold get the insurance policy?"

KiKi and I exchanged glances.

"I told her she'd need it." Odilia slammed the door, end of discussion.

KiKi stepped off the porch, and I followed. Without saying a word we walked back to Madison Square, sat on a bench, and took a deep breath. "Visiting Odilia isn't all colored stones and eggplant. There's financial planning involved, and if followed, it pays off really well."

"Especially if you have a hand in making it pay off?"

"You really think Marigold would do that?" KiKi asked, both of us having a hard time getting our minds around the possibility.

"Marigold sure wasn't with us last night, and the woman's mad and desperate. She knows the lumberyard well enough. We should go talk to her."

"What are we going to say?" KiKi wanted to know. "Here's a fruit basket, sorry for your loss, and did you knock off your husband for financial gain?"

I did the double-eyebrow arch, thankful I actually did sort of have eyebrows. "Think about it, she could have knocked off Scummy, too; he was driving Butler nuts. Marigold gave Mamma the bottle of honey bourbon, and then she left for her bridge club soon after Mamma left to talk to Scummy. Scummy was bleeding Butler dry; maybe Marigold had had enough of being broke and got rid of them both."

"And bought insurance thanks to Odilia, the icing on the cake. Parker's deli is a few blocks over. Let's get a fruit basket. That's perfect condolence food and will get us into Marigold's."

"Kind of sneaky."

"These are sneaky times."

Fifteen minutes later KiKi and I stood on the porch of the Philbrick-Eastman House. I had the fruit basket, and KiKi raised the pineapple doorknocker to Marigold's not so humble abode that needed a sprucing up bad. "I don't know about this," I said to KiKi. "Mamma's going to kill us for barging in on Marigold this way; she's got to be devastated."

"Your Mamma can't kill us in someone else's house. It's not mannerly. Your mamma's big on mannerly."

Mamma yanked open the door on the second knock, took one look, and yanked KiKi inside then came back for me. "Oh, thank God you're here. I don't know what to do. Listen. Do you hear that?"

"Crying?" KiKi asked as I handed over the fruit basket. "Poor Marigold. Maybe a pear will help or a kumquat. Maybe we should call the doctor and get her a sedative."

Mamma poked herself in the chest. "I'm the one who needs a sedative. What you're hearing is laughter. Marigold's been online all morning shopping. In two days this place is going to look like Macy's threw up, and Marigold's supposed to be in mourning. This is not mourning; this is the Home Shopping Network on steroids. Where's the decorum, the manners? What will people think?"

"Insurance?" KiKi asked

Mamma gasped. "How did you know? Marigold went and took out a huge policy on Butler just last week. It's like hitting the jackpot."

"Unless you're Butler," KiKi added, and we all made the sign of the cross.

"Last night Marigold spent the whole evening having drinks and God knows what else with the new owner of the Southern Peach Hotel down by the river. They hit it off, she swears she's in love, and then she wakes up this morning to no husband and boatloads of money."

Okay, where was Odilia when I was getting my divorce? Where was my rich guy and hotel owner? I didn't need an attorney; I needed Odilia. "Marigold was with this guy all night?"

"Half the city saw them making goo-goo eyes at each other at the Southern Peach bar till the sun came up. Shameful if you ask me."

"I'm not asking you," Marigold's voice drifted down from upstairs. "I'm rich. I'm rich, rich, rich!"

Mamma insisted on staying on, and even though it was just nine, KiKi fixed Mamma a double Bloody Mary with a lot more bloody than Mary. I turned the TV to reruns of *I Love Lucy*, then KiKi and I hoofed it back to the Soap Box to retrieve the Beemer. KiKi fired up the engine, and we turned onto Bull then Charlton Street, passing by Money-Honey's house.

"Stop," I said to KiKi on a whim. "I think we need to take a look around Money-Honey's house."

KiKi eased the Beemer to the curb. "Why sure, let's just mosey on up to the front door and say we've stopped in for a spot of tea, what the heck were you doing at the Haber lumberyard, and by the way isn't this your scarf we found there?"

"Money-Honey's not home. Her car's always parked in

the drive 'cause it's too big for the carriage house. Honey's still our best suspect for polishing off Seymour outside of Dozer. The maid is probably in. I'll tell her I'm with Cuisine by Rachelle who did the catering the other night for Honey's campaign bash, and we forgot a tray and could we look around for it."

"You think she'll buy it?"

"It's a maid; she doesn't care. I'll take my time and see if I can get upstairs to look for the suit that matches our scarf. Then we can take the information to Ross."

"Seems kind of flimsy."

"Flimsy is all we've got right now, and it's better than nothing. The worst thing that can happen is she recognizes me from the Fox then slams the door in my face." Before KiKi could think of another excuse or I lost my nerve, I crossed the street to the William Battersby House. I raised the pineapple knocker and out of the corner of my eye spied KiKi heading toward the carriage house. She looked back at me and grinned; I returned the look, shaking my head violently *No*!

"What?" Money-Honey barked when she opened the door.

"You're not supposed to be here," popped right of my big mouth.

"I live here. Go away."

So much for getting upstairs, but the good news was Money-Honey didn't recognize me with short brown hair and fake brows. "I wanted to tell you . . ." I said to Money-Honey. "Actually I wanted to tell your maid because I know how busy you are that you are an amazing candidate, never seen anyone quite like you on the podium, and with you being an alderman, I'm absolutely sure Savannah will never be quite the same."

"Why thank you kindly. What did you say your name was?"

"Ann Taylor"

"Ann Taylor, you are so sweet. Now I really must go. My driver will be here any moment."

"Going on a trip? How nice for you."

"I have an election to win, dear. I'm not going anywhere till this thing is in the bag. Some idiot backed into my car and busted the taillight out of all things. It's in the shop. Now I really must go."

Money-Honey closed the door, and I crept around back by the carriage house, looking for Savannah's version of Nancy Drew. I ducked behind an azalea bush and a line of oleander bushes and a bed of withering impatiens, begonias, and foxgloves all in neat rows except for one open empty space. An obvious empty space because there was a hole in the ground. I stopped dead, staring at the dirt. Someone had been digging in the garden, digging foxglove plants. Not digging with a big shovel but a small hand shovel at just one plant.

"Pssst," sounded from the Beemer, KiKi already there making hand gestures for me to get a move on, and she was right. If Money-Honey's ride came along and she came out and saw me poking around her house, there'd be another encounter with the cops. I backed out of the garden and took shotgun in the Batmobile.

"What happened to Honey not being home?" KiKi fired up the engine, and we continued on down Charlton.

"Her car's in the shop. Things didn't exactly go as I planned. Did you find anything?"

"There were gas cans in the carriage house, but everyone has gas cans with lawn equipment. The maintenance people probably keep it on hand. Honey, and my guess is Valley too, are guilty as a priest in a whorehouse, and we both know it, and we can't prove a darn thing."

It was after ten when I opened the Fox, two frustrated customers waiting on the porch. I offered the 20-percent-discount apology, and all was well, but I hated starting off the workday late.

I wrote up a sale for a blue wool skirt and two pairs of jeans as a cruiser pulled to the curb, Detective Ross rolling up the sidewalk. How could anyone get so big in one week? I sucked in my gut and swore to start jogging . . . tomorrow. Yes, definitely maybe tomorrow.

"I need some blue suits and maybe a brown one," Ross said, taking a look around the Fox, powdered sugar trailing down her front. "That dry cleaner went and shrank all my clothes, do you believe."

"These things happen." I came around the checkout door and led Ross over to suits.

"You know," she said, picking up a white blouse that would hide the powdered sugar dribbles quite nicely, "I'd like to talk to you about the fire out there at the lumberyard. They got me covering fender benders now, me a full-fledged detective doing uniform cop duties."

Ross sniffed and dabbed her eyes with her sleeve. "I used to be on the front-burner homicide cases and now this. That detective from Atlanta has the whole police department convinced I'm no good, but if I can come up with some new evidence on this case, I can get my credibility back. You got any leads?"

I could tell her about Honey and Valley being at the lumberyard and about the scarf, but then Ross might go charging after Honey, and without real proof she'd look worse than ever. "I just saw what the firemen saw," I said to Ross. "Did they find anything?"

"The theory is Butler came out from his office, got whacked, then was dragged into the warehouse. Seems Butler was selling bad wood at inflated prices, and someone got ticked off about it. All they have are pieces of a broken taillight they found up by the office. It's new, not been rained on or driven over. Do you know how many busted taillights there are in this city?"

"Taillight? Really?"

"The thing on the back of a car. Are you okay? You look kind of funny?"

"How would you like to take a little ride with me? I'll buy you a doughnut."

"It is after ten, and my blood sugar is dropping. It might be a right fine idea to get a doughnut."

Chapter Twenty-one

I GRABBED Old Yeller from behind the checkout door, ran to KiKi's and told her and Bernard to mind the Fox, then jumped in the cruiser, wedging myself into the mound of empty pastry bags.

"Cakery Bakery here we come," Ross said, gunning the engine.

"We have to make a stop first. It has to do with a fender bender."

I got a pouting lower lip.

"It's about that taillight that's busted out at the lumberyard. We might . . . maybe . . . God willing and a little bit of luck . . . have the match. Honey Seymour's car has a busted taillight, and she was at the lumberyard last night. I even have her scarf, and it's a perfect match for one of her expensive suits hanging right there in her closet. Mary Kay over at the Soap Box confirmed it."

I told Ross about the spots on the skirt and the scattered pills and the empty pill bottle and poodle girl and the foxglove in Honey's garden and about the wood and the Butler/Seymour connection.

"Delray Valentine wants this election as much as Honey does," I added. "They both have motive and last night before the fire I was at the lumberyard doing an Odilia thing for a friend." Only in Savannah could you make that statement to a cop and not wind up in the slammer. "I saw Honey Seymour and Delray drive up in the Lexus. They had words, and Butler flattened Delray. The Lexus was fine then; now the Lexus is at the dealer."

"Maybe for an oil change?"

"It's the taillight. Honey told me herself this morning that it was broken. Said someone backed into her. I don't think so; I think she backed into something out at the lumberyard, and the taillight pieces the police have are a match for Honey's car."

Ross slowly sat up straight, dusted off her doughnut crumbs, eyes clear, and a little snarl in her voice when she said to me, "It's all circumstantial. Honey could have broken the taillight the first time she was out at the lumberyard."

God help us all, for better or worse, Ross was back. "She didn't. I saw the Lexus, and it was fine when it drove off, and there was someone else at the lumberyard besides me. My guess, he's an employee because he and Butler wore the same shirt. He can tell you the same thing. He owns an old red Ford pickup. It shouldn't be hard to find him, and he'll tell you what I just did."

"Maybe she broke the taillight here in town?"

"And maybe she didn't, but we need that busted taillight.

It's concrete evidence and worth a shot. It puts Honey Seymour and probably Delray at the scene of the crime. They had the motive. They want to save the reputation of Seymour Construction and win the election. My guess is Honey would throw the municipal insurance policies Delray's way, making him a rich man."

"What about Kip Seymour? You think they killed him? Why?"

"He was sleeping with the volunteers, and it was about to go public, ruining his chances at getting elected. Honey and Delray were desperate. This all lends to reasonable doubt if Mamma goes to trial. Planting the honey bourbon bottle with Mamma's fingerprints in my garbage can would not be hard."

Ross floored the cruiser, hit the sirens, and tore down Gwinnett. Cars pulled to the curb, traffic parting like the Red Sea for Moses as we raced through the city, the Lexus dealership suddenly looming just ahead in a matter of minutes. Ross squealed to a stop in front of the double garage doors marked *Service*.

Ross jumped out, nearly giving herself a hernia, and flashed her badge. "You have a Lexus here getting a taillight repaired. I need to see it and the light you repaired right now."

"You got a warrant?" a big burly mechanic, oil stains on his pants and shirt, said, swaggering his way toward Ross.

"Don't need one if you invite me in, which I'm sure you'll do since I'm doubting you got a permit for that fence out front or that new garage you just added on, and I would just hate to have building inspectors crawling all over this place."

"We just fixed the light," swagger guy growled, hands on hips.

"Got the old one you took out?" Ross growled back, hands on hips.

Swagger guy went to a recycle bin and pulled it out.

BY FIVE O'CLOCK I WAS ON PINS AND NEEDLES waiting to hear from Ross. Did the taillight pieces fit? Did they find the employee with the pickup? A lot was riding on that taillight. I wrote up a sale for a yellow jacket and charged the woman the wrong amount; my brain was total mush.

"Did you hear anything?" KiKi asked, wringing her hands as she bustled in the back kitchen door.

"Nothing. Where's Mamma?"

"I got her teaching the teens. She's taking her frustration out on them. Maybe they'll learn something."

The Fox was empty, customers home doing the Dolly Domestic thing. As I tagged the clothes I took in for consignment that day, KiKi hung them up, BW following her around the shop to make sure she did it right. I had just handed KiKi a cute polka-dot jacket for a display when Honey Seymour barged through the front door. Her eyes were wild, hair on end, and there was a big gun in her hand.

"You!" she scowled, looking right at me. "You little good-for-nothing troublemaker. I didn't recognize you at my house with that stupid haircut and bad dye job." Honey waved the gun. "You and your crazy aunt and mother have the police out looking for me all over a stupid broken taillight and sawdust on the bottom of some gasoline cans in my carriage house."

She aimed the gun at me. "Get out from behind that

counter. You all have ruined me, and I'm going to ruin you both, then I'm going after that holier-then-thou judge Gloria Summerside. I was winning this election by a landslide. I was going to be the next alderman and then mayor and then who knows how high I'd go. The barmaid makes good. I was on my way to sitting on Savannah's city council and running this here city."

Money-Honey aimed the gun and pulled the trigger, the blast echoing off the walls and the bullet zinging by my left ear and hitting the stairs. Holy crap!

"That's just a little sample of what's coming. I'm finished, and it's not my fault. I didn't do that fire at the lumberyard," she sobbed. "You're setting me up for that, and killing Kip was nothing but an accident. I didn't kill him on purpose. He was having an attack, and I gave him one of his pills thinking it would help, but it just made things worse, and then he stopped breathing, and I slapped him around a few times, but it didn't do any good. It never did any good the other times either. Blast that man!"

"And since he was already dead," I said, playing for time, "you put the pills in the honey bourbon bottle so you could frame Mamma and take your husband's place and win the election." Lord have mercy, where were nosy neighbors when you needed them? Where were the sirens? The police? They were there fast enough when I was at Dozer's.

"Framing Gloria was Delray's idea, all Delray," Honey said. "And maybe a little mine. We put so much work and effort into the campaign, and Kip was just ruining everything with his fooling around and poking anything in a skirt. I swear that man never did know how to keep his pants zipped."

"You had every right to be upset," I said to keep Honey focused on me and not KiKi. I hoped the police would get here soon; anytime now would be good.

I caught some movement by the kitchen door. The police? No! It was Mamma charging into the hall like the marines and yelling, "No one holds a gun on my daughter and sister!"

Money-Honey spun around, fired another shot that hit the ceiling as Mamma whacked her over the head with a campaign sign, knocking her to the floor. KiKi kicked the gun under the checkout door, Mamma and I pounced on top of Money-Honey, and I tied her hands roughly behind her back with her very own cream-colored Chanel scarf that matched her suit perfectly.

"You're really not going to run for alderman?" I said to Mamma the next morning over coffee at her house, Auntie KiKi off picking Uncle Putter up at the airport.

Mamma took a sip and shook her head. "I couldn't win. Even though Honey's confessed to killing Kip and there's overwhelming evidence she and Delray knocked off Butler and set the fire at the lumberyard, there's too much that's gone on. A hint of scandal is all it takes to kill a campaign, and this time it was a lot more than a hint. Besides, I like being a fulltime judge, and I think Archie Lee is going to do a pretty fair job on city council. I ordered a big bouquet of flowers from Flora's Flowers, and I was going to drop them off in person to wish him luck."

I put down my coffee. "You're kidding?"

"I want to make peace with him, Reagan. If he has

problems, I want him to feel free to ask me for help. It's what's best for Savannah; that's why I was running for alderman in the first place. I love this city. I want to take care of it and keep it strong and vibrant."

Mamma checked her watch. "I have a meeting down at the courthouse to get my chambers in order and my cases rescheduled." She beamed. "Guillotine Gloria is back."

I wished Mamma luck then headed off to talk to Mavis Lee Hornback who planned to redecorate and wanted to consign furniture at the Fox. Her lovely late-Federal clapboard two-story faced Crawford Square, taking me past Colonial Park Cemetery and the Cemetery. My steps slowed the closer I got to the bar.

If Mamma was big enough to make amends with Archie Lee, so was I. Right? He might just toss me out on my behind, but it wouldn't be the first time, and I'd survive. If I made peace too, maybe Archie Lee would bury the hatchet and contact Mamma if he needed something. I had to do what was best for the city.

"Hi," I said, moseying up to the bar stacked with boxes. The Cemetery was quiet this early in the morning, lights on to clean the place up but no one around except Archie Lee clearing out a big crate.

Archie Lee looked up, a snide grin on his face. "Go away."

"I came to wish you luck in the election," I said all cheery and sweet and trying my best to be sincere.

He stopped working and swiped his forehead. "Well, ain't that special. The thing is, I don't need your luck or anyone else's. I've got this election wrapped up. I've got everything under control. I'm the new alderman, and I'm going to do it right. I'm getting new clothes and a new car and maybe a new house if I get the urge. Here, let me show you something."

Archie Lee took a white box from the bar and pulled off the lid. He set aside the bill from Spanish Moss Printers and took out a lovely embossed invitation. "Feast your eyes on this little gem. I'm having myself a celebration party the night of the election over at the Old Pink House. Archie Lee, the big man in town for a change. Guess no one will be snubbing me anymore, will they?"

He handed me the bill. "Just the invitations cost a lot of money. I'm a man who knows how to get what he wants."

"Those are expensive," I said, using up every bit of nice I had in me. I smiled and handed back the bill, then stopped. I took another look, a closer look at the bill this time. The date the invitations were ordered was the very day after Money-Honey declared her candidacy. There was no way Archie Lee could have known he was going to win the election then. Fact is Money-Honey had the lead, a really big lead.

"You know, don't you?" Archie Lee said in a too-sweet voice, making every hair on my head stand straight up.

"I don't know anything," I said, tossing the bill in the box and backing toward the door.

Archie Lee reached under the bar, brought out a shotgun, and pointed it right at my middle. "You and your buddy in the back are just too darn smart for your own good, you know that?"

Chapter Twenty-two

"WHAT buddy?" Archie Lee laughed and hitched his head toward the back. "Move it and don't try anything funny. This is my pappy's shotgun, and it don't miss."

Mamma? Did Archie have her in the back? Did she beat me here and figure it all out, too? Oh, please, not Mamma. But I didn't see her flowers. KiKi was with Uncle Putter. Mercedes? It must be Mercedes; maybe she'd figured it all out.

I wound my way through the tables heading toward the hall; the kitchen door was closed. "Open it," Archie Lee ordered.

The big cauldron sat cooking on the old black stove, fragrant aroma of Old Bay Seasoning and Guinness fi the room, and Walker Boone was tied to a chair i corner. He looked at me and sighed. "Great. What the heck are you doing here?"

"*You* knew about the dates on the invitations, too?"

"Butler's books. He sold lumber to Archie Lee, and the delivery was to the house on Blair. I figured there was a connection."

"You bet there's a connection," Archie Lee said. "That there was my granny's house. I bought the wood and fixed her steps for her, and she fell straight through and broke her hip and her back. That fall put her in a wheelchair. Haber burned down her house to get rid of the evidence, but I knew what happened, and I wasn't about to let him get away with it. Seymour Construction was doing the same thing, hurting innocent people by using bad lumber, and they were going to get away with it, too."

"So you took care of them both," Boone said, giving me a weird look. "With Honey Seymour accused of murdering Butler, it would all get front-page attention. Otherwise, it would be buried in the courts forever." This time Boone gave me a piercing look. Either he had gas or something was up. I gave him a *what* look back, and he rolled his eyes.

"And it was easy enough to pull off," Archie Lee continued in a smug voice. "The night Honey had her rally I slipped in like a delivery guy and snatched one of her fancy scarves. My rally didn't start till six so I had plenty of time."

"And then you planted the scarf at the lumberyard when ʝou knocked off Butler and set the place on fire," I said, ̣ing it all fall into place. "Why the taillight?"

̣Brother said I needed more to connect Honey than just ̣ꝼ, so he busted the light out late last night and planted it at the fire. With all the commotion going on no one noticed him there. He even put sawdust from the lumberyard on the bottom of the gas cans in Honey's garage."

"Nice touch."

"Now I get to be Savannah's new alderman." Archie Lee grinned ear to ear. "Not bad, if I do say so myself. I'm a lot smarter than people think I am."

"Wait a minute, back up," I said, things starting to sink in. I glared at Boone. "Why are you here?"

"Bad timing?"

I parked my hands on my hips. "When the lumberyard went up in flames, you knew it wasn't Honey who set the fire all along. You knew it was Archie Lee?"

"I suspected."

"What happened to looks like a duck and quacks like a duck?"

"I didn't want you to wind up exactly where you are now, but in true form you wound up here anyway."

"You wanted to handle it."

"Something like that."

"And look where it got you. You are a rotten, no-good, two-faced—"

"Archie Lee," came Popeye's voice from an open door in the corner. "I almost got that hole dug down here like you wanted."

Keeping the shotgun on me, Archie Lee backed to the doorway. "We're needing another hole. We got more company."

"What company?"

"That Summerside girl."

A sinister laugh floated up the stairs, sending chills clear through my body.

Archie Lee stood on one foot, a sly smile on his face. "We're going to bury you two in the basement with those Yankee soldiers everyone's always talking about around here. I got one crate cleared out front, and I'll get another, or maybe I'll just jam you both in the one and save time. What do you think about that?"

"I think it sucks," I said to Archie Lee. "I think all this sucks." I glared at Boone. "I'm so pissed off at you. And I'm fed up with having guns pointed at me, and I absolutely, positively refuse to be buried with a bunch of damn Yankees."

I kicked the two-by-four out from under the stove, the boiling caldron flipping over, scalding water and peanuts sailing right for Archie Lee and the open door.

Archie Lee jumped out of the way, dropping the shotgun, and Boone decked him with a solid left hook as I whacked Archie Lee in the gut with the oar and slammed the door to the basement closed, Boone flipping the lock.

"Nice going, Blondie." Boone grinned. "Glad you got my message."

"What message? There was no message. I thought you were having an attack of something, and don't you Blondie me you double-dealing piece of crud. You lied to me; you always lie to me. I never know what to believe."

"How about believing this?" Boone picked me up and kissed me, and for a second I forgot about being mad. Okay, maybe for a lot of seconds I forgot about being mad. I couldn't breathe, my heart raced, and I really did see stars, lots of 'em. He let me go, setting me back on the floor.

"You . . . You think that makes up for the duck thing?"

The grin grew. "Maybe a little."

"It doesn't, not one bit."

This time Boone laughed. "Worth a try, and I wouldn't have it any other way." And then he kissed me again.

From *New York Times* Bestselling Author

Jenn McKinlay

Cloche and Dagger

THE FIRST IN THE BRAND-NEW HAT SHOP MYSTERIES

Not only is Scarlett Parker's love life in the loo—as her British cousin Vivian Tremont would say—it's also gone viral with an embarrassing video. So when Viv suggests Scarlett leave Florida to lay low in London, she hops on the next plane across the pond to work at Viv's ladies' hat shop, Mim's Whims, and forget her troubles.

But a few surprises await Scarlett in London. First, she is met at the airport not by Viv, but by her handsome business manager, Harrison Wentworth. Second, Viv seems to be missing. No one is too concerned about it until one of her posh clients is found dead wearing the cloche hat Viv made for her—and nothing else. Is Scarlett's cousin in trouble? Or is she in hiding?

"A delightful new heroine!"
—Deborah Crombie, *New York Times* bestselling author

jennmckinlay.com
facebook.com/TheCrimeSceneBooks
penguin.com

M1340T0613